D.T. BELLA

A Pinch of Distrust

First edition

ISBN: 978-0-646-86907-0

Cover art by Mousam Banerjee

This book was professionally typeset on Reedsy.
Find out more at reedsy.com

I would like to dedicate this book to my family & friends, without whose support this would not have been possible.

Contents

Acknowledgments

I would like to thank my mother, Maureen, for her help with this book - her input was invaluable. I would also like to thank my wife, Alisa, and my friends Christian, James and Jaimi. Their feedback was incredibly helpful with refining this novel. I'd also like to thank Lee Bradford, for designing the series logo.

1

A Disturbing Discovery

Yaetherim blinked, but the sight below him didn't change. That was another fairy lying prone on the shore of Verbore Island. Dead, or at least close to it. Below the body, a growing patch of purple stained the moss. A smear of blood led up from the murky water.

Yaetherim swooped down towards the stricken fairy. Curse words slipped from his lips. The locals had invited him here, to the Isle of Origin, to find peace. So much for that now. He swung his feet down. They slapped against the stones. A grunt escaped him. Not the neatest of landings, but style could wait. Only a hand's width separated him from the bleeding fairy. He examined the prone fairy's injuries. Stab wounds, no mistaking them. They were fresh.

Yaetherim's head whipped around, running over the clearing. To the right, some leaves rustled. Yaetherim's heart raced. Cold sweat broke out on his brow. His arm shot out. Energy crackled along it. A loud snap came from a nearby tree. The branch he'd summoned landed in his fist with a satisfying slap. A second spell sharpened its end into a point.

"Somebody there?" he barked. More rustling greeted his words. Another fairy emerged from the forest between two palm trees. Lizard-like wings, charcoal-black hair, a firekind. She wore the armband of a protector. A dagger dangled from her belt. Its sheath could hide a bloodied blade.

He held his other hand above one of the injured fairy's wounds. This time, the magic drifted out. Just a familiar tingle, starting from the crystal clasped in his belt buckle. Beneath his fingers, a smooth milky-green sochar leaf materialised. Carefully, Yaetherim began wrapping it around the remains of the wounded fairy's wings.

"What are you doing?" demanded the protector. She hovered closer, her hand on her dagger. Her voice shook, but she tried to hide it. No surprise there. Unlike Yaetherim, she probably knew this poor fellow. Yaetherim aimed his makeshift spear at her.

"Tending to his injuries. They're stab wounds. You're the only one here who's armed."

Her eyes widened. A frown creased her brow. Yaetherim shifted to show her his belt.

"Can't exactly cut him with just a crystal, can I?"

She pointed to the satchel slung over his shoulder. Like most fairy garments, it was woven from leaves and other plant materials.

"Your bag's big enough for a dagger."

"Oh, so I'm undoing what you believe I've done?" Yaetherim snarked.

"He was lying there, with you standing over him! What did you expect me to think?"

"You were hiding in the trees while I tended to his wounds," Yaetherim retorted. "What did you expect me to think?"

A dash of annoyance flavoured his words. He did not need this now.

The protector glanced down, then to where the injured fairy's belt should have been. Slowly, she drew her blade. Yaetherim didn't take his eyes off it. She held it towards him. The late afternoon sunlight reflected off the unblemished steel. Yaetherim frowned.

"That's only one side of it."

She turned the dagger over. No marks stained this side either. Yaetherim tossed his improvised spear aside. The protector landed next to him.

"I am Yaetherim of South Alken Forest. Your elder Paeyelin invited me," Yaetherim said.

"I am Taegithi of Verbore Island and that is Paetobim," replied the protector. Yaetherim nodded. Beneath his hand, the leaf finished forming. A faint salty

2

aroma wafted up from it. Yaetherim checked his crystal. Still opaque and full of energy. He moved onto Paetobim's next largest wound and cast again. A gasp came from behind him, but he didn't turn around. He sighed.

"Aye, I have scars," he said, "you can gape at them later."

"Sorry, I-"

"I'm used to it. Please fetch help. We should get that unclean water off him."

He'd spoken curtly. They could converse afterwards. Merely drinking unfiltered water was enough to make anyone sick, let alone swimming in it. Just the odour hanging in the humid air turned Yaetherim's stomach. Even now, an antidote may not aid Paetobim.

"Aye, ah, of course," Taegithi replied. She took off. Yaetherim watched her go. Despite the clean dagger, suspicion lingered. She had been close by. But so had he. Yaetherim dismissed his suspicions and finished conjuring the leaf. He turned Paetobim over to tend to the other injuries. The latter's arm flopped out. A crystal rolled out of his right hand, stopping against a nearby rock. Yaetherim ignored it. It wasn't the first spent crystal he'd seen.

Each wound sliced through Paetobim's flesh with no rip or tear. Only the blood showed their location. No blade or crossbow bolt could cut that neat and deep. Yet Yaetherim knew such injuries. He didn't need to check the scars on his own arms. They were just as clean and thin, with no sign of tearing or twisting.

A groan drifted through the air. Paetobim opened his eyes and tried to sit.

"It's all right, Paetobim. You're safe now," Yaetherim said. His tone belied his words.

"Nay... Rychillans in Cerrane..."

"What?"

Yaetherim frowned. His breath caught in his throat. Rychillans were banned from visiting Cerrane. Another moan interrupted his thoughts. He shook his head. Paetobim needed help. The rest could wait. With a few more spells, Yaetherim dressed Paetobim's wounds. A flick of his hands summoned some soft leaves, upon which he rested Paetobim.

Yaetherim stepped over and picked up the crystal Paetobim had dropped.

3

If stood on end, it would reach his knee. Human-sized, much too large for a fairy. Several vertical scratches marred the sides. Such marks only came from Rychillan jewellery. Only a hint of blue remained within it, the shade of a waterkind. A cold sweat crossed Yaetherim's brow. With his hands trembling, he reached into his satchel. He withdrew another crystal. As he held the two side-by-side, his suspicions solidified. Both were identical.

Something touched Yaetherim's shoulder. The crystals fell from his grip. He turned. One arm whipped up. His wings flicked out. A spell shot from his lips. The makeshift spear jumped back into his other hand. He brought it down, aiming it like a dagger.

Another fairy stood behind him. The newcomer held up his hands. Large eyes stared at him over a set of thick, callused fingers. Traits of a groundkind fairy. Not the most useful magic when healing. Perhaps he had just been the next nearest protector. No, that wasn't it. The armband of a protector captain sat on this groundkind's forearm. Again, annoyance seasoned his speech.

"You startled me, Captain Kae-"

"Kaetarpen of Mirost Village, Verbore Island. My apologies. That was not my intention."

He'd spoken sincerely. Yaetherim dropped the spear and took a deep breath. His wings relaxed and drooped.

Kaetarpen's eyes flicked over Yaetherim's right shoulder. Yaetherim waited. He counted off the heartbeats in his head. Three, while Kaetarpen stared at the hole in his wing. Then one heartbeat each for the scars on his arms and legs. Seemed correct. That's how long most people took. Kaetarpen's expression shifted.

"That is airship skin on my wing. Had it stitched in place by a Rychillan healer," Yaetherim explained, "everyone asks."

Yaetherim leaned over and looked around Kaetarpen. Taegithi had indeed brought help. She and a waterkind tended to Paetobim, while two more protectors stood guard behind them. All four had their wings extended, ready to fly at a heartbeat's notice.

"They attacked his wings this time too," Yaetherim said.

"Who?"

"The Rychillans Paetobim saw in Cerrane."

Kaetarpen's eyes widened. He spun on his heel. Firmly and quickly, he issued orders.

"Taegithi, I need you to go back to the village. Gather up all the protectors who aren't on patrol. Bring them to Cerrane, the southeast corner. Inform Paeyelin too."

Taegithi nodded and departed.

"You said this time?" Kaetarpen asked. Yaetherim picked up the spent waterkind crystals and handed them to Kaetarpen.

"He was holding one of these when I found him."

Kaetarpen held the crystals side-by-side.

"Where did you get the other?"

"Oato Clearing, South Alken Forest," Yaetherim replied. "It came with my scars."

His voice had shaken on that last sentence, even though he'd spoken softly.

Kaetarpen glanced over his shoulder. Yaetherim followed his gaze. Beside Paetobim lay an improvised stretcher. Nothing fancy, just palm fronds wrapped around two branches.

"It's all right, sir. We should be able to move him to the village," said one protector. Kaetarpen nodded and turned back to Yaetherim.

"You should go with them."

"Where are you going?"

"To Cerrane."

Yaetherim tilted his head.

"On your own?"

Kaetarpen couldn't be that stupid. It took a certain measure of intelligence to reach the rank of captain.

"The others are meeting me there," Kaetarpen replied tersely.

"Will there be archers amongst them?"

"Those who aren't on patrol, aye."

Yaetherim cracked his knuckles. Each pop got a wince from Kaetarpen. Good, he had his attention. Kaetarpen needed to understand what he'd be

5

facing. Yaetherim held his right arm out, showing the three scars along it.

"Do these look like the work of a blade?"

Kaetarpen leaned forward.

"Not torn... smooth..."

His eyes widened and flicked over to the waterkind crystals. Yaetherim nodded. Memories shot into his mind. A thin jet of liquid, flying towards him. Then pain, blotting out everything else. His wings shuddered and his fingers tensed.

"A dagger made of water?" Kaetarpen asked.

"A focused and directed stream of it. Very narrow. More of a lance than anything," Yaetherim said, his voice wavering. "Paetobim didn't even get his own weapon out."

Kaetarpen looked over to the stretcher. He stroked his chin.

"Yaetherim, could you accompany me to Cerrane? Your knowledge of this situation may prove useful."

Yaetherim's heart started racing. The Rychillans who'd attacked him could still be there. Yes, a chance of finding them was what had brought him here. But this was not what he'd expected. At least he wasn't alone this time.

"You sure we'll meet up with the other protectors first?"

Kaetarpen folded his arms.

"That is what I said," he replied. He spread his wings and lifted off. After looping round, he hovered and waited. Yaetherim flexed his right wing. Most fairies could just take off without a second thought. He didn't have that luxury anymore. Each stitch around the patch tugged in a familiar pattern of twinges. A few chafed the wing itself. But all stitches held. That done, Yaetherim tucked the waterkind crystals into his satchel and took flight.

They weaved through the forest, Kaetarpen in the lead. Branches and leaves flicked past. Yet despite the wind chill, sweat formed on Yaetherim's forehead. This wasn't about advising any longer. He was flying to Cerrane to intercept those who'd attacked him. They'd escaped last time. This was a chance to rectify that. He thought back over his training as a protector. Spotting and tracking poachers had been a large part of it. He'd need those skills now.

A curt gesture from Kaetarpen caught Yaetherim's attention. Both fairies pulled up into a hover. Just ahead, the forest almost vanished. Vines and moss covered the remnants of buildings. Not that much still stood. Cerrane hadn't seen residents for over two centuries.

"That's Cerrane," Kaetarpen said, his voice low, "we'll stay behind the trees. Keep an eye out."

Yaetherim nodded. His right hand dropped to his belt. It grasped air where he'd once worn a dagger. Kaetarpen gestured and moved off. Yaetherim followed. He kept glancing towards Cerrane. All he got were glimpses of the overgrown buildings. No signs of movement. But several walls still stood. Enough to hide a few humans, be they Rychillan or another race.

"Our patrol path comes through the trees just west of where we stopped," Kaetarpen said, "then skirts the clearing until it reaches the southern shore."

"Does it go into the ruins at all?"

"Nay, but Paetobim would've checked if he thought something amiss. He's quite devoted to his duty."

They reached the edge of the forest and perched on a branch. From here, the former town lay visible before them. A couple of structures still stood somewhat intact. To the southwest, the remains of a stone dock jutted out into the ocean. Again, no sign of movement. But tracking required more than sight alone. Yaetherim sniffed the air. His throat heaved. He coughed.

"Are you all right?" Kaetarpen asked.

"Just the stench of the water. None of that human odour."

While promising, it was hardly conclusive. Perhaps the breeze had been blowing the wrong way. Kaetarpen nodded. He glanced towards the ruins.

"We'll be careful, though. Anything we should know?"

"They were burying something when I came across them," Yaetherim said.

"What sort of thing?"

"Papers of some form. I can't recall more. That attack stole a few memories too. They'd dug a hole under a rock."

He sighed.

"We sent protectors to Oato Clearing two days later, but they found that hiding spot empty."

A flurry of movement caught his attention. Taegithi emerged from the forest to his right, a dozen fairies behind her. Five carried crossbows, the rest wore daggers on their belts. Yaetherim almost smiled with relief.

After the protectors landed, Kaetarpen stepped forward. While he briefed them, Yaetherim looked back at Cerrane. Something dull-silver dangled off the edge of the dock. Probably steel, yet somehow devoid of rust. No boat, for what that was worth. Paetobim's attackers could have come ashore elsewhere.

"Finally, if you see anything out of place, speak up," Kaetarpen finished. Yaetherim cleared his throat and pointed to the dock.

"I have. Either someone's left that behind, or the Rychillans have forgotten an effective metal preservation treatment."

Fourteen pairs of eyes looked over. A babble of conversation broke out. Kaetarpen clapped his hands twice. Silence fell.

"Well-spotted. We'll head that way first," Kaetarpen said. He turned back to the other protectors.

"Any questions?"

"Sir, you mentioned these Rychillans were using a water lance. What sort of range does that have?" asked an archer. Kaetarpen glanced over at Yaetherim. All eyes fell upon him. He gestured to a half-fallen wall in the middle of the clearing.

"From about there to here."

A few hands reached down to daggers. One or two fairies mumbled, but no more questions came. Kaetarpen took off, waving for the others to join him. They formed up, flanked by the archers.

"Yaetherim, could you please bring up the rear?" Kaetarpen asked.

"Of course."

After his preflight checks, Yaetherim joined them. They flew towards the dock, eyes peeled for any signs of movement. About halfway there, a movement amongst the bushes caught their attention. A protector on the right brought her bow up. A small, scaly brown animal skittered out into the daylight. The archer lowered her bow. She let out the breath she'd been holding.

"It's just a lizard," she said, relieved. It scurried along between trodden bracken and broken branches. Yaetherim frowned. Between the damaged plants, not around them, on suspiciously smooth soil and stones. Only a few ancient arrowheads littered the track. Even those lay to the sides.

"That's a path down there," he called. A few of the protectors looked down.

"We'll check that next," Kaetarpen replied from the front.

They reached the dock. Several stone bollards stood along its edge, each covered in moss and lichen. A steel ladder, with two handrails curving over onto a metal plate, dangled over the edge. No fairy would need such a thing.

Yaetherim looked out over the bay. Town buildings on the far shore interrupted the line of the forest. One towered above all others, a terminal for those Rychillan airships. But the rest of Alkentoft blurred into a salad of bricks and corrugated iron. No boats floated in the bay between there and here.

Kaetarpen joined Yaetherim. He glanced out over the water. His eyes narrowed.

"See anything?" he inquired.

"Nay, they must've gone in a hurry. I mean, they left that ladder behind. Chances are they're already back in Alkentoft."

Yaetherim slumped. He closed his eyes and took a deep breath. His attackers weren't here. They couldn't harm him now. But his chance to catch them had departed along with them. He opened his eyes to find his hands balled into fists. He unclenched them. Kaetarpen turned to the other fairies.

"Spread out," he ordered, "stay in pairs. We're looking for Paetobim's belt and something to identify those Rychillans. Start with that path Yaetherim spotted and work outwards from there. Taegithi, you'll coordinate. Report anything you find to me."

The protectors took to the air. Yaetherim glanced at Kaetarpen.

"We should check those structures that are still standing," suggested the latter.

Yaetherim nodded. They flew off and headed towards the ruins. Doubt clawed at Yaetherim. Unlike Oato Clearing, Cerrane presented plenty of potential hiding spots. A deep breath steadied his nerves. Fifteen fairies were searching this time. That should be enough.

He turned his attention downward. That path ran along what had once been a street. His eyes flicked side to side. Nothing stood out until he reached a sharp bend in the trail. With a flick of his wings, Yaetherim looped around to double-check. He blinked, surprised.

"What is it?" Kaetarpen asked.

"There's a junction there."

Two paths diverged through the broken plants, one towards each side of the street. Both ended at relatively undamaged structures. Kaetarpen swooped down and took a closer look. He ordered the nearest pair of protectors to investigate the structure on the right. That done, Kaetarpen veered left, through the hole in that house's roof. Yaetherim followed him in. The building held less than a clean saucepan. Only a few scorch marks marred the bare wooden walls, and moss dotted the floor. A faint scent of smoke hung in the air. But no aroma of food, so not a cooking fire.

Yet an instinct tugged at Yaetherim's thoughts, that gut feeling that had served him well. The product of details seen but not noticed. On one occasion, it had led to the capture of a trio of poachers. So he landed for a closer examination. Most of the moss sat in the gaps between floor stones. But two slabs lay encircled, with not a hair's width left clear. Yaetherim cast a simple movement spell. Just a gentle tug. The minimum needed to dislodge anything unrooted.

But both solid rings of moss jumped up. A flick of Yaetherim's hand sent them out of the way. He curled his finger, bringing a single piece to him. It had been compressed, mashed in place by fingers. They weren't dealing with a florakind, then. Or at least, someone who didn't want to show they were one.

Yaetherim gestured to the stones and looked at Kaetarpen.

"Can you raise those?" he asked. Kaetarpen frowned. He stepped over and crouched down.

"Aye, I can lift it with the dirt below. But my crystal's running low."

10

"Right," Yaetherim replied. With another spell, he broke a chunk of wood off the door. He levitated it in mid-air.

"Ready."

Kaetarpen cast his magic and the nearest edge of the stone rose. After a few heartbeats, the clump of soil lifting it up came into view. As soon as it was high enough, Yaetherim wedged the wood under it. The stone thudded onto the wood. Beneath it, a hole cut through the dirt. Kaetarpen strode over, poking his head under the rock to get a proper look. His wings twitched. After several moments, he spoke. Disbelief dripped from his voice.

"It's full of human-size crystals. All firekind and waterkind."

Yaetherim checked the stash. About three dozen crystals lay within. He stepped back, his eyes wide. Such a hoard would fetch a couple of hundred kerlum in Alkentoft, or fill a fairy's ledger of favours. Yet they just sat there, hidden but unguarded. These Rychillans must be rich, too.

He reached in and pulled out one of the waterkind crystals. Although full, it sent no tingle of energy across his bark-brown skin. It wasn't his element. He turned the crystal over and scrutinised it. No scratches or spots sullied its surface. Yaetherim returned it.

He and Kaetarpen moved over to the other suspect stone. They raised it the same way. This time, a shallower hole held just a fragment of paper. With a movement spell, Yaetherim brought it to him. He floated it in front of his face. Rough edges showed where it had been torn from the rest of the sheet. It bore a geometric pattern, but not a recognisable one.

"Is that it?"

The words escaped before Yaetherim could stop himself. His fist clenched. Several heartbeats passed before he relaxed his grip. Someone thought this paper worth maiming over. He wanted to know why. That was owed him for all he'd suffered.

"What's it say?" Kaetarpen asked. Yaetherim held the page up.

"Can you make that out? It's not Fairic or Rychillan. Druhlashi, maybe?" Kaetarpen peered at it. He shook his head.

"Nay, their writing's blocky."

"Right," Yaetherim muttered. He handed Kaetarpen the paper. While the latter examined it, Yaetherim inspected the holes. Several somewhat straight lines ran down each side. Shovel marks, so these weren't the product of groundkind magic. He pursed his lips.

"Speaking of Rychillans, it seems they've been coming here for quite a while. Paths like that don't make themselves. Yet they were only spotted today?"

Kaetarpen frowned. He handed the page back to Yaetherim. A hint of annoyance flavoured his words.

"We've been seeing likely signs of trespassers for a while. I suspect that's why Paeyelin invited you here. Have you noticed anything more?"

"Not here, nay. There's still that other building."

Yaetherim lowered the paper onto a spare stone. A simple spell summoned a large leaf through the gap in the roof. Another incantation folded it into an envelope. He tucked the page into it, being careful not to damage it. After all, it was their only clue to his attackers. He placed the envelope in his satchel and secured it.

With that done, they flew over to the other building they'd noticed earlier. One protector emerged from the doorway and stopped about an arm's length away.

"Sir, I was about to get you. There are letters in here."

Kaetarpen raised an eyebrow.

"Letters?"

"The remains of them, anyway. You'd better have a look."

Yaetherim pushed the door open further with a spell. It swung without resistance or squeaking. Once through, he flew around behind it and checked the hinges. He called Kaetarpen over and pointed to the hinges. Just like the ladder on the docks, they bore no blemishes.

"They don't appear a century or two old, do they?" he asked. Kaetarpen leaned in and frowned.

"Nay. Nor do they have a maker's mark on them."

"Nor any signs it's been removed," Yaetherim replied. He filed that observation for later and turned his attention to the rest of the building. Unlike the first, only a musty smell filled the air. Patches of sunlight dotted the floor from several small holes in the roof.

A short stool of Rychillan design stood in a corner. Next to it, a mat rested on the ground. Someone had woven it from palm fronds. Some green and freshly picked, others almost completely dry and brown. From a distance, it would resemble a jumble of leafs. A protector nodded to it.

"We had to move that off the fire."

He punctuated his words with a flick of his thumb. A pile of ash sat near the far wall. Several singed pieces of paper lay atop it. Yaetherim stepped over. Each sheet bore writing, in one of two different sizes. The larger was mostly Rychillan, with Fairic sprinkled amongst it. The smaller scrawl was the opposite. Another protector leaned over the papers, studying them. Kaetarpen landed beside her and picked up the page on top. It came apart in his fingers. Yaetherim suppressed a sigh of annoyance. This was evidence, they needed it intact.

"Allow me," he said. He levitated the next letter into his palm. Blotches and stains covered the paper, some still wet.

"Did it rain here this morning?" he asked. The protector nodded. Yaetherim scrutinised the few legible words left.

"Can you read Rychillan?" he asked Kaetarpen.

"Some," Kaetarpen said, "what's that word there?"

"Beloved," Yaetherim replied. That term held a lot of meaning for Rychillans. He turned to the protectors.

"Did you check the rest of those? Are there any names?"

"Nay. One of them already fell apart in my hands."

With a wave of his fingers, Yaetherim summoned the surviving fragments from the top of the ash. Another few motions laid them out across the floor. Most contained 'beloved' amongst the text, in both languages. Kaetarpen had spotted that too. His expression made that clear. Some colour faded from his face.

Yaetherim pursed his lips. Such a cross-species relationship was not a new idea to him. He'd heard of it once or twice, on visits to Alkentoft. But each human stood as tall as five or six fairies. That size difference would bring disquiet to some aspects of courtship, at least for the fairy. A kiss could resemble the last thing a morsel of food saw before being consumed.

Kaetarpen regained his composure a few moments later. He and the protectors stepped from fragment to fragment, examining each. While they did so, Yaetherim turned his attention to the mat. He frowned. Unlike the crystals in the other hut, a lot of effort had gone into hiding these letters. A simple movement spell could have woven the fronds together. But the execution would have required patience. The labour of someone used to waiting.

Yaetherim closed his eyes, thinking over what he'd seen so far. Images flicked through his mind. That steel ladder and the unmarked hinges. Moss and the woven mat. His eyelids snapped open.

"Is that dock outside the only one on this island?" he asked. A protector nodded. A smirk curled Yaetherim's lips.

"Captain Kaetarpen, is your quartermaster a florakind, by any chance?"

Kaetarpen turned with an eyebrow raised.

"Yaemetan? Aye. Why do you ask?"

Yaetherim gathered his thoughts.

"We know two Rychillans attacked me and Paetobim. If they were using this building for trysts, why would they have letters written in Fairic? Why bother sneaking over here? I doubt it's more convenient than finding somewhere in Alkentoft. Then there's the smoke."

Kaetarpen sniffed the air.

"I can't smell any smoke."

"Neither can I," Yaetherim replied, "not here. But there was in the other building. That must be where the attackers were."

Kaetarpen nodded.

"Very well," he said thoughtfully. "Go on."

Yaetherim pointed to the mat. Kaetarpen peered at it, then fixed Yaetherim with an inquiring gaze.

"Must've taken a while to make that," Yaetherim observed. "It's not the type of thing one can just smuggle under their clothes. Who else visits here regularly? Aside from your florakind quartermaster who receives deliveries through the only dock on the island."

"I understand your reasoning, but Yaemetan doesn't unload alone."

Yaetherim stroked his chin.

"No, but it's probably how they met. Either that or he may have gone to Alkentoft to arrange purchases. I presume you patrol the shoreline?"

That question earned him a nod from all three protectors.

"No alarm raised," he continued confidently, "so nobody spotted any boats. But those Rychillans were here today. Paetobim's wounds and that ladder prove it."

His hand shot out. An accusing finger pointed at the letters.

"Perhaps his attackers discovered how the blacksmith was sneaking over here and copied that method."

One protector frowned. A single word spilled from her lips.

"Blacksmith?"

"Those hinges have no maker's marks," Kaetarpen said. Yaetherim nodded.

"Aye, exactly. That violates their guild rules, I believe. Either they wanted to face punishment, or they didn't want it traced to them. They're usually firekinds. Hence the fire to destroy those love letters, and the mat to hide the ash. Unless Yaemetan is a dualkind?"

Kaetarpen shook his head.

"Nay. The only dualkind in our village is Taeperra, Paetobim's sister. She's a teacher of magic."

"Returning to my earlier question," Yaetherim said, "does Yaemetan have the patience to weave a mat like that?"

Kaetarpen's expression darkened. He folded his arms.

"Aye. But he should know better than to have such an affair."

Going by Kaetarpen's tone, Yaemetan would be in for a stern conversation. Kaetarpen glanced over at the papers.

"We need to bring these to Mirost Village."

From his satchel, Yaetherim drew the envelope he had made earlier. With a movement spell, he added the surviving letters to the fragment already in it. After returning it to his bag, he strode out of the building.

While Kaetarpen rounded up the other protectors, Yaetherim flew over to the dock. A quick look around confirmed the path he'd spotted ended here. No other broken branches or crushed leaves led away from it. So, the trespassers had only made the one path. He turned his attention to the ladder. Just as suspected, no signs of a maker's mark marred it.

He looked up as Kaetarpen joined him.

"May I see your dagger?"

He'd asked as though requesting someone to pass the salt at dinner. Kaetarpen handed his weapon over. Yaetherim turned it in his hands. Merely a simple Rychillan-made blade, a design known as a 'stinger'. Nothing fancy, but well-balanced with a maker's mark embossed on the pommel.

"Is this the standard-issue dagger here?" Yaetherim asked.

"Aye. Is there something wrong with it?"

"Nay, not at all. Who produced it?"

"Yaemetan has an arrangement with an armourer in Alkentoft."

Yaetherim handed the stinger back. A smidgen of sarcasm seeped into his voice.

"I'm sure he does."

By now, the rest of the protectors had joined them. Their search had found nothing else of note. They took flight. Yaetherim followed at the rear of the formation. Before long, familiar aromas drifted through the air. Eggplant, potatoes and nistyr root, none cooked enough to eat yet. Yaetherim's stomach rumbled. It had been an exhausting day.

Ahead, huts nestled amongst the tree branches. Walkways made of rope and wood boards ran between them. Several landing platforms jutted out around the edge, each with two protectors standing guard. Pretty standard for a fairy village. It looked almost identical to his own, on the east side of South Alken Forest. This half-familiarity brought relief to Yaetherim. He'd be safe here, properly safe.

The protectors broke off to the left. Kaetarpen gestured for Yaetherim to follow him. He led him to the right, to a landing platform in the shadow of an overhanging fern. An airkind fairy stood waiting, his face wrinkled by age. Kaetarpen landed and bowed his head towards the elder. Yaetherim did the same. They met the elder's gaze a heartbeat later. Yaetherim took a deep breath, held it for a moment and let it out. Now wasn't the time for anger.

"I am Yaetherim of Riala Village, South Alken Forest."

"I am Paeyelin of Mirost Village, Verbore Island," replied the elder. After a few brief words, Kaetarpen departed. Paeyelin turned to Yaetherim.

"Thank you for accepting my invitation, Yaetherim. Are you still of mind to do a juko meditation?"

Yaetherim's eyes narrowed. An exercise of reflection and prayer, fairies traditionally did such introspection on their birthday. Undergoing that here may have brought Yaetherim peace. This was the Isle of Origin, after all. That's why Yaetherim's elders had arranged this invitation for him.

"Is that the only reason you invited me here? I mean no disrespect, but Captain Kaetarpen mentioned you've had signs of trespassers."

Despite his words, he'd spoken calmly. Paeyelin glanced over his shoulder towards a hut. Through its door, Yaetherim caught sight of Paetobim. The wounded fairy lay on a bed inside, the sochar leaves over his wounds now stained purple. Paeyelin's voice dripped with worry.

"I had hoped you might provide some acumen to help prevent an incident like this."

"You wanted two berries from the one branch," Yaetherim replied. He folded his arms. A juko contemplation could very well have provided the peace of mind for such insight. But he wouldn't have time for that now. Not with this fresh information about his attackers.

"Well, I came here for answers," he observed, "but I guess they won't be coming from within."

"I understand," Paeyelin replied. "I-"

"NO!"

Yaetherim's head snapped over. He'd never heard so much anguish in a single word. That shout had come from Paetobim's hut. Yaetherim jumped off the landing platform, swooped around, and hovered outside it.

A young fairy, her hair the colour of charred wood, stood over Paetobim. Tears streamed down from her ember-red eyes. Next to the firekind crystal on her belt sat another, groundkind brown. Yaetherim froze. Kaetarpen's earlier words came to mind.

"The only dualkind in our village is Taeperra, Paetobim's sister."

Taeperra's grief could only mean one thing. Paetobim was dead. This was now a question of murder.

2

Racing to the Rescue

A blue sedan blasted through the intersection. Tenora jerked the steering wheel of her speedster to the side. Its tyres skidded. Invective shot from her mouth. For a moment, she locked eyes with the other vehicle's driver. Her lips fell silent. She'd never seen such terror. This was not just careless driving. That other vehicle was out of control. It had three people in it. She had to do something.

Tenora yanked the regulator. Steam surged through her car's engine. Exhaust beats merged into a roar. Her car jumped forward. Tenora steered after the runaway.

She grabbed the whistle lever. An earsplitting shriek sounded out through the streets of Alkentoft. She brushed a lock of natural navy-blue hair from her eyes. Her hands flicked over the control levers on the dashboard. Regulator, brakes, steam pressure, she played them as one plays an instrument. Inch by inch, she gained on the runaway sedan.

Up ahead, the street ended at a T-junction. Tenora leaned forward, willing her car onward. She had to catch them. At speed, they wouldn't make the turn. Tenora caught up mere yards from the intersection. She veered left and brought herself alongside the runaway. With a flick of the steering wheel, she steered into it.

Both cars skidded round the corner. Tenora's bounced off brickwork. The side mirror snapped off and smashed on the pavement. That didn't matter. They'd made the turn. From the sedan, its terrified driver looked over. Beside him sat a woman and a young boy, both stricken by fear.

"You need to disengage the runes!" Tenora called.

"I've tried! It's not working."

"Then pop the safety valve. Red knob in the middle."

The man's eyes widened.

"Look out!"

A lorry bore down on Tenora. She braked, swore and wrenched the steering wheel. Tyres squealed. The wheel bucked in her hand.

"Oh, no you don't!"

Knuckles white, she wrestled with the steering. Her car skidded over behind the runaway. The truck whooshed by. A sharp rebuke blasted from its whistle. Tenora ignored it. Whilst that manoeuvre had kept her alive, it had cost her distance.

A pop sounded out. Steam shot up from the runaway's boiler, carrying the brass safety valve. Tenora smiled. The hole it left should vent the engine and slow the runaway sedan. Now to stop it.

She reached for the gear lever. She hesitated, her fingers clasped around the cool metal handle. Gearbox testing had set her upon this test drive. But this was an emergency. With a flick of her hand, she downshifted. The engine surged.

Within seconds, she caught up to the other vehicle. She pulled alongside and flung out her left arm. Firekind energy crackled from the ring on one finger. A spell shot from her lips. More than enough to extinguish the engine's fire. Steam ceased spewing from the engine. Its driver braked hard. The car dropped back.

The woman passenger jumped out of the sedan, the boy wrapped in her arms. Several bystanders ran in to catch them. Tenora breathed a sigh of relief. Two safe, one to go.

Steam belched from the sedan's funnel. Tenora blinked. 'Twas an extinguishing spell she'd cast. That fire should still be out. A loud crack sounded out. The other vehicle sped up. Tenora spun the steering wheel to the right. Her car skidded over into the runaway's path.

Ahead, the street curved sharply into the harbour. Beyond the dock loomed the ocean water. Tenora had to finish this now, lest they both end up drowned. Her eyes flicked from the mirror to the road. Carefully, she matched the other car's speed.

A clang rang out, the impact of bumper on bumper. Tenora bounced out of the seat and slammed back down. She wrenched the brake lever. It bucked in her hand. She kept her grip. Lives depended on it.

Squeals and squeaks filled the air. Both cars skidded over the cobblestones. The runaway threatened to break free. But they slowed down.

The water drew closer and closer. Tenora held on. A dull thud came from behind her. She hoped it was the other car's door. But she didn't look away from the windscreen.

She steered left at the last moment. Her car swung around. The rear wheels slid out. The vehicle juddered and stopped. Tenora leapt out. Sweat plastered hair to her brow. She pushed it aside.

A loud crunch sounded out. Tenora's heart jumped. The runaway car bounced off a merchant ship moored in the harbour. Some sailors dived for cover. Others ran to peer over the side as the vehicle sank below the murky water.

Tenora dashed over, her gaze locked on the car. No sign of movement came from within it. Beside it, something round broke the surface of the ocean. Either a seat cushion or someone trying to come up. Before Tenora could tell, it vanished beneath the waves.

"Did you see anyone in there?" she called up to the sailors. A discordant cacophony of voices replied. Several arms pointed behind her. A Rychillan man lay motionless on the cobblestones. Tenora frowned and dashed over. He stirred and blinked twice. Again, that terrified look met hers.

"My wife and son, they jumped out earlier. Did you spot them?"

Tenora shook her head.

"No. We can go and check. My car's still drivable. It was just two streets away. Are you injured?"

"Only some cuts and bruises, thank Luxanke."

Tenora leaned down and helped him to his feet. Out of habit, her eyes flicked to the terax marks tattooed along his left arm. She felt his gaze upon her own symbols. Nothing remarkable stood out amongst his. She'd saved a baker with a few accomplishments under his belt. Like most Rychillans, he only bore the mark of a rynil. No movement to another class.

"I owe you my thanks, Arch-Mechanic…"

"Tenora. Tenora Perskel."

Before she could ask his name, running footsteps filled the air. A young boy slammed into the baker's leg and wrapped his arms around it.

"Daddy!"

The baker laughed and picked up his son, then turned as his wife joined him. Tenora moved aside to give them some privacy. Neither mother nor child bore severe injuries.

As she watched them, Tenora weakened at the knees. She stepped back and leaned against a warehouse. Her hands trembled. She slid down the wall. What she'd just done, well, she had never driven like that. She was a mechanic, for Luxanke's sake, not a guard constable. She could have died several times over during that chase. But as she sat there now, watching the family smile and laugh, she didn't regret it at all.

Tenora reached into the right pocket of her overalls and pulled out a metal case the size of her palm. Her hands still trembled as she pulled it open. From within, she drew a small cylinder of loose tobacco leaves rolled in paper. She placed the tip in her mouth and snapped her fingers. A single flame flared up at the other end.

She inhaled, then blew the smoke out. As usual, her stress dissipated with it. Yes, she could have died, but she hadn't. Nor had the family walking towards her. Tenora pushed herself off the wall. She dropped the cigarette and scrunched it out with her boot. They stopped just an arm's length away. Before they could say anything, a shout sounded out from one ship.

"The water, look!"

Several bystanders ran over. Tenora joined them. She blinked and bit back a profanity. Before her, the ocean rolled and splashed. Steam rose from it, above the sunken car. A few strange creatures with oval bodies and wide, flat appendages bobbed to the surface. They floated on their side without moving. A pungent odour came from them.

Most of the bystanders stepped back, noses pinched. Questions and speculation filled the air. Tenora leaned forward. She'd never seen such animals. They must have come from within the water. But she knew what had killed them. Somehow, flames still burned within that car's engine. Just like when she'd tried to extinguish it earlier. Such an occurrence belied all she knew of runes. Yet she couldn't dispute the testimony of her own eyes and nose.

A woman spoke from behind the crowd. Her words escaped Tenora's notice, but carried a note of confidence and authority. Silence fell upon the chattering bystanders. A few of them moved apart. Someone clad in maroon stopped next to Tenora. That pushed Tenora's thoughts aside. Only those on the king's business, most often the town guard, wore the royal colour.

She fiddled with her ring and swallowed the lump in her throat. One hand reached for another cigarette, but she interrupted herself. Rules of driving flew through her mind. She'd committed five violations, at least. That wouldn't do her reputation for caution any good.

"Is anyone in that car down there?" asked the newcomer.

Whilst Tenora didn't recognise the voice, she had seen that face somewhere before. It belonged to a woman with silver hair, maybe seven or eight years older than Tenora. Terax marks ran the length of her heavily tanned arm, stopping just short of her shoulder. Out of habit, Tenora read them. Halfway up, Tenora stopped. Her breath caught in her throat. Not merely a town guard, this newcomer was a veritor. The highest rank amongst the guards, charged with investigating threats to the peace of Rychilla.

Tenora cleared her throat. Out of Alkentoft's three veritors, only one woman held that position. Veritor Karis Relinda. Rumours about her stirred in Tenora's memories. Some claimed she was part-Druhlac. Others stated she was actually a dualkind. All Tenora knew for certain was that they called her the steel veritor.

With that thought, Tenora swallowed. She looked up into a pair of dark sunglasses.

"It was empty, Veritor Karis," Tenora said. She turned and pointed to the family she had rescued.

"They were aboard it."

Karis pushed her sunglasses up on top of her forehead. Her grey eyes bore into Tenora's, like a drill through wood. Little wonder she'd earned her nickname.

Tenora reached up and tucked her hair behind her right ear. But she didn't look away. Karis looked behind the crowd.

"Is that damaged green car yours?"

Tenora nodded. Karis raised her hand and beckoned over the three guard constables waiting nearby. When they joined her, she pointed to the people crowded around.

"Get their accounts of what happened. Include the sailors on those ships. Do not allow witnesses to leave without giving statements."

While the guards did so, Karis gestured for Tenora to follow her. They headed for Tenora's car. Neither spoke, and Tenora took the chance to gather her thoughts.

"You must be Arch-Mechanic Tenora Perskel," Karis said. Tenora blinked.

"Yes, but I don't think we've met before."

"Not formally."

Karis drew a notebook from her left trouser pocket. She flipped through it and stopped on a page covered with elegant handwriting.

"Fourteen weeks and three days ago, you broke up a brawl at Cropper's Crony with a wall of fire between the two belligerents."

Tenora frowned and thought back.

"Yes, one of my friends accidentally offended a Druhlac. Didn't want either of them to come to harm. But it was a guard constable who settled it down after that."

"I was dining a few tables away. You acted quickly to prevent trouble."

Tenora nodded.

"That's what happened today too, I guess."

They reached Tenora's car. Tenora crouched down and winced at the sight. Anyone would think it had met a farmer's plough. Gashes exposed bare metal in several spots. The front-right mudguard curled around like

24

the claw of a roosting chicken. On the bumper, the number plate was bent lengthwise. She straightened up and found Karis waiting with notepad and pencil poised.

"What did happen today?" Karis asked. Tenora recounted the chase. Karis said nothing and just took notes.

"Send any bills for damages to my workshop," Tenora finished. "I'll see them settled."

Karis nodded curtly.

"That will be arranged. But you may already have the largest one."

From a pocket of her overalls, Tenora drew a pair of pliers. She gripped the curled mudguard and bent it away from the wheel. Not quite into shape, but enough to keep it well clear of the tyre.

"Steel's more flexible than people think. We do these sorts of coachwork repairs at my workshop."

"I see."

"Aside from the damages, what fines can I expect?"

Karis glanced at the rescued family. With her left hand, she fiddled with a brooch pinned to her shirt. Her expression softened for a moment, then she turned back to Tenora.

"It is too soon to tell. We are yet to interview all witnesses."

"Oh."

Karis checked her notes.

"One thing of note. You said the fire re-ignited itself after you extinguished it."

"Yes."

With the pliers, Tenora pointed to the floating corpses of those round creatures.

"It boiled the water after sinking, Veritor Karis. Such immersion should have swamped the flames and exhausted the firekind crystal."

"Can you explain how that may have happened?"

Tenora shook her head. A note of concern seeped into her words.

"It bothers me. No rune sequence ought to have such an effect."

"Have you heard of such an occurrence before?"

Tenora went to say no, but the word died on her lips. A snippet of memory stopped her, something mentioned recently. Her eyes widened, and she fiddled with a lock of hair.

"I must confess, I'm not sure. Perhaps, but I'll need to check. I'll arrange to have that car salvaged."

Karis made a note in her notebook.

"Let me know if you require help with the salvage. We will also have to discuss this further. Can you visit my office at the ninth hour tomorrow morning?"

"Yes."

"I shall see you then."

Tenora watched Karis stride away. A sigh escaped her. Like goatgrass, the question of penalties had already taken root amongst her thoughts. It would prickle them until dealt with. She'd have to do her best to ignore it until then. Perhaps it wouldn't be bad. Despite breaking traffic laws, she had saved three lives. That must count for something.

However, another concern had also sprouted in her mind, one which did deserve cultivation. She strode over to the edge of the water, through the dispersing crowd. Below her, the brown ocean lapped against the stone wall. Beneath it lay a car which had nearly killed its passengers. Even without the threat to life, it had ignited her curiosity. Firekind and waterkind runes generated and regulated steam, which then drove the wheels via cylinders and a gearbox. All of it proven technology, refined over decades. Yet she could not escape the fact this runaway had happened.

Tenora turned to find the baker and his family waiting a few steps away. They beckoned her over, and she joined them. After expressing their gratitude, they departed. She watched them leave. Once more, that faint memory of something she'd heard tugged at her thoughts. Other such incidents had occurred and may happen again. Next time might not go so well.

But she could sort that out later. Right now, she had to see inside that car's engine. Given this vehicle's current location, that would be a bit of a problem. Options cascaded through her mind, none of them satisfactory.

She'd need help from waterkinds and florakinds, the latter to lift the car by its coachwork. After a brief conversation with a sailor, Tenora strode over to the warehouse. As it turned out, the Merchants' Guild had a salvage team for these occasions.

As she approached, the three people standing watch outside eyed her. One stepped forward. His hand hovered near the dagger sheathed on his belt. His eyes ran over Tenora's terax. Tenora explained what she sought, and the guards exchanged a dubious look.

"Can't hurt to ask, I suppose," said the nearest. "Wait here."

He disappeared into the building. A few muffled words drifted out from within. Another man emerged, his wheat-yellow sash marking him as a merchant, especially from a distance. His lips twisted up in an expression Tenora often wore herself. Polite, professional, and sincere. Although in this case, that last element didn't carry to the purple eyes that poked out from beneath his brown, neatly combed hair. Tenora matched his smile with one of her own. As the warehouse manager, Rynach Reulo was just the person to help her out.

"Arch-Mechanic Tenora, good to see you again. I understand you are after the aid of our recovery crew?"

"That's right, Merchant Rynach. Did you hear that accident? A car sank in the water. I want to arrange for its salvage and delivery to my workshop."

"I presume it wasn't yours? Doesn't sound like you at all."

"You're correct," Tenora replied, and she told him what happened. By the time she finished, a concerned frown had replaced Rynach's smile. He stroked his moustache.

"Ah, that's what that hullabaloo was."

"I wish to get it out. I suspect something may be amiss with its rune panels."

Rynach raised an eyebrow. It almost disappeared underneath his fringe. After a few moments, he turned his attention to the ocean.

"Could you show me exactly where it is?"

"Of course."

Tenora led Rynach over to the harbour wall. His nose crinkled as they approached. He peered into the water. Doubt sprouted within his words, growing as he spoke.

"Florakinds are usually enough. The crates float. But I can sort it out for you. You're sure the coachwork will lift the rest of it? I mean, it won't separate from the chassis or anything?"

"We often raise cars like that in my workshop. It's useful for aligning them over inspection pits."

Rynach nodded.

"Very well. We'll need crystals to work with."

"I'll bring enough of each type and some kerlum for their efforts," Tenora assured.

"This'll take some hours to prepare. A Brial ship's due in later, but we should have time before then. Can you meet me here at the nineteenth hour and a half? I should have everything arranged then."

Tenora nodded, and a grateful smile curled her lips.

"I appreciate it. Could you please engage a lorry to deliver it to my workshop, too?"

"Of course."

"Thank you."

With that, Rynach returned to the warehouse, and Tenora headed to her car. She climbed in and flicked two of the control levers. A soft crackle signalled the ignition of the engine behind her. Tenora leaned into the seat as she waited for the steam pressure to build up. While examining the runaway vehicle may provide some information, it wouldn't hurt to get as much as possible. She closed her eyes and thought back. Arch-Mechanic Thirer came to mind, something he'd mentioned in passing at last week's guild meeting.

A shift in the engine note interrupted Tenora's thoughts. The pressure gauge confirmed it. Enough steam to move had built up. Tenora turned the car around. The steering wheel moved smoothly in her hand and the vehicle responded as expected. So the axles weren't damaged. She listened for any other signs of trouble. Upon hearing none, she drove it back down the street from whence she'd come. Unlike her drive to the harbour, she reached her workshop without incident.

She steered the car through the familiar doors, parking it in the bay designated for it on the right. She opened the door, smiling at the chorus of clangs, hisses, chatter, and running footsteps. Wait, that couldn't be correct. It wasn't safe to run on a shop floor, unless it was an emergency. Every mechanic knew that.

"Chief? Are you injured?"

Silence fell. Tenora held up her hand, causing her second-in-command to slow to a walk.

"I'm uninjured, Somath."

She had never seen Somath Koljon so worried. Even after he reached her car, a frown still creased his brow. Tenora looked past him, to the rest of her mechanics.

"Please, as you were."

They nodded and returned to work. Upon turning back, she found herself on the receiving end of a concerned look. With her voice lowered, she recounted the day's events. By the time she finished, some colour had drained from Somath's face.

"Thank Luxanke you're still alive. Chief... Tenora, please tell me you shan't do something like that again."

"Hopefully, I won't have to. I recall hearing mention of similar situations last week. Have you heard of any such incidents?"

Somath glanced down. His eyes flicked off to the left, then met Tenora's.

"Two or three nights ago, while dining at the Envelope & Propeller. Mechanic Seralyn mentioned something about a lorry losing power."

"Anything mechanical?"

"Their examination found nothing amiss with the engine."

Tenora nodded thoughtfully. A few seconds passed, then realisation slammed into her.

"Did you say Mechanic Seralyn?"

An apologetic smile crossed Somath's lips.

"Sorry, Chief."

"Not your fault," Tenora replied. Sorrow-tinged memories of smiles and affectionate moments seeped into her mind. A sigh escaped her. Best to get this done, rather than contemplate what could have been. With that, Tenora strode over and pulled a lever mounted on the rear wall. It clanked into position. A glance through the glass panel in the ceiling showed a single flame burning in the call lantern above it. Tenora released the lever. It moved back to its original angle, retracting the ignition rune in the lantern. That sorted, Tenora retreated to her office in the corner.

Four minutes later, she lay down her pen. Two notes sat on the desk before her, identical save for the salutations. She'd tried to write neatly, yet the letters still looked as though a chicken pecked them out. That would have to do. The messenger summoned via the lantern would arrive at any moment. She crossed to the office door.

There. Just inside the workshop's double doors hovered a fairy, an airkind whose cream-coloured hair stood out against the grease, wood and metal surrounding him. A pouch, woven from plant leaves, hung off his shoulder. Tenora waved to get his attention, then beckoned for him to join her.

"Good afternoon, Arch-Mechanic Tenora. I trust you are well?" he said when he reached her.

"Very well, thank you," Tenora replied in Fairic. She handed him the first note.

"Please take this to Arch-Mechanic Thirer."

Her fingers closed around the other letter. Words caught in her throat. The family she'd saved earlier came to mind. Three lives could have ended today, one a child too young to even use magic. Were these malfunctions due to a definite reason, they could easily cause more pain and suffering than a failed courtship.

"This message to Mechanic Seralyn," Tenora mumbled, "of Arch-Mechanic Warrett's workshop."

She reached into a small pocket in her overalls. From within, she pulled a coin purse. After counting out three kerlum, Tenora held the coins out. The messenger shook his head.

"It's only one kerlum and two kerlo per message. Two and a quarter kerlum total."

Tenora flicked her free hand towards the door.

"It is quite a lot of flying around. I mean, Seralyn's all the way down by the riverfarer docks."

He folded his arms, but smiled.

"All part of the job, Arch-Mechanic Tenora. Besides, I do like a long flight to stretch my wings."

Tenora returned one of the three octagonal coins to the purse, and replaced it with a smaller, square kerlar.

"Thank you," the fairy said. He placed both money and letters into his pouch, then flew out. Tenora watched him go.

* * *

Five minutes before the eighteenth hour, Tenora strode into Cropper's Crony. Chatter and pleasant aromas wafted through the air, the latter tinged with cigarette smoke. Rychillans, Fairies and some Druhlac occupied almost all the tables around the ground floor of the inn. Even the couches in the middle were mostly filled. From behind the bar, the proprietor shot her a grin. His gaze lit up.

"Evening, Tenora."

"Good evening, Rynroth. May I please see your Fairic menu?"

He handed it over, and his smile changed. A knowing look came into his eyes.

"You won't need to worry about a drink. Mechanic Seralyn's already bought your usual mug of mead."

Tenora blinked. 'Twas not just the clammy air causing the sweat upon her brow.

"By the left front window," Rynroth said.

"Thank you. Can you please send Arch-Mechanic Thirer over, if you spot him?"

Rynroth's smile gave way to a puzzled frown.

"Arch-Mechanic Thirer?"

"It's a mechanical matter we're to discuss, and I very much hope I'm wrong. I see you've added a few dishes to this menu."

"Our adviser visited again a couple of weeks ago."

"You have a consultant for Fairic food?"

Rynroth grinned.

"A forest fairy who's an avid cook in his spare time. Recipes and advice are how he pays for his dining and board here."

Tenora raised an eyebrow. Sounded like a convenient arrangement. For a moment, she wondered what had led to it. Then she examined the menu. After a few moments of consideration, she placed and paid for her order.

That done, she weaved through the patrons towards the front window. After a few minutes, she spotted the face she sought. Even now, those storm cloud-grey eyes caught her attention. Tenora stopped next to Seralyn's chair and took a deep breath.

"Hello Seralyn."

Seralyn blinked, looked up and brushed a lock of chestnut-brown hair aside.

"Tenora, hello, I, ah, I got you a drink."

She dropped her hand towards the mug on the other side of the table. Tenora sat down behind the mead and sipped it.

"Thank you, but you didn't need to do that."

Seralyn reached up and twisted her hair around her finger. A habit of hers, born from worry.

"Your letter mentioned you wanted to ask about something mechanical? I mean, you're more senior at this…"

Seralyn trailed off, and Tenora stifled a sigh. The latter drew out a cigarette and lit it. Silence and smoke hung in the air between the two women.

"I also asked Arch-Mechanic Thirer to join us," Tenora replied, "as I think we have all witnessed similar incidents recently."

"What sort of incidents?"

Tenora sipped her mead and marshalled her thoughts. Between sips of mead, she recounted her earlier drive to the harbour. Her food arrived when she got to the part about the boiling water and those strange creatures killed by it. She cut herself a piece of cauliflower loaf and ate it. A well-balanced blend of cashews and spices complemented the vegetable. Tenora made a mental note to order that again at some point.

"So animals can live in the ocean," Seralyn observed. Tenora paused, her mouth full of food. Perturbed by the engine problem, she'd overlooked that.

"I suppose so. But they're not threatening the peace of the kingdom. That fire re-ignited itself underwater. Runes should be predictable. That's why we use them. Would you have expected that?"

Seralyn shook her head. Before she could reply, a man strode up to their table. Like Tenora, he had natural navy-blue hair, but that was where the resemblance ended. A few faint wrinkles lined his face, and his hands bore several minor cuts and scars. In one hand he carried a glass of white wine, and a newspaper in the other. He nodded to Tenora, then to Seralyn.

"Good evening Arch-Mechanic Tenora, Mechanic Seralyn."

Tenora pushed out a spare chair at the table.

"Good evening, Arch-Mechanic Thirer. Thank you for joining us."

Thirer sat down and placed the newspaper between them. Today's evening edition, with a headline proclaiming an afternoon of chaos at the harbour.

"Is this what you want to discuss? Your note mentioned an accident."

Tenora scanned the newspaper's front page. Despite the dramatic headline, the report itself just stated most of the facts. It omitted any mention of the underwater fire and those creatures it had killed. She handed the newspaper back to Thirer and filled him in on the rest.

"It brought to mind those malfunctions you mentioned last week, after the guild meeting," she said, "and I fear they may be related. Arch-Mechanic Thirer, I believe you approached Veritor Jorryn about this?"

Thirer leaned forward and pinched the bridge of his nose. A distinct note of annoyance entered his voice.

"I did. He listened, but didn't see it as a threat to the peace. Seemed eager to put it down as an isolated incident."

"So what happened?"

Thirer sipped his wine.

"It was a tractor, one of the older ones. Good when built, not so efficient today."

Tenora nodded. Looking after such equipment on her parents' farm had first steered her towards becoming a mechanic. She took a mouthful of mead and Thirer continued his story.

"First we heard was when a messenger arrived with news of a breakdown at Chealey farm. I sent Jotol up to take a gander at it. He usually looks after them."

Tenora nodded. Seralyn leaned in.

"What did he find?" she asked.

"He had it towed to the workshop," Thirer replied. "We found the engine had blown out one cylinder."

Both Tenora and Seralyn sat up straight. The former slowly set down her mug of mead.

"Blew out a cylinder?" Tenora asked.

"But... they're made of steel," Seralyn added. Thirer nodded.

"Yes, shattered the engine block. Must've had quite a surge of steam. We gave it a full inspection before replacing it. Nothing obviously wrong, no damage to the rune panel or the crystals. Jotol replaced the panel, just in case."

"Was that the last of it?"

"I believe so. We've not made repairs on it since then."

Tenora leaned back and sipped her mead. She rolled it around her mouth while considering Thirer's words. Steam pressure could do some nasty things. But whence it came was the question. She swallowed her mead and turned to Seralyn. The other woman glanced down and took a sip of her beer.

"Ours was a lorry which lost power on the road into town," she began. "It got towed into our workshop. Arch-Mechanic Warrett inspected it personally. The boiler was ruptured, and the firebox full of water."

Tenora's frown deepened.

"Any sign of metal fatigue in the boiler itself?"

"No, 'twas almost new. I'd helped replace it three weeks previously." Seralyn leaned in.

"When we drained it, we found the waterkind crystal completely clear."

"Any damage to the rune panel itself?" Thirer asked. Seralyn shook her head. Tenora tapped her fingers on the table, a steady beat over and over.

"So we have a surge of steam, a surge of water and a surge of fire. You're both certain the rune panels were undamaged?"

Both of the other mechanics nodded. Tenora leaned back. Her eyes lost focus as possibilities ran through her mind. Nothing mechanical could cause such behaviour. But it couldn't be the rune panels. Governed by tight regulation, only the College of Mages could legally make them. Yet that eliminated all engine components from consideration. Tenora shook her head. Such apparent impossibilities indicated a lack of information, that was all.

"I'd like to check both those vehicles. Can you arrange that?"

Thirer nodded.

"I'll have Jotol meet you at the Chealey farm tomorrow morning."

Seralyn cleared her throat.

"I'm not sure if Arch-Mechanic Warrett would take too well to that," she said apologetically. Warrett had never liked Tenora, since she'd reported him to the Mechanics' Guild for using reconditioned parts. Nothing wrong in itself, but he hadn't disclosed that fact to his clients.

"Don't worry about it too much," Tenora replied. "I shall approach him myself."

After discussing some details, their conversation diverted to other matters. Tenora turned her attention to her meal, lying half-forgotten in front of her. Between the sedan she'd chased down and these other vehicles, she should be able to find answers. Hopefully, it would be before anyone got hurt.

* * *

A short while later, Tenora steered her car onto the street leading down to the harbour. This time she drove her personal vehicle, instead of her test speedster. A cool, crisp breeze ruffled her hair. Despite her concerns, Tenora couldn't help but smile. An evening this pleasant deserved to be enjoyed in the open. So she'd taken down the roof of her banana-yellow two-seat roadster before leaving Cropper's Crony.

Soon, the aroma of the ocean mingled with the others in the air. A series of whistling and clicking sounds reached her when she got to the harbour. A nasty suspicion crossed her mind. Sure enough, another ship sat between the ones she'd seen earlier. Instead of the angular, vertical sides of a Rychillan craft or the nimble shape of a Druhlac riverboat, the curved lines of this vessel flowed smoothly. Several tall bird-like figures stood on its deck. Their plumage and beaked faces confirmed Tenora's fear. Those Brial merchants had arrived early.

Normally Tenora would welcome the chance to see a Brial ship close-up. Their design verged on artwork. However, this one brought naught but disappointment, not due to form but to position. It lay moored above where the runaway had sunk.

Tenora parked out of the way. She climbed out of her car and put up the roof. After locking it, she walked over to the dock. Several people stood nearby. All wore the sashes of merchants, along with waterkind or florakind crystals. Presumably the salvage crew, yet no lorry waited. Two of them looked over. Most kept their eyes on Rynach. At the base of the ship's gangplank, he conversed with one of the Brial.

"I thought they weren't arriving until later," Tenora said, a note of disappointment in her voice. A merchant glanced back at her. His face seemed familiar. They may have crossed paths in the market hall.

"That's what we heard too," he replied. "Apparently they had some engine trouble."

Before Tenora could reply, Rynach joined them. He shot Tenora an apologetic smile. Like before, it didn't quite reach his eyes.

"Arch-Mechanic Tenora, it seems I owe you an apology. They arrived earlier than expected."

Tenora folded her arms.

"Do they have to remain there?"

"Unfortunately, yes. They've already started unloading. Only one other berth can hold a ship this size. It's currently occupied by another vessel."

Tenora sighed and stifled the expletives on her lips. No course of action would recover that car tonight. A prayer to Luxanke wouldn't help. Praying had never helped her. Hopefully, that truck and tractor would yield something useful.

"Do you still require payment for their time?"

Rynach shook his head.

"Don't worry about it, Arch-Mechanic Tenora. I've cancelled the lorry too."

Tenora nodded. She strode over to the harbour wall and pulled out a cigarette. One of the Brial stood nearby, adjusting the mooring ropes running from ship to bollard. They turned, and Tenora found herself transfixed by speckled green-and-brown eyes either side of a carrot-orange beak. She stepped back.

The Brial opened their beak, and whistled softly. It sounded like they were asking her something. Tenora shook her head.

"I'm sorry," she said apologetically. "I don't know Brialish."

The Brial clicked their beak twice. A whistle from the ship cut through the air. The Brial on the dock turned and whistled a reply. They glanced back at Tenora, then headed for the ship's gangplank.

Tenora stepped away and placed the cigarette in her mouth. With a snap of her fingers, she lit it. Another sigh escaped her. Yet more goatgrass to prickle her thoughts. After finishing her cigarette, she extinguished it and tucked the butt into a pocket of her overalls. For now, she could do naught but rest. Tomorrow had the makings of a busy day.

3

Planting a Seed

A short while after Paetobim's death, Yaetherim followed a protector along the walkways of Mirost Village. Not a single note of music reached his ears. Conversations, when overheard, were in hushed tones. 'Twas not the first time he'd seen this. Back home, they'd been on edge for weeks after his assault. But while he had survived, Paetobim had not. No wonder the entire community mourned.

Even the protector escorting him had barely spoken. She'd only said the village council wanted to speak to him. He could guess why. His village had already gone through this. That's the insight they now needed.

They reached the chapel, and Yaetherim's escort stepped aside. She gestured for him to enter. He nodded thanks and did so. Several other fairies stood around the altar, below the glass-domed roof. Save for Kaetarpen and one other, all bore the marks of old age. Yaetherim pursed his lips. This would be the village council. Dominated by elders, like back home. Hopefully, this lot would actually listen.

"They appear to be love letters. But we are yet to confirm whom this affair involves," Kaetarpen finished. A few murmurs of discontent came from the others. He paused and looked around. Upon spotting Yaetherim, he beckoned him over. He performed introductions. As suspected, this was the village council.

"Yaetherim has already been of aid to us earlier this afternoon," Kaetarpen said. Paeyelin smiled wryly.

"Although not quite the help I had in mind, we will still be grateful for whatever insight you can provide."

Yaetherim nodded. Expectant eyes fell upon him. His thoughts flew back to Cerrane.

"Well, for starters," he replied, "the lovers did not kill Paetobim."

A few frowns greeted his statement.

"From where do you draw such certainty?"

That question came from an elder named Paeteris, who stood with her arms folded and an eyebrow raised.

"Both buildings contained piles of ash. Yet I only smelled smoke in the one without the letters of courtship. Hadn't had time to drift away," Yaetherim replied. He jerked his shoulder. His satchel swung around and bounced off his hip. From it, he drew the two spent waterkind crystals. He placed them on the altar. The elders leaned in for a closer inspection.

"Paetobim was holding one of these when I discovered him," Yaetherim explained.

"And the other?" Paeyelin asked. Yaetherim made sure to speak casually.

"Found next to me in Oato Clearing, eight months ago. Only thing my attackers left behind. So no love letters."

"No jeweller can make two pieces that are identical," Paeyelin observed. Yaetherim nodded. No machine existed to fabricate jewellery. Instead, they were crafted by hand.

"Exactly."

Paeyelin examined the crystals, then looked at the other elders. Her gaze went from one to the next. None spoke, but understanding passed between them.

"We take your point, Yaetherim," Paeyelin said. "Kaetarpen, we will need to send a messenger to Alkentoft."

Kaetarpen bowed his head, spun on his heel and departed. Outside the door, someone moved out of his way. Yaetherim frowned. It wasn't Yaemetan, but a fairy with the leathery skin of a firekind. Yaetherim turned back and stifled a sigh. This conversation sounded disturbingly familiar. He tried and failed to keep a note of annoyance out of his voice.

"I hope you'll do more than simply ask the Rychillans to investigate this," he said. Paeyelin nodded.

"Aye. Patrols will be conducted in pairs. We shall also raze what's left of Cerrane. That's long overdue."

Yaetherim pinched the bridge of his nose. This time, he did not attempt to mask his annoyance.

"Do you think my village council didn't make such a request? They contacted the highest authority. The Governor assigned it to one veritor, Jorryn Lorem."

Yaetherim spat the name and folded his arms. Silence fell. After a heartbeat, Paeyelin spoke.

"There's already a veritor investigating this? But surely…"

Yaetherim's left fist clenched. His fingernails dug into his palm.

"Surely he'd have something by now, aye. That's what I expected."

"What happened?" Paeyelin asked.

"Nothing! I've visited Alkentoft three times since. Most recently, a couple of weeks ago. Each time, I met Veritor Jorryn and demanded updates from him. His excuses have all the strength of a dead flower's petals. Handled at the highest authority, aye, but not with the highest priority."

Yaetherim's right arm shot out in the direction of Alkentoft. His next words dripped with frustration.

"I know the reply Veritor Jorryn will give you. He'll tell you he's doing all he can, but he has limited time, other cases, and not much information. So I'll ask again. What else will you do about this?"

Silence hung in the air. Paeteris folded her arms. A frown creased her brow.

"You seem to suggest our own investigation. The Accord of Reiksoft-."

"Says crimes are to be investigated by the species of the perpetrator," Yaetherim interrupted. "Rychillans when they're suspected, and Fairies when it's us. I've read it at least thrice. But it leaves some things unmentioned."

As his own village's council had pointed out, multiple times, it wasn't a treaty to be taken lightly. That document had ended the civil war a couple of centuries ago. Since then, both Rychillans and Fairies had abided by its provisions. Peace had ensued. But the accord only outlined things in broad strokes. Describing the forest without specifying the trees. A question from Paeteris interrupted Yaetherim's thoughts.

"Even so, where would you start? We know nothing about these killers."

"They've been doing this for at least eight months and one of them is good with waterkind magic. Money or access to crystals is no obstacle to them, judging by the size of their stash. They're doing something with fire and have sneaked over here multiple times undetected. Aside from all that, you're right, we know nothing about them."

A smirk curled Yaetherim's lips. He'd delivered that last sentence as though talking to a youngling. Although perhaps a youngling would have considered their words, rather than making assumptions. Paeteris frowned.

"There is no need to put it so rudely," she replied. Before Yaetherim could reply, Kaetarpen returned with another protector in tow.

"Please give us a moment, Kaetarpen," Paeyelin said. "Yaetherim has provided some additional information."

Kaetarpen shot an inquiring look at Yaetherim. The latter filled him in while the elders conversed. By the time Yaetherim finished, a frown sat upon Kaetarpen's brow. Paeyelin joined them.

"Yaetherim, thank you for sharing your insight. It's given us cause for discussion."

Yaetherim folded his arms and almost flared his wings. He'd have preferred his words to give them cause for action. Paeyelin turned to Kaetarpen.

"Captain Kaetarpen, we'll send you Alkentoft tomorrow. There are a few things we'd like you to mention to Veritor Jorryn Lorem. Thank you for your help, Yaetherim."

Paeyelin led Kaetarpen over to the rest of the council. The other protector departed, presumably to deliver a message to Jorryn. Yaetherim strode outside. He paused and peered around. No sign of that firekind he'd spotted earlier. Tantalising aromas drifted over from the kitchen. He had taken two steps before a voice called out.

"Yaetherim?"

Yaetherim looked back. He halted and waited for Kaetarpen to catch up.

"I've requested a meeting with Veritor Jorryn tomorrow morning," Kaetarpen said. "You've dealt with him before. What should I expect?"

Yaetherim turned and continued along the walkway. Kaetarpen matched his pace.

"Excuses," he growled, "they all boil down to two things. Not enough information or time. Apparently, the merchants' guild has some urgent thefts he's working on. As if catching some thieving connil is more important."

"Paeyelin said you mentioned a few facts we've learned?"

"Aye. They've been at this for eight months. One's a skilled waterkind. Either they have money or access to a source of crystals. Surely that would prune some possibilities. Then there's also their means of getting-"

Yaetherim broke off. He stopped and tapped his fingers together. Kaetarpen went a few more steps before realising.

"We know someone who might have seen them. A pair of someones. Yaemetan and his lover," Yaetherim said. Kaetarpen raised an eyebrow. His wings flared, and a hint of doubt flavoured his words.

"You think they witnessed Paetobim's murder?"

"No, just the killers. Consider it. The Rychillans are coming over by boat, you saw the bollards. An airship's too big and noticeable. Two groups, sneaking to the same place. They must have crossed paths at one point. Perhaps in Cerrane, maybe on the water."

Yaetherim cracked his knuckles. Kaetarpen winced. Yaetherim ignored him. He rubbed his wings. They ached where they met his back. No surprise there. He had done a lot of flying today.

"Would you have some soothing balm in your storehouse, by any chance? You did say Yaemetan is your quartermaster."

Kaetarpen's eyes widened. Yaetherim cleared his throat.

"You wouldn't mind if I try to get him to open up?"

"You?"

Yaetherim lowered his voice.

"You're his commander. Do you think he'll admit anything to you?"

"Very well. Just tell me how it goes."

"Of course," Yaetherim replied. A smirk flitted across his lips. Now he was a fairy investigating another. No treaty violations there.

When they reached the end of the walkway, Kaetarpen took the lead. A couple of walkways later, they rounded a broad tree. Ahead, a building of wood and woven leaves ran completely around the next trunk. Much larger than the other huts, it lacked the usual louvres below the windows. Kaetarpen led him straight into the doughnut-shaped structure.

Shelves ran round both the front and rear walls. All held a decent selection of weapons and tools. The metal ones bore the same maker's mark as Kaetarpen's dagger. A fairy sat on the floor to the right, holding a written list. He sprung to his feet as Kaetarpen closed the door. His frond-like hair bobbed. Words poured from him like juice from a jug.

"Sir, thank Galarus you're here. I have heard rumours about Paetobim..."

His voice trailed off. His gaze ran over Yaetherim. Kaetarpen nodded. His wings drooped, and he slouched.

"I'm afraid so," he murmured. Silence filled the storehouse for few heartbeats. Kaetarpen straightened up and spoke again.

"This is Yaetherim, a protector from South Alken Forest. He's helping us find who's responsible."

"I've met Paetobim's killers," Yaetherim remarked. Yaemetan's eyes widened and flicked over Yaetherim's right shoulder. Yaetherim gestured over his shoulder.

"Captain Kaetarpen mentioned you had some soothing balm?"

"Huh? Oh, of course."

Yaemetan strode off and returned with a jar. Kaetarpen nodded.

"Thank you, Quartermaster. Yaetherim, I'm afraid I must leave you for the moment. You should be able to sort yourself out."

Yaetherim suppressed a smirk.

"Thanks, Captain Kaetarpen."

Kaetarpen departed. Yaetherim opened the balm. A pungent odour hit his nose. Not as eye watering as Naeviol's version back home. Like most Fairic garments, his shirt had two buttons at the bottom-rear. He undid the top one. Both sides of the slit around his wings fell loose. With one hand, Yaetherim took some balm and applied it to the base of his wings. He felt Yaemetan's gaze upon him. It wasn't difficult to guess what the quartermaster wanted to ask.

"Aye, they were the ones who wounded me," Yaetherim explained, "eight months ago."

Yaemetan gaped at him.

"Eight months? But did you report it to the Rychillans?"

"Aye."

Yaetherim recalled the flimsy excuses he'd received from Veritor Jorryn.

"But they only had a spent waterkind crystal. A veritor's investigation needs more than that."

Yaetherim finished applying the balm. Already, the ache had started to fade.

"It'll have more, now," he added, "we searched Cerrane. It happened there, by the way. Found a stash of crystals and a few papers."

"What sort of papers?"

Yaetherim shrugged.

"Couldn't read the one from the first hut. Only got a fragment there. It's not Rychillan or Fairic. In the other building, it was merely a pile of letters. You know, with signatures and all that."

Yaetherim shot a glance at Yaemetan. It may have just been the fading light, but the other fairy's bark-brown skin seemed to have paled.

"Letters? Do you think they're from the killers?"

There had been a slight tremble in the quartermaster's words. Yaetherim shrugged, as though he hadn't noticed.

"Perhaps, or it could be two separate lots. You wouldn't know anything about that?"

Yaemetan jumped. His wings twitched. He tugged on the bottom of his tunic.

"Why would I?"

He'd almost said that normally. But his voice had definitely shaken this time. Yaetherim peered at Yaemetan. Sweat soaked the other fairy's brow. Could be from the humidity.

"I was a protector, before encountering those Rychillans. Our quartermaster knew all the gossip. Just thought it might be the same here."

"Oh. Oh, that. No, I've heard nothing."

"It may not involve the letters. But whoever left them there could have seen the killers. I mean, Cerrane is small."

Yaetherim handed the jar back to Yaemetan.

"Thank you."

Yaemetan took the container and strode off quicker than before. Yaetherim waited for him to return.

"Is there anything else?" Yaemetan asked.

"Nay," Yaetherim replied. He spun and walked out of the storehouse. He found Kaetarpen on one of the landing platforms, discussing patrol arrangements with the other protectors. When finished, Kaetarpen stepped over to Yaetherim.

"I gave him a chance. He denied it."

"Did you believe him?"

Yaetherim scoffed.

"Would you trust a poacher with his hands full? He's a terrible liar. You'll want to have him watched."

"I see."

Kaetarpen turned and beckoned over the fairies to whom he'd been talking. As Kaetarpen issued additional orders, Yaetherim headed for the visitor's hut they had given him. It had been a tiring day.

He strolled along the unfamiliar walkways. Only lanterns and patches of moonlight lit the way now. He found himself lost in thoughts. Someone considered that fragment of paper worth killing for. They'd taken a lot of risks to hide it, too.

A voice drifted through the air, little more than a whisper.

"Excuse me, are you Yaetherim?"

Yaetherim stopped and turned. One hand dropped to his belt, to draw a dagger no longer there. A fairy stood halfway up the walkway behind him. Her face glistened in the lamplight. At least, what was visible through her dishevelled, charcoal-black hair. Bags sat under her eyes. Eyes he'd seen

45

crying earlier. Yaetherim relaxed his wings. He met her gaze.

"Aye, that's me. You must be Taeperra?"

She nodded.

"Aye. I, ah, can we talk?"

"Of course," Yaetherim replied. She joined him on the platform.

"Kaetarpen told me what you did for Tobi. I want to say thank you."

Yaetherim blinked.

"You don't owe me anything, if that is what you're thinking."

Taeperra shook her head. When she spoke again, her voice trembled.

"I heard you talking at the chapel."

"Was that you watching by the door?"

"Aye, my mind swarmed with questions. I went to pray to Galarus. What you said about that veritor…"

Yaetherim's heart sank. He had spotted someone waiting outside, yet had still allowed his anger to best him.

"It wasn't the first time I'd had that conversation, but I am tired of it," Yaetherim confessed.

"Galarus creates each of us with a purpose," Taeperra said, her voice trembling. "That's what the priests say."

A tear rolled down from her eye and joined the others on her cheek.

"But I am struggling to find the purpose in my brother's murder."

"It's not anybody's purpose to be murdered," Yaetherim replied. Taeperra sighed. Her wings flopped. She sagged on the platform's railing, like palm fronds during a storm. But it was grief that weighed her down, not rainwater. Yaetherim had seen his brother in a similar state eight months ago.

He closed his eyes and thought back, seeking anything that could bring her comfort. Memories flicked through his mind. The ladder. Two holes under rocks, one full, one empty. Paetobim bleeding on the shoreline. His own actions in Oato Clearing. His eyes snapped open a moment later.

"Paetobim could swim, couldn't he? That's the only way it makes sense."

"Aye, Tobi enjoys, um, enjoyed swimming. There are pure springs near the middle of the island. He often went there."

A tear broke free and ran down her left cheek.

46

"Then I think he scared those Rychillans off," Yaetherim said. Taeperra blinked.

"What? You, you know how he died?" she asked, her eyes wide.

"Some things in Cerrane told the tale. Would it help you to hear it?"

Taeperra took a deep breath and glanced into the forest.

"Aye," she breathed. Yaetherim explained what they'd found earlier.

"I think your brother noticed the boat and ladder when on patrol. As a diligent protector, he investigated. The Rychillans saw him arrive and fled like cowards."

Yaetherim paused. This next part would be painful.

"Go on," Taeperra whispered. Another tear rolled down her cheek.

"When they realised they wouldn't lose Paetobim, they lashed out. He fell into the water. Managed to get to shore. That's where we found him."

Taeperra reached up and wiped her eye.

"So he died protecting us."

Her lips twitched upwards for a heartbeat.

"I can see how that fits together. But you worked the other way around. From clues to an explanation."

"Well, I was a protector."

"So was Tobi, but he never mentioned such a manner of thinking."

Her gaze flicked over to Yaetherim's wings. When she spoke, her voice carried an undergrowth of disappointment.

"Perhaps that's why you survived, then. Galarus had another purpose for you, mayhap. To put things together like that."

She'd spoken softly, but Yaetherim snapped his reply.

"Then he could've come up with a less painful method."

A sharp movement caught Yaetherim's eye. His head flicked around. Two protectors stood on a platform, a couple of trees away. Their hands flew, conversing in signed Fairic. No, arguing in that language.

"How did you lose Yaemetan? The captain told you to watch him like a poacher."

"He ordered **us** to follow him."

Yaetherim's eyes narrowed. They'd been following Yaemetan. So he should be nearby. Yaetherim's gaze drifted down. Something moved in the shadows below the platform. He leaned in for a better view.

"What's going on?" Taeperra whispered. Yaetherim raised a finger to his lips and beckoned her over. He held his hands up and signed his next words.

"Can you move one of these lantern flames? I'd like to get a discreet peek under there."

Taeperra frowned. She looked from Yaetherim to the platform. Her fingers reached out for the nearest lamp. Slowly, she curled them. The lantern's flame flickered. She raised her hand. The fire moved with it, as though held on a stick. Once clear of the lantern, Taeperra brought it down and across.

Yaetherim leaned in closer. Yaemetan hung beneath the platform, his arms wrapped around the beams supporting it. So, he was trying to get away. Yaetherim smirked. That seed he'd planted had borne fruit. Now to harvest it. He got Taeperra's attention and signed again.

"Thank you, I've seen what I need. Can you please tell those protectors Yaemetan is beneath the platform? Make sure he hears you."

"What?"

"Don't mention I'm here."

Taeperra tilted her head, then nodded. After returning the flame to its lantern, she walked over to the two protectors. Yaetherim stepped back. He flexed his wings, his usual pre-flight check. His eyes remained on Yaemetan.

"Are you looking for Yaemetan?" Taeperra asked.

"Aye, did you see where he went?"

"He's hanging under this platform. We-I spotted him from over there."

A thunk punctuated her words. From under the platform came a flurry of movement. Yaemetan pushed himself off the tree trunk. He soared upwards. The protectors shouted. Yaetherim banked around after the fleeing Yaemetan. Each beat of his wings shoved him forward. He couldn't let the other fairy lose him.

Darkness loomed, broken by patches of moonlight. A shadow flitted across one. Branches whipped by. Some scratched Yaetherim. Ahead lay only shadows. This wouldn't work. He'd only get injured, and Yaemetan would escape.

Yaetherim swooped up through the next gap in the forest canopy. Leaves brushed him. He kept climbing. Moonlight bathed the treetops below him. It reflected off the surrounding water. Across the bay, a few clusters of flames flickered within the trees. Fairy villages, including Riala Village. Yaetherim turned right, towards the brighter orange lights of Alkentoft. He glanced down.

There.

Off the shore of the island, something flew on a beeline toward the town. Yaetherim couldn't make out the details. But it appeared the same size and shape as a fairy. Yaetherim's heart jumped. With a flick of his wings, Yaetherim adjusted course. Maintaining his altitude, he matched the other fairy's speed. That wasn't a problem. Despite his injuries, Yaetherim remained a fast flyer.

They approached the south side of Alkentoft. Not anywhere notable. Just one of the town's cobblestone streets, its end marked by a street lamp at the edge of the water. The other fairy landed upon the lamppost and looked back. As suspected, it was Yaemetan. Yaetherim overshot and touched down on top of the nearest house. He ducked behind its call lantern. His heart raced and wings twitched. Only now did his thoughts catch up with the situation. He had merely meant to push Yaemetan into confessing. Now here he was, alone. No other protectors around like in Cerrane. Some deep breaths steadied his nerves. This could lead him to his attackers. He'd have to be careful.

Yaetherim peered round the call lantern. Yaemetan took off. Yaetherim pursued a heartbeat later. He flew higher than the other fairy and behind. Keeping in his blind spot, as though tracking a poacher.

They followed the street for its entire length. It ended at a T-junction at the other end of the town. Yaemetan turned left. Yaetherim did likewise. He swung wide above the houses on the far side of the intersection. Yaemetan flew low over the verandah roofs. Any lower and he could have walked along the corrugated iron below him. To the right, a creek marked the border between cleared land and forest. Fences between each building divided the backyards. Behind the furthest house stood a small brick shed. A chimney emerged from the roof, like a tree pushing through the canopy. That made it the workshop of a potter, blacksmith or armourer.

Yaetherim allowed himself a slight smile. Kaetarpen's earlier words came back to him. Yaemetan did indeed have an arrangement with an armourer in Alkentoft. Yaetherim landed atop the house in front of the workshop.

A knock sounded out from below. Yaetherim crept to the edge of the roof. He lay flat, his wings pressed to the tiles. Only his eyes poked over the side. He flinched as the window below him flew open. Yaemetan entered. The wooden shutters slammed closed. Voices spoke behind them, too muffled to hear. Magic tingled over Yaetherim's skin. With a movement spell, he slowly opened one shutter. Not too wide. Just enough to listen in. Two voices drifted up, both worried.

"You're not supposed to come here, Meti."

"It's an emergency. They've discovered us."

"What? How?"

Yaemetan told his lover what had happened. Silence fell once he'd finished.

"Dinsec," he said, "you haven't seen any other Rychillans around when you've visited, have you?"

A sigh came in reply.

"No, but, well, I think someone's found the boat. I've noticed it disturbed and even wet when I have not yet launched it."

Yaetherim nodded to himself. So the killers had borrowed Dinsec's method of sneaking to Cerrane. Yaemetan hadn't considered that possibility, if the shock in his voice was anything to go by.

"Someone else is using it?"

"I hoped not, then I discovered this."

Floorboards creaked. Yaetherim stretched out further.

"What? But you're not a waterkind," Yaemetan said.

That settled it. Yaetherim needed to see what was happening. Slowly, to avoid making a sound, Yaetherim climbed down off the roof. Fortunately, this was an older building. No groundkind magic had fused the bricks together. Instead, mortar gaps between them provided plenty of handholds. The rough edges cut into his skin. It was worth it. This was the best lead he'd had in eight months.

Yaetherim stepped out onto the verandah roof and turned around. He checked his crystal. It had more than enough energy left. He raised his hand and cast a simple spell. This needed delicacy. Like approaching an injured bird.

"Where did you find that?" Yaemetan asked.

"In the boat, before our last tryst."

"What? You didn't mention that."

"I did not want to worry you, Meti."

Yaetherim finished casting. He stepped up to the gap between the shutters. He leaned over and balanced with one palm on the bricks. It wasn't the best angle. Aye, he could see a Rychillan arm. The terax marks gave that away. But it held something out of sight. He shifted his position to get a better view.

His hand slipped.

A gasp escaped him. His other palm slapped against the shutter. Yaetherim pushed himself back onto his feet. He stabilised himself with his wings. The window banged shut.

"Meti, someone's outside!"

Yaetherim's wings flicked out. No time for pre-flight checks. He had to get away now. He launched himself into the air. Something slammed into him. Pain shot through his body. He tumbled. His hands scrabbled for grip on the corrugated iron. He flapped fiercely. For a moment, he regained control. Then he ran out of roof.

He swung his legs down. Cobblestones smashed into him. He staggered forward a couple of steps. A salty liquid seeped into his mouth. Blood, but not too much of it.

A bang sounded out. Yaetherim spun around. Yaemetan swooped through the now-open door of the house. Behind him strode a Rychillan woman. Moonlight glinted off the dagger in her hand. Yaetherim didn't wait to see more.

He turned and ran, his feet slapping on the cobblestones. One, two, three steps, then he took flight. With hard, rapid flaps of his wings, he climbed.

His heartbeat pounded in his ears.

"Stop, we only want to talk!"

Yaetherim glanced backward. Yaemetan flew behind, trying to catch up. Further back, the Rychillan woman stood watching.

"I didn't know Rychillans needed a dagger to talk!"

Yaetherim veered left and swooped down into the next street. A bus approached, the beat of its engine growing louder. Yaetherim banked into its path. Steam threatened to surround him. His hand shot out. Magic crackled along it. The tethering spell latched onto the vehicle's wooden body. It jerked Yaetherim around. He pulled himself in as though climbing a vine. Several fairy-size handles ran across the top of the vehicle. Yaetherim grabbed the nearest one and held on.

A glance back showed no sign of Yaemetan. Yaetherim took a deep breath. His heart raced. He'd expected a rose bush and got kudzu. But he could still harvest something from this. He would need to talk to Yaemetan and Dinsec. He would just have to prepare first. Fortunately, he had some friends in Alkentoft. He knew where he could lie low.

4

Semi-Official Inquiries

D
awn the next morning found Tenora travelling north from Alkentoft, heading for one of the farms surrounding the town. Once again, the roof was down on her yellow roadster. Wind shoved at her driving goggles and blew her hair over the back of the seat. Fields and forest passed by, a tapestry of nature and crops, backed by the ocean and the distant Druhlash mountains. Farm driveways punctuated the side of the road, marked with signposts bearing the names of the owners.

Before long, she spotted one that read 'Chealey'. Her hands moved without thought and guided the car along the driveway. At the end, a mustard-yellow four-door sedan stood beside the farmhouse. A young Rychillan man leaned against it, reading. Steel trim and oversized but elegant mudguards marked it as an older vehicle, yet the lack of blemishes or rust showed it to be well-maintained.

Tenora parked next to it, disengaged the runes, and climbed out. She tossed her goggles onto the passenger seat of her car. The young man lay his book aside. His terax mirrored Tenora's own, with marks showing he'd been apprenticed straight out of school.

"Good morning. I take it you're Mechanic Jotol?"

"That's right. Arch-Mechanic Tenora?"

She nodded and glanced towards the barn at the rear of the farmhouse. Jotol followed her gaze.

"It's in there, ma'am. I've already spoken to Farmer Tuson. He's milking the cows in the back paddock at the moment. So we've time to examine the tractor."

Tenora tucked a strand of hair behind her ear. She walked to the front of her car and pulled a small toolbox from the boot. A familiar clank came as she hefted it. They headed for the barn. Jotol's gaze flicked from the building to Tenora and back again. With her free hand, she brushed her overalls and the shirt under them.

"Did I pick up some bugs on the drive?"

While she enjoyed the wind through her hair, such driving carried risks.

"No," Jotol replied. "But I've heard Arch-Mechanic Thirer mention you a few times. You're not quite what I expected."

"Should I be older?" Tenora asked. She stifled a sigh. Embers of that doubt burned within some of her colleagues. Despite the rules of the mechanic's guild stating promotion was to be based on skill and merit.

"Not really," Jotol replied. "I only noticed you'd broken your nose at some point. He described you as careful."

"It was a workshop accident during my apprenticeship. That's why I'm cautious now."

They reached the barn, and Jotol pushed the doors open. Straw and dirt lay scattered over the stone floor, highlighted in a few spots by the early morning light from the windows. To the left, shelves held old but well-maintained farm implements. At the rear, facing them, sat a tractor. Grime and scrapes covered its body, a testament to years of hard work.

Tenora didn't miss a step as she strode towards it. It had been a while since she'd last inspected such a vehicle. They did not get many tractors in the middle of town. But she had worked on the ones at her parents' farm. Only two key differences separated them from cars. They had their engines at the front and gearboxes set up for strength instead of speed.

"I understand it blew out a cylinder?"

Jotol nodded. He gestured to a panel on the bottom-left of the tractor. Unlike the rest of the vehicle, this bodywork bore no blemishes.

"Ripped a hole right through that, it did."

Tenora stepped around beside the tractor. After tying her hair into a ponytail with string, she tucked it into the back of her overalls. With that done, she needed to take another safety precaution. Two screw caps protruded from the top of the engine, just ahead of the steering wheel. Beneath one, a firekind crystal sat in a small compartment. The other held a waterkind crystal. Tenora removed both crystals and lay them on the ground next to her toolbox. With the engine now safe, she could work on it.

She had it open moments later. As expected, its layout matched what she knew from car engines. A rune panel beneath the crystal compartments, a boiler in front of that atop the firebox, and a steam pipe leading to the cylinders. At the rear, several rods connected control runes to levers in the dashboard. Nothing appeared out of place. She'd have to examine it end-to-end.

"Have you found anything amiss, ma'am?" Jotol asked.

"Not yet," Tenora replied, and she leaned into the engine compartment. The rune panel bore no signs of damage or age. Only five slight scratches marred it, the result of spent crystals being changed out. She tapped it and glanced back at Jotol.

"Arch-Mechanic Thirer said you swapped this out. Do you still have the original one?"

"I'm afraid not. But there wasn't any difference between them. Just replaced it as a precaution."

Tenora grabbed a screwdriver and removed the side of the firebox, laying the steel sheet aside. Firebricks lined the base. Whilst standard, to retain heat, these brought a frown to her brow. Those in the middle lacked charring and were of uniform colour. She leaned in and twisted her head up towards the boiler. Discolouration marred its underside, much more so than from regular use.

"How damaged were the firebricks when you found them?"

"Quite a few of them were cracked. I replaced them as a precaution."

Tenora nodded. A suspicion had already taken root amongst her thoughts. But she wouldn't water it yet. Not until she'd completed her examination. From the boiler, she moved along the pipe to the three cylinders connected to the gearbox via the driveshaft. She found naught unusual here, nor on the valves used to regulate the engine's timing. Only some wear and tear, as expected. It seemed there was nothing amiss. But somehow, this engine had caused a surge of steam powerful enough to rip a steel cylinder block wide open.

A second examination proved as fruitless. She ran her left hand along the side of her head, as though tucking aside an errant strand of hair.

"How long ago did this accident happen?" she asked.

"One week and a couple of days."

"Before that, when did you last work on this tractor?"

Jotol shrugged and glanced down.

"About ten weeks ago, just regular servicing. Saw nothing unusual then, either."

"And it hasn't played up again?"

"No."

Tenora pursed her lips. Some temporary anomaly may have caused that surge while leaving no trace. Perhaps something in the magic itself. Even mages, with all their studies, didn't know everything about these elemental forces they'd harnessed. But Tenora knew one thing for certain. She wouldn't find any answers here.

After reassembling the tractor, she thanked Jotol for his help and returned to her car. On the drive to Alkentoft, her thoughts remained with that vehicle. A surge of heat would account for the excess steam and firebox damage. It also tallied with what she'd seen yesterday morning, when that other car's fire had flared back into life. But that was merely speculation on her part. Perhaps she would find something more substantial at Arch-Mechanic Warrett's workshop. If he spoke to her, that is. Best to get that over and done with.

She reached Warrett's shop and parked outside. It was still quite early, and the aroma of freshly baked bread filled the air. Messenger fairies flew about, delivering newspapers and the morning mail. A few Rychillans strode along the footpath. The beat of an engine drifted over from another street. Probably a farm lorry, going by the time and pitch of it.

Tenora climbed out of her car and walked to the workshop. Her knocks echoed on the large barn-like doors. No sound came in reply.

"What are you doing here?" demanded a voice from behind her. She spun around. Arch-Mechanic Warrett stood between her and her vehicle, his arms folded. A familiar frown creased his brow, his usual expression when talking to her. Tenora stepped away from the door. She twisted her ring so that the crystal faced her palm, and curled her fingers. Triggered by the extra contact, firekind energy tickled her skin. Better to have it ready and not need it than vice versa.

"I wanted to talk to you," Tenora said.

"About what?"

"Farmer Polren's lorry."

Warrett's frown deepened.

"Is this an official inquiry?"

"No, but I think it's connected to that runaway car yesterday."

Warrett opened and closed his mouth twice, almost as if gathering his words.

"I saw the newspaper. I'm surprised a cautious mechanic like you didn't just try shutting the engine down," he snarked. Tenora blinked and flicked a lock of hair back.

"What makes you think that? We disengaged the runes and popped the safety valve. Then I put out the fire. It reignited moments later."

Warrett's eyes narrowed.

"Without an ignition rune engaged? I find that hard to believe."

Tenora's right hand shot eastward, toward the harbour.

"If you read the newspaper, then you know how it ended."

"Yes, it bounced off a trade ship. You got the driver and passengers out, I'll give you that. But it was rather reckless."

Tenora took a step towards Warrett. It was rich of him to call her that, when he'd claimed the opposite almost every time they spoke. But she replied in a calm, professional tone. The one she reserved for talking to upset clients.

"Am I cautious or reckless, Arch-Mechanic Warrett? You've said the former enough times, even just now. And whenever I've put forward a motion at the guild meetings."

Her gaze met his and didn't waver. She'd often suspected he used that as an excuse to attack her. Caution was hardly a bad thing, especially when the lives of others rode on your doing a good job.

"You've got no official standing," Warrett said, "but I'll tell you, anyway. We did not find anything amiss with Farmer Polren's lorry."

He stepped aside and pointed towards Tenora's car.

"Now please leave."

Tenora did so. She let out a sigh. That could have gone better. But it could have gone worse, too.

She leaned over the roadster and put up the roof. It slid up without a hitch. A sharp click sounded out, but Tenora checked it had latched into place, anyway. With that done, she climbed in and fired up the engine. While it built up steam, Tenora smoked a cigarette. As the wisps of smoke drifted upwards, she considered what had been a fruitless morning. The image of three frightened faces trapped inside the runaway car came to mind. Just that alone brought a cold sweat to her brow. She pursed her lips. Everything happened for a reason, however obscure.

Tenora leaned forward. She could trust Jotol and Warrett, despite the latter's manner. They were still rynil, like Tenora and most other Rychillans. Their teraxes showed that. So, assuming they weren't mistaken, whatever had caused these malfunctions had vanished shortly afterwards. She'd need to get to a malfunctioning vehicle just as quickly. Doing so would require a bit of authority. Which, as Warrett had pointed out, she didn't have.

Tenora took a drag on her cigarette. These breakdowns could present a threat to the peace of the kingdom. All Rychillan vehicles, from cars to riverboats to airships, relied on rune-powered steam engines. She checked her pocket watch. Her gaze lingered on the gears behind a circular cutout in the face. They'd never played up, nor missed a beat when wound. Driven by a spring, they simply did their job with no runes or crystals to worry about.

A hiss sounded from the engine. Tenora flipped the timepiece shut and pocketed it. 'Twas just after the eighth hour. Karis had asked her to visit around the ninth. A short drive brought Tenora to the town hall. After having breakfast at a nearby bakery, she headed to her appointment. After a brief conversation at reception, she was sent straight up. Two flights of stairs later, Tenora emerged into a corridor. Oak panels lined it, punctuated by doors on either side. She stopped halfway along, immediately before the staircase to the governor's office. Three brass plates screwed to the door on her left displayed the names of Alkentoft's veritors.

Voices drifted out from within that room. While not a heated discussion, Tenora couldn't help but overhear them. One belonged to Karis, the other she didn't recognise.

"... you are not the only person to investigate multiple cases at once. A good veritor knows how to manage what time they have."

"Well, yes, but these thefts... the merchants have been quite insistent."

"Yet you attach more importance to them than this assault. An attempt to end someone's life, and you prioritise the theft of goods and kerlum. I am starting to doubt my decision to endorse your promotion to veritor, Jorryn Lorem. It has been 320 days since then. For over 250 of them, you have let this case languish."

Tenora paused, her hand halfway to the door. Karis hadn't raised her voice, yet her words had been as pointed and cutting as a dagger. No wonder they called her the steel veritor. Tenora shook her head a moment later. Although unintentional, she shouldn't eavesdrop like this. With three quick flicks of her wrist, she knocked. Behind it, Jorryn fell silent mid-protestation.

"Come in," Karis said. Tenora did so. She found herself surrounded by bookshelves and the faint aroma of coffee. Opposite the door, the shelves met a large window. It provided a view over the town to the ocean. Most of the buildings didn't reach this height. Only the mail towers and airship terminal stood taller.

A tidy desk stood in front of the window. Karis sat behind it, her back to the glass. To Tenora's left, several semi-organised stacks of paper covered the desk occupied by a young veritor. Another desk completed the triangle. Both veritors looked over. Tenora cleared her throat. Karis got to her feet.

"I'm Arch-Mechanic Tenora Perskel. You asked me to report to you at the ninth hour, Veritor Karis. About that incident in the harbour yesterday."

For a moment, Tenora found herself on the wrong end of a steely stare.

"We have completed our inquiries," Karis said, "and while you caused damage, it is nothing irreparable. Furthermore, you saved three lives, and there is no record of your involvement in any past crimes. I will not be pressing any charges against you."

Tenora's shoulders slumped, and she smiled.

"Thank you, Veritor Karis."

"However, we may reconsider this should you be involved in any such incidents in the future."

"I understand, Veritor Karis."

Karis nodded, then sat down. She pulled a notepad from the nearest stack and flicked through it before putting it down. Her eyes met Tenora's again, and she gestured to the chair in front of her desk.

"Please sit. You mentioned other malfunctions yesterday?"

Tenora took the seat.

"Yes, and I've been looking into them."

Karis looked up. Her left hand fiddled with the brooch pinned below her shoulder.

"I see. What have you found?"

Tenora glanced down and rubbed the side of her neck.

"Not much so far," she admitted, and she recounted what had happened that morning. Both veritors listened, and Karis took notes.

"... so I think that whatever's causing this may be some sort of temporary effect."

"Is such a thing likely?" Karis asked. Tenora pulled her watch out and held it up. Sunlight from the window highlighted the scratches and dents on its case.

"Mechanisms work predictably. A gear is a gear, that remains constant. Take this pocket watch, for example. I know that the cogs within will advance one step every second. That hasn't changed since the day I bought it, despite the knocks it's picked up in my workshop."

Karis nodded.

"Yet steam engines draw on magic to power them," Tenora continued, "and that is a bit more nebulous. Some unknown factor may be behind this."

"What sort of factor?"

That question had come from Jorryn. Both Karis and Tenora shot him looks.

"Engines rely on runes to regulate firekind and waterkind energy. Sudden changes of these elements caused these malfunctions. It could be worth consulting a mage," Tenora explained.

"Is there any possibility these are due to a mechanical fault?" Karis asked. Tenora paused and considered the question. Both of the vehicles she'd inquired about this morning had been repaired several days earlier.

"I can't say for certain," she replied. "We weren't able to salvage the car from the harbour."

"What happened?" Jorryn asked. Tenora explained about the miscommunication with the Brial. She turned to Karis when finished.

"I must see one of these cars while it's playing up, or as quickly as possible afterwards. May I please have your aid with this, Veritor Karis?"

"What help do you need?"

"If the town guard could send any malfunctioning vehicles to my workshop, as soon as they identify them, that should provide the opportunity I seek."

Karis nodded.

"I shall give the order. Please keep me informed of what you find."

"Of course," Tenora replied. With that, she bade them farewell and departed. Hopefully, this approach would bear fruit.

* * *

A short while later, Tenora pulled herself out from under a roadster in her workshop. She took care not to graze the bodywork with the wrench in her hand. Once steady, she turned and offered her free hand to the Apprentice-Mechanic she'd been teaching. He slid out from under the car, and she helped him to his feet.

"The key to valve timing is-"

A shrill whistle pierced the air. Her spanner slipped from her fingers. She broke into a run before it hit the ground. Her heart raced. Each breath came fast and shallow. That tone, that warble, meant only one thing. A boiler had reached its limit.

A loud pop greeted Tenora outside her workshop. The whistling stopped. She cursed and spun on her heel. A safety valve had just popped. Too much steam. Behind her, another set of footsteps slapped the cobblestones. Ahead, a sedan approached. Steam shot up from the engine, from the hole left by the safety valve. Tenora's right hand flicked up, palm forward.

"Stop! You need to get out, NOW!"

She twisted her ring and closed her hand. Firekind energy skittered over her skin. The car braked. Tenora didn't wait. An extinguishing spell leapt from her lips.

"Chief?"

Somath stood just behind her. She nodded to the waterkind crystal hanging from his necklace.

"We have to cool that car's boiler before it explodes."

"Understood."

The sedan stopped. Its driver jumped out. He ran to Tenora.

"What happened?" she asked.

"It started playing up. A town guard patrol ordered me to take it to Arch-Mechanic Tenora Perskel."

Tenora nodded.

"That's me."

A flash of maroon caught Tenora's eye. Two guard constables joined them.

"Ma'am, sirs, you need to step back."

Tenora shook her head.

"That engine will explode if we stop casting."

A heartbeat later, the flow of magic stopped. She flicked her fingers out. A clear crystal lay in her ring. She swore. Her hand jumped from pocket to pocket, searching for a spare. Neither the guard constables nor the driver could help. Two wore airkind crystals, and the other constable a groundkind one.

"Chief, I don't think I can hold it much longer," Somath said. Beside him, the airkind guard cast a spell of his own. The air between them and the car turned opaque. Just a simple walling spell, but it'd do the trick. It had to. The groundkind constable pointed at the driver's crystal.

"Cast up a wall over the other side, quick!"

The driver did so. A dome of solid air surrounded the car. Tenora cupped her hands around her mouth.

"Take cover! Take cover!" she called and repeated the warning in Fairic. Fairies and Rychillans dived aside. The groundkind constable tapped her on the shoulder.

"That should confine it. You can stand down now."

Somath glanced at Tenora. She nodded. He lowered his hand and stepped back.

"Chief, we'd better-"

A boom interrupted him. The car's rear jumped. Flames and water blasted out. Shards of wood and steel flew off in all directions. Most of them slammed into the air walls. Some got through. A few bounced off nearby cars, others shattered windows.

One fragment shot towards Tenora. She shoved Somath aside and dived clear. It whooshed past her left ear. Water splashed onto her shoulder. Her head snapped around. The debris hit the street and skittered along the cobblestones.

Tenora jumped to her feet. The shouts of confused bystanders filled the air. Fairies and Rychillans emerged from the cover they'd sought. Two bled from injuries, from flying fragments. Tenora slumped and took a step back. Despite the explosion, nobody had been killed.

"It's alright, Chief," Somath said from behind her. "A constable's gone to get a healer."

Tenora nodded. She turned to the driver and the remaining guard.

"Could you please stop casting the walls? I'd like to examine that car."

They just stared at her. Tenora blinked. She glanced down at her overalls. Somath stepped forward and put his hand on her right upper arm.

"Tenora."

She looked up. Somath seldom called her that. Worry crossed his face.

"Is something amiss?" Tenora asked.

"You're injured."

"What?"

Tenora raised her left hand to her shoulder. When she took it away, she found it covered in red blood. Human blood. Her blood. She felt the side of her head. There it was. A nick on the outside of her ear, about the size of a single kerlo coin. She gritted her teeth. It wasn't her worst injury.

"It can wait. It's just a slight cut."

Somath shot her a doubtful look. Tenora pulled a clean rag from the front pocket of her overalls. She tore off a piece. With a few quick motions, she untied the string holding her ponytail. Several seconds later, she had the impromptu bandage tied over her injured ear.

"That should hold it," she said. Somath chuckled, and Tenora turned back to the wrecked car. She needed to examine it now. Whatever had caused the explosion may have already vanished.

The walls of air faded away. Twisted metal and splinters lay scattered. Only some larger components remained recognisable. Each wheel pointed in a different direction. A chill went through Tenora and she shuddered. It was one thing to know the power steam could provide. 'Twas another to see it demonstrated in such a violent manner.

She leaned down; her gaze flicking from piece to piece. She ignored the body panels. The engine parts should hold the answer. A piston lay within arm's reach. She crouched next to it. A brief examination revealed just normal wear and tear, along with damage from the explosion itself.

A short distance away, a wood board rested on the cobblestones. It had once been this engine's rune panel. Half of it, anyway. Its size and shape showed that. She picked it up, and a frown crossed her brow. An intricate design covered the board, with lines crossing each other and intertwined. Those were not runes. She turned and beckoned Somath and the constable over.

"Did you find something, Chief?"

She handed Somath the panel.

"Do those look like runes to you?"

"No," Somath replied after a moment's examination. Tenora spoke to the guard constable.

"Could you please tell Veritor Karis about this? She's expecting to hear from me."

He nodded.

"Certainly, Arch-Mechanic...?"

"Tenora, Tenora Perskel."

The constable strode off. Somath handed the half-panel back to Tenora. She gestured at the strewn debris.

"Can you please find the rest of this?"

Somath nodded and went to do so. Tenora examined the board again and ran her finger over the engraving. They didn't match any rune sequence she'd seen. Perhaps rejoining the other half would clarify things. But one thing was already quite clear.

Tenora pulled out a cigarette. With her hands shaking, she placed it in her mouth. After two attempts, she lit it. Yet the familiar sensation did little to quell her worries. Someone must have made that rune panel and swapped it with the original. Not the sort of thing that happens by accident.

5

Answers in the Forest

Yaetherim's eyes snapped open. He sprang to his feet. A hand reached for the crystal on his belt. The other closed around empty air where his dagger would have been. He'd gone three steps before thought caught up with instinct. He was in a fairy room at Cropper's Crony, one of the most reputable inns in Alkentoft. A place of safety. No Rychillans loomed over him. Something had just exploded instead.

Yaetherim's eyes widened. He hadn't dreamt the blast that had woken him. Shouts and babble from outside confirmed that. He strode to the window and flung it open. No signs of damage greeted him. Everyone on the footpath below looked away from the inn. A few pointed in the same direction. That explosion had happened on another street. It didn't pose a threat to him.

Dinsec and Yaemetan, however, could do so. Yaetherim thought back to last night. He'd been busy fleeing for his life and all that. But now, the significance dawned upon him. Dinsec had found something unexpected in her boat. She'd mentioned that before he had given his presence away. So she hadn't said that for his benefit. Somehow, the killers had discovered Dinsec's skiff and borrowed it.

Yaetherim cracked his knuckles. While reasonable, it remained mere supposition. He'd need to know for sure. Could be risky, considering the events of the previous evening. An idea came to him. A smirk twisted the

66

right side of his lip. Perhaps it wouldn't be too perilous after all.

A pencil and notepad lay on the bedside table. Yaetherim sat on the edge of the bed and wrote for several hundred heartbeats. When finished, he had a detailed note to Kaetarpen. Some specifics stayed secret, for now. Such discretion should be worth a large favour.

Yaetherim's stomach growled. He put the letter aside. It could wait for a few minutes. He exited the room and locked it behind him. A brief walk brought him to the spiral staircase at the end of the corridor. Yaetherim descended it and emerged in an alcove set high in the wall of the ground level.

An array of appetising aromas filled the air. Below, tables and couches covered the floor like stones in a clearing. Two billiard tables stood on the far side of the room, unused. Too early in the morning for that. Fairies and humans, both Rychillan and Druhlac, occupied most of the furniture. But neither Dinsec nor Yaemetan sat amongst them. Yaetherim smirked. He had indeed given them the slip last night.

Yaetherim spread his wings and glided down to the bar. Behind it stood a familiar Rychillan man. He wore a brown tunic, like the other staff. But the gold edging on it marked him as one of the inn's two owners. Yaetherim landed and found himself on the receiving end of a warm smile.

"Yaetherim? I didn't know you were here. Just your usual?"

"Aye, please Rynroth. Could you turn on the call lantern? I've got to send a letter."

Rynroth nodded towards a nearby table. He spoke as though indulging in a private joke.

"That won't be needed. Naeliya had to stay overnight again."

Yaetherim turned and spotted a mop of dishevelled red hair with a friend beneath it. He'd usually seen that face across mugs of beer, on his previous visits. Most of them were hers. But he had never seen Naeliya with such a pallor before. He flew in for a closer view. Her skin appeared almost grey, instead of the usual blue of a waterkind fairy. She sat slumped forward, cross-legged, atop the table. Her head rested on one hand. With the other, she picked at the slice of toasted banana loaf before her. She didn't look up when Yaetherim landed beside her.

"I hope the food's not that bad. I mean, it's my recipe," he joked.

"Your recipe?"

Blue eyes met his own. They narrowed for a moment, then shot open. She blinked and her wings twitched. Perhaps she'd forgotten how he paid for his accommodation here. Cooking was just a pastime for him. But Rynroth and Chef Tarlon had found Yaetherim's knowledge in that area valuable. He'd mentioned this to Naeliya on his last visit, but she had been quite drunk by then.

"Yaetherim? I didn't... were we drinking together yesterday? I usually recall who joins me."

"Nay, we weren't. I got here late, from Verbore Island."

Yaetherim peered closely at Naeliya. A concerned frown creased his brow.

"You sure you'd remember? Looks like you had more than usual last night."

That was saying something. Naeliya normally went through two or three human-sized beers, when drinking. Guilt flicked across her face, and she picked at her banana bread.

"Maybe, I... wait, did you say Verbore Island?"

"Aye."

Now she met his gaze. Curiosity blossomed in her eyes.

"But you're not... hold on, what brought you here? Did Veritor Jorryn make some progress with your case?"

Yaetherim sighed and pinched the bridge of his nose.

"Nay, I've an update for him. That isn't how it's supposed to work."

Naeliya's face lit up, and she smiled. Yaetherim shook his head.

"Not like that," Yaetherim added. "They've struck again. In Cerrane, another protector. He didn't survive."

Naeliya's smile vanished. Her wings shot out, and her jaw dropped. She stared at Yaetherim.

"Please tell me you jest."

"Nay," Yaetherim replied. Before he could explain, his breakfast arrived. Once the waiter had gone, Yaetherim filled Naeliya in. Bites of sauteed kudzu and cashews punctuated his recount of the previous evening. Naeliya paid attention, leaning forward over her forgotten food. Silence fell when he'd finished. Naeliya blinked twice. She murmured something, a snippet of unfamiliar Rychillan.

"It's a lot to take in," she added. Yaetherim nodded.

"Do you know who Yaemetan's lover is?" Naeliya asked.

"Aye, but that's staying between me and the trees for the moment. I'm hoping they'll reward that favour with another."

He punctuated that sentence with a wink. Naeliya raised an eyebrow and leaned in. Her gaze didn't waver.

"But you're telling me this much. Is there some way I can help?"

Yaetherim nodded. Naeliya smiled. Her wings shot up. One flicked forward and slapped the shawl on her shoulder.

"It'll be more interesting than flying around town delivering messages. What do you need me to do?"

"I need you to fly around and deliver a message to Verbore Island."

Naeliya tilted her head.

"I've never been there before. Is it for that Protector Captain you mentioned?"

"Captain Kaetarpen, aye. I have the letter upstairs."

Yaetherim finished his breakfast, then retrieved the note from his room. Naeliya departed with it. With that sorted, he headed outside. Now to get some answers.

* * *

The streets of Alkentoft slipped past the windows of Yaetherim's taxi. Although he had found his way to Cropper's Crony, he didn't know the route to Dinsec's house. So he'd harvested some local knowledge. Before long, his ride reached the street he had fled the previous night. Yaetherim had the driver drop him a few doors down.

He flew straight up and looked along the houses. A fairy stood on the roof of Dinsec's house. Despite the distance, their palm-frond hair and woven clothing betrayed his identity. Yaetherim stopped two buildings away. He hovered high and whistled. That got Yaemetan's attention. He spread his wings and bent his knees, ready to fly. Yaetherim flung his arms up. He signed rapidly.

"Stay there!"

Yaemetan froze. He held his hands up, palms forward, and let his wings droop. Yaetherim didn't take his eyes off him. With slow, deliberate motions, he conveyed his next sentence.

"Protector Captain Kaetarpen is expecting me to meet him later this morning."

"You will be there. As I said yesterday, we just want to talk," Yaemetan signed back.

"That's not the impression I got."

Yaemetan strode up to the peak of the roof. He held his hands out and slowly turned around. Then he signed again.

"You can see I'm unarmed. Could you please land? My arms are getting tired."

Yaetherim flew closer. His heart pounded. His fingers grabbed air where a dagger would be. Yaemetan did appear disarmed. But he had stayed overnight with an armourer.

Yaetherim landed on the roof next to Dinsec's and strode to the gutter. Close enough to converse while maintaining distance. Yaemetan stepped towards him.

"You'll want to stay back from the edge. It's a rough landing," Yaetherim warned.

"Sorry about that. I panicked. Didn't mean to get you with the shutter. Dinsec thought it might've been a thief."

Yaetherim folded his arms. So that's what had hit him. But Yaemetan had spoken sincerely, and there'd been a pinch of regret in his voice.

"Right. As I said, Kaetarpen is expecting to meet me later. I've also sent him a letter explaining what happened last night."

Yaemetan sighed, and he sagged.

"Understood," he muttered.

"However," Yaetherim continued, "I haven't told him who you're courting.

Nor anyone else."

"You didn't tell him that, but you mentioned what I did?"

Yaetherim scoffed.

"You couldn't have been more obvious, fleeing like that. I expected you to conjure up some excuse to visit Alkentoft this morning. Sneaking off in darkness, you may as well have written a letter of confession."

Yaemetan ran his fingers through his hair.

"I panicked."

"I'm not surprised. This is a question of murder."

Yaemetan's eyes widened, and his jaw dropped.

"We had nothing to do with that," he protested. "All we did was meet up! We just-"

Yaetherim cut him off with a wave of his hand.

"I am not interested in that. I heard you discussing the discovery of a boat?"

"Aye. Is that what you're after?"

"It would be helpful," Yaetherim replied dryly. Yaemetan took flight. A few brief flaps brought him to where Yaetherim stood. Yaetherim stepped back to keep clear air above him. Yaemetan gestured for Yaetherim to join him. The latter did so, but maintained his distance.

"I'll check she's okay with this," Yaemetan said. He flew over to the workshop. Steam drifted up from its chimney. Within it, a silhouette moved about in the orange glow spilling from the door. Yaemetan's shadow joined it, and both remained still for a few moments. Then Yaemetan emerged and gestured for Yaetherim to join them. He swooped down.

Warm air rushed over Yaetherim as he flew inside. A metallic odour, almost identical to burning dirt, assaulted his nose. Some form of fireplace sat below the chimney. Dinsec stood in front of it. Several minor burns and cuts covered her hands. Some blended in with the terax marks on her arms.

"I'll be back. Need to get something," Yaemetan explained. Before Yaetherim could reply, he flew off. Yaetherim found himself alone with Dinsec.

Yaetherim's gaze lingered upon her terax marks. He thought back, over what he'd read while recovering. Rychillans had four classes, based on trust and honesty. The arm before him only bore the mark of a rynil. It was the class in which all Rychillans started. So, she was somewhat honest. At least, she hadn't been caught doing anything dishonest.

"Meti, ah, Yaemetan mentioned you thought we might know about a murder," she said in Fairic. She turned to Yaetherim. Firelight glinted off the dagger in her right hand. Yaetherim's heart jumped. He dived left and took cover under a workbench.

"What? I won't hurt you," Dinsec said.

"Would you mind lowering the weapon, then?"

"Oh. Of course."

A soft 'clunk' followed Dinsec's words. Yaetherim poked his head out. The blade lay upon an anvil near the fireplace. Dinsec stepped back from it. With her hands raised, she turned to him. A hint of annoyance coloured her words.

"That's what I was working on. Your arrival distracted me."

Yaetherim emerged, flew up, and sat on the edge of the workbench. Dinsec glanced down.

"My trade is making weapons," she stated, "not using them."

Yaetherim flung his arms out, scars upward. Dinsec recoiled.

"Do you know a blade capable of leaving these, then?"

Dinsec examined them. A tear came to her eye.

"Clean edges," she said softly. "It must have cut deep to scar like that."

"One of them reached the bone."

Dinsec shuddered. She stepped over to a cupboard and returned a few heartbeats later. In her hand, she carried a fairy-sized dagger of classic stinger design. But unlike a traditional weapon, a translucent edge, the width of a finger, surrounded the blade's steel core.

"Is that a spent crystal blade?" Yaetherim asked. He'd heard of such, but never laid eyes upon one.

"Yes, it cuts finer than metal," Dinsec replied. Her gaze flicked from it to Yaetherim's arms. After a few looks, she shook her head.

"No. Any wounds that deep would be wider. The shape of the blade guarantees that."

"Then you know I'm not here about the weapons."

Before Yaetherim could say more, Dinsec held out the stinger. Yaetherim jumped aside. His wings flared. A dive off the workbench would give him the speed to beat Dinsec to the exit. He turned back. She'd stepped away.

"Didn't mean to startle you. I just thought this might help with your nerves."

Yaetherim looked down. Dinsec gripped the dagger by the point, offering him the handle. Yaetherim's cheeks flushed. He took the stinger and examined it. The faint green shade of the blade showed she had made it from a florakind crystal. The handle's wood inlay would act as an anchor for that element's magic. A perfect weapon for a florakind fairy like him.

It fit well in his hand. With a couple of quick movements, he felt the balance of the dagger. His heartbeat slowed. Knowing he could defend himself steadied his nerves.

"Thank you. Now, I have been working with Veritor Jorryn on this. I realise that the Accord of Reiksoft-"

Dinsec leaned in and spoke softly.

"Forget about that. I'd rather this be kept to as few people as possible, Yaetherim. What do you want to know?"

"You visited Verbore Island frequently. But you weren't the only trespasser."

"I do not expect you to understand," Dinsec muttered. She picked up the weapon she'd been working on and resumed her work.

"I don't need to," Yaetherim replied. "I just thought you might have seen the killers."

Dinsec lay the dagger on the anvil. She strode over to the tool rack in the corner.

"I suspect we have crossed paths, but not in the manner you think. On multiple occasions, I have found my boat disturbed. I suspected it to be the work of wild animals. Yet it was too consistent. Then I discovered a spent crystal in it on my last visit."

"A waterkind crystal?"

A clang rang out, metal against a stone floor. Dinsec's head snapped around.

"How did you know?" she demanded.

"It's not the first one to show up."

"It shouldn't have been surprising. That skiff uses runes to move. They're engraved on its sides. Same rune sequences we use to pump liquid through pipes, in fact. But I usually take the spent ones with me."

Yaetherim frowned.

"You mean they try to push water through it?"

"Past it. But because there's more water, the boat moves instead."

Yaetherim couldn't help but smirk in admiration. That method of movement would be silent. Little wonder the Verbore Island protectors hadn't noticed Dinsec's visits.

Before he could say more, Yaemetan returned, a spent waterkind crystal in his hands. He thudded down next to Yaetherim and staggered. Yaetherim reached out and steadied him. Yaemetan dropped the crystal. It tumbled onto the workbench. As it rocked, the scratches on it caught the light from the fire. Yaetherim picked it up. He didn't need a close look. That pattern was etched in his memory, just as it was in this crystal. He tucked it into his belt. It pressed against his stomach, but he'd suffered worse.

"Same markings as the other crystals," he observed. "Mind if I ask a few details?"

Dinsec nodded, and Yaemetan yawned. Dinsec leaned in towards Yaemetan. The latter stood up on his toes. Then he stepped back and held up his hand.

"We've got company, remember?"

Dinsec stopped and gently ran a finger down Yaemetan's wings. Yaetherim looked away. Such intimacy belonged to those involved in it.

"You should get some rest, Meti. It was a long night for you."

Yaemetan rubbed his eyes and nodded. He glided down to the floor of the workshop and walked out. Yaetherim found himself on the end of a stern look from Dinsec.

"He was rather worried when he arrived here."

"Consequences can do that," Yaetherim retorted, "and it could've been other protectors who followed him."

Dinsec glanced down.

"I take your point."

"Thank you. Now, where do you have this boat of yours hidden?"

"How familiar are you with North Alken Forest?"

Yaetherim's eyes widened.

"A little," he replied. Dinsec retrieved a notepad and pen from a drawer. After a few minutes of sketching, she ripped off the page and handed it to him. Upon it was a map. He recognised a few of the features marked on it.

"You'll find it there," Dinsec said, and she pointed to a dot on the shoreline. Yaetherim ran a finger across the paper.

"Not a bad hiding spot. But there may be protector patrols near there."

"I noticed a few, just in the last dozen weeks. Didn't think there were any fairies in that area."

Yaetherim shrugged.

"There weren't. Those patrols were from South Alken and Elori Forests, a joint stewardship. One of my good friends helped set it up. Someone needs to look after North Alken Forest, too. Anyway, have any protectors seen you?"

"It's possible. I try to remain casual. As far as they know, I'm testing weapon designs on fallen trees."

Yaetherim nodded.

"I take it you've not told anyone about this?"

"Of course not," Dinsec snapped.

"Not even when drunk? I mean, alcoholic drinks loosen one's tongue."

Dinsec shook her head.

"I don't drink often. When I do, it's only one or two at most."

Yaetherim cracked his knuckles. Several small pops sounded out. He tapped the crystal delivered by Yaemetan.

"Yet someone discovered your boat. This proves that."

A suspicion sprouted amongst his thoughts. He picked up the stinger from where he'd laid it to take the map and hefted it.

"Is there another way somebody could've spotted it? Perhaps a fairy hitched a lift on your car?"

It was a common practice. Rychillans put handles on the roofs of their vehicles for just that reason.

"No, I walk. So there's nothing parked beside the road to attract attention."

"Someone following you, then?"

"I'm careful about that, too. Usually I use one of five different routes to the edge of town. We also vary which days we meet."

Yaetherim smirked. His fingers tightened around the handle of the stinger. More precautions meant fewer chances of discovery. Either Dinsec had missed something, or she was lying to him now. He only had her word for where she'd found that crystal.

"You've been very cautious with this," he observed.

"Obviously not careful enough. If you figure out how they knew, I wouldn't mind knowing."

Yaetherim stroked his chin. His wings moved back and forth, as though trying to push his thoughts around.

"There must be some way they noticed. Do you go over after dark?"

"No, in the late afternoon. My shopkeeper usually collects my day's work at the seventeenth hour. If I'm going to visit Meti, I'll head over after that. There's enough light to navigate over. We-"

"I don't require those details," Yaetherim interrupted. Dinsec shot him a look which could have withered a sunflower.

"We only have limited time together. I need to return before dark, too."

"Did you fix up a hut in Cerrane at all? I noticed some rather new hinges on one door."

Dinsec glanced at the fire.

"Our guild's rules state specialists should remain within their area of expertise."

Yaetherim folded his arms. He'd seen fairies avoid mid-flight collisions with less evasion.

"I take it you'll be heading to the boat next?" Dinsec asked. Yaetherim nodded and thought back to his conversation with Taeperra last night.

"Aye. I think the killers panicked. They might have dropped something else in it."

Yaetherim folded the map and tucked it into his belt. He offered the stinger to Dinsec. While it had been of comfort, it wasn't his. But she didn't take it.

"You may need to defend yourself," she warned. "These people you're after are willing to kill."

Yaetherim blinked. The few kerlum in his satchel wouldn't cover this. It would be like trying to feed a village with a single apple.

"But it's, I mean, I can't pay-"

Dinsec cut him off with a wave of her hand.

"You could destroy my reputation with a few sentences, Yaetherim. Rychillans also consider relationships such as ours unsavoury. One of my best daggers is sufficient payment for your silence, I hope?"

"Well, aye. But I just wanted to trade that for information about your boat."

"I provided that to clear our names. Now, what do you say?"

Yaetherim hefted the stinger in his hand again. It fit nicely.

"Alright. I promise I won't tell any Rychillans about this," Yaetherim said. Dinsec's posture sagged, and a small smile crossed her lips.

"Thank you," she replied. She gave Yaetherim a scabbard. After putting it on his belt, Yaetherim departed.

As he flew south, he considered inviting Veritor Jorryn to join him. But that would have to be after their meeting. By then, the killers could have returned to the boat and covered their tracks. Surely there wouldn't be any harm in looking on his own.

* * *

Wind buffeted Yaetherim. Trees and bushes whipped past on either side of the road. Below him, the lorry rocked and bounced over the cobblestones. Yet Yaetherim didn't let go of the handle on its cab roof. It had come up behind him just as outside Alkentoft, and he'd hitched a ride.

Ahead, a charred palm tree stood beside the thoroughfare. It marked the boundary between North and South Alken Forests, and was one landmark on Dinsec's map. Yaetherim rolled over and pushed himself off the side of the lorry. He stabilised himself with his wings and hovered above the cobblestones. He glanced at the plume of steam rising from the truck's funnel at the rear of the cab. Burns were always a risk when hitching rides in that manner. He had no idea how town fairies did it with ease.

The rhythm of the lorry's engine faded into the distance. Familiarity took its place. Birds chirping, the faint buzz of insects, and the aroma of forest flowers. Yet his heart still beat like a drum and his right hand clasped the hilt of his dagger.

Dinsec's directions were clear, and he soon found a simple wooden skiff. It leaned against a tree, with one end tucked into a bush. Branches and palm fronds covered it, concealing it from view. A movement spell cleared them out of the way. Runes ran along the side of the boat. Aside from the first, the sequence just had two runes alternating, all the way to the back.

Yaetherim landed in the skiff. Several twigs and leaves lay scattered across its floor. An airkind crystal sat amongst them, cut to a size and shape needed to fit in a fairy's buckle. Its opaque, pale grey colour showed it still contained most of its energy. That made a disturbing amount of sense. Paetobim wouldn't have had much time to defend himself.

Yaetherim went to tuck the crystal into his belt, but stopped. It was already stretched tight from the waterkind one Yaemetan had given him. Adding any more threatened to burst it. A banana tree stood by the edge of the clearing. With a blast of magic, Yaetherim ripped off a large unbroken leaf. Another spell folded it over and sealed the edges. He tore a hole at the top, barely wider than a single hand.

After tucking both crystals into his makeshift pouch, Yaetherim continued his search. Several leaves woven together turned out to be a belt of traditional Fairic design. It bore a straight slice, just a hand's width to one side of the buckle. A few spots of purple blood blemished it. Yaetherim thought back. When worn, that cut would match the wound across Paetobim's stomach.

Yaetherim folded the belt and tucked it into the pouch. He'd need to return it to Taeperra once this was over. But right now, it was exactly what he needed to show Jorryn.

A twig snapped.

Yaetherim pressed himself against the inside of the boat, his heart racing. He peered over the edge. A lizard ran out of the undergrowth. It stopped beside the skiff and sniffed the air. Yaetherim cursed under his breath. Even with his stinger, he didn't like his chances. That creature's legs almost matched his wingspan. Such a creature could leave a fairy with nasty wounds. Yaetherim already had enough of those.

With a flick and a spell, he sent a nearby branch flying into the undergrowth. It rustled against the leaves and grass. The lizard turned. Yaetherim launched himself straight up. A few flaps of his wings brought him into the tree's branches. The reptile hissed and snapped its jaws. After a few heartbeats, it ambled away. Two deep breaths calmed Yaetherim's nerves.

He returned to the boat. It yielded nothing more of note. Yaetherim perched on the bow and surveyed the clearing. Those Rychillans hadn't even cleared out this vessel. They'd been in a hurry and had dropped that waterkind crystal in it. Perhaps they had left more behind. He didn't spot anything, except a conspicuously clear path through the forest. The only gap large enough to allow humans through.

Yaetherim launched himself off the bow of the boat. He swooped low. Several blades of grass brushed his legs. Broken bushes and trampled turf marked the start of the trail. Yaetherim landed and drew his stinger.

On each side, untouched grass reached up to his knees. Ankle-height for a human. They wouldn't even have noticed the damage they did as they trespassed. Yaetherim pursed his lips and moved on.

With each step, he examined the ground before him. In some places, tangled undergrowth crossed the trail, as high as his waist. Footprints indicated the Rychillans had simply stepped over these. His stinger made quick work of these obstacles. Not quite the intended use, but still a welcome aid.

Halfway to the road, he stopped beside a semi-rotted coconut. A pile of leaves covered the path before him. Gaps between them showed something white beneath. With a spell, Yaetherim cleared them away. Once done, a sheet of paper lay before him. He picked it up and examined it. Like the one from Cerrane, half had been torn off. It bore similar markings, yet they didn't match those on the other page.

Yaetherim put it into his pouch and continued his search. He reached the road, finding nothing more of interest. He looked along the cobblestones, towards Alkentoft. No other roads passed through this part of the forest. All of Dinsec's routes must lead here. A single common location, which could be observed.

One set of possible observers should be nearby. Yaetherim raised his fingers to his mouth and whistled twice. After a heartbeat, he did so again. Identical whistles drifted through the trees in reply. Yaetherim turned towards them. Two fairies emerged from the forest, each wearing the armband of a protector. After getting directions, Yaetherim took off.

He swung left after passing a grove of wild tomato plants. A few heartbeats later, buildings came into view amongst the treetops, the remains of Taselo Village. Moss and vines covered most of them. One half-fallen hut even had a fern growing out of it. But three stood out due to their newly built walls and neatly thatched roofs. Clear, tidy walkways connected them and a landing platform of similar construction.

Several fairies moved about, a fraction of the protectors who'd volunteered for the stewardship. Yaetherim's eyes flicked from one to the next, seeking a nokind fairy with blue wings and hair the colour of dry grass. After failing to spot her, he caught a protector's attention. With a few words of signed Fairic, Yaetherim explained who he sought. The protector asked him to land, then strode off along a walkway.

Yaetherim landed and sat on the platform. His legs dangled over the edge. He checked the pouch. Nothing had fallen out. Yaetherim frowned. This should be ample evidence. Yet Veritor Jorryn may still take refuge in excuses. He had the gumption of a boulder.

"Therry?"

Yaetherim jumped to his feet and turned. The newcomer's hazel eyes twinkled. Her grin revealed a cute gap between her front teeth. A slight smile flickered across Yaetherim's lips. It vanished after a heartbeat. Although he'd asked for his friend by name, this was not a social visit.

"Thank you for seeing me, Protector Captain Charlys. Can we speak privately?"

A worried frown replaced her grin. No surprise there. He hadn't addressed her with such formality since they were younglings.

"Of course, Yaetherim. The mess hall should be empty."

"Is there somewhere more private?"

That got her attention. An eyebrow shot up. Her wings flared and one hand went for her dagger.

"The tomato grove, then. We're not harvesting from it at the moment."

Yaetherim nodded and took off. He waited for Charlys, then followed her. They soon reached the tomato vines and sat on a tree branch above them. Charlys leaned forward and put her palm on Yaetherim's knee. He didn't flinch. She wouldn't hurt him.

"Therry," she whispered, "what's happened? Last I heard, you'd been invited to Verbore Island."

Yaetherim pulled out the crystal Dinsec had given him. He handed it to her. She turned it over. It nearly slipped from her hands. She fumbled, caught it and scrutinised it.

"This, this isn't the one we found with you in Oato Clearing."

"We didn't find it with Protector Paetobim in Cerrane yesterday, either."

Charlys looked up. Her wings twitched. She frowned.

"Protector Paetobim?"

Yaetherim explained the last day's events. Silence fell once he'd finished. Charlys handed him the crystal and brushed her hair out of her eyes. Yaetherim took her hand. It trembled. Yaetherim contemplated his next words.

"It'll be alright," he assured her. "Even if I have to do Veritor Jorryn's job for him. I think the killers spotted the armourer passing through here to her boat. Who's in this part of the forest regularly?"

Charlys let out a low whistle. She leaned forward. Her right wing brushed Yaetherim's left. A pleasant tingle, similar to magic, followed the touch. Again, a smile flickered across Yaetherim's lips. He shook his head. This wasn't a moment for distraction.

"We keep watch on the foresters who harvest in this area. They usually return to town around the time your armourer heads out. There's the College of Mages, too."

Yaetherim perked up. He hadn't considered that institution. It was a Rychillan thing. Amongst other things, their younglings went there for lessons in magic.

"That's near here, is it?"

"Aye. It's between Alkentoft and that burnt tree you mentioned."

Yaetherim cracked his knuckles. A disapproving frown flicked across Charlys' face.

"How do I get there from here?"

Charlys stared at him.

"You think they're involved?"

"Skilled mages with access to crystals. It seems to fit."

"It does, when you put it like that," Charlys replied. Her grip on Yaetherim's hand tightened.

"Therry, please be careful."

"I will."

She pointed through the trees.

"If you fly straight up, you'll spot a gap in the forest canopy over there. It's a large building, two levels with a verandah and a balcony. A stream runs across the clearing behind it."

Yaetherim did his pre-flight checks. Charlys pushed herself off the branch and hovered a few arm lengths away.

"I shall check our reports from last night," she said, "in case any patrols saw something."

"Thank you, Sunbird," Yaetherim replied. The nickname brought a smile to Charlys' lips, for a heartbeat.

"I'll owe you a couple," Yaetherim added. Charlys nodded and left. Yaetherim took off and flew straight up, weaving through the branches and leaves. After a few moments, the forest lay spread before him. To the right, the building and cobblestone streets of Alkentoft interrupted it. Halfway to the town, a gap cut through the canopy. Yaetherim swooped down towards it.

Just as Charlys had said, a single structure stood centred in the clearing. Yaetherim landed on the peak of its corrugated-iron roof. Rychillan voices drifted up from within. Most belonged to younglings. They weren't of any interest to him.

To the right of the building sat a cobblestone slab with five cars parked upon it. Nothing special there. At the front, it met a driveway wide enough to allow a lorry through. Pruned trees flanked it, their branches slightly wilted. It entered the forest and joined the road Yaetherim had travelled to find the boat. He hadn't paid attention to it earlier. His worry had been finding the landmarks from Dinsec's directions.

Yaetherim strode to the front of the roof and peered down the driveway. A lizard scurried across the far end. Yaetherim frowned. If he could spot that, so could anyone in the building below him. The more he considered it, the more it made sense. These mages had skill enough to teach magic. Casting a complex spell, like a water lance, would come simply to them. They also had easy access to crystals and a clear view of the road Dinsec travelled to reach her trysts. A perfect opportunity for someone less than honest.

A bus turned into the driveway, steam billowing from its funnel. Below, hinges creaked. A cacophony of conversation almost drowned out the vehicle. Mostly the voices of younglings, with adults asking them to move along.

Yaetherim glided onto the bus while the younglings boarded. Just like the lorry, handles ran across the cab roof. Yaetherim grabbed one of them. After several heartbeats, those who'd been aboard headed into their class. Those who'd just had a class climbed aboard. Now laden, the bus moved off to return to Alkentoft.

Yaetherim looked back over his wings. Two mages stood on the balcony of the college. He did not know if they'd seen him, but that didn't matter. He had evidence and a case with more than enough facts to root it firmly. When he returned, it would be to get answers. Now, he just needed to ensure Jorryn would actually investigate.

6

A Question of Runes

Tenora's hands shook as she placed a cigarette in her mouth. Shortly after the explosion, the town guard had moved the wrecked car into her workshop. In the couple of hours since then, she had inspected it twice. Only the rune panel, now reassembled via florakind magic, stood out. Save for a seam across the middle, it clearly displayed the runes engraved in it. Three of them, each carved small enough to fit a printer's block. Obviously the engraver had tried to conserve space. Any smaller and they wouldn't work. The initiator and terminator were as expected. But the engraving between them was a different story. Tenora had never seen one like it before, and she'd dealt with quite a few in her career.

A snap of her fingers conjured a flame at the end of her cigarette. But the familiar taste did little to steady her nerves. No suspicion took root amongst her thoughts this time. Instead, knowledge bloomed. She knew the purpose this panel attempted to serve. 'Twas a goal Tenora sought herself: getting more work from the energy within crystals. But while her approach focused on improving mechanical efficiency, this panel's creator had chosen a much more dangerous road.

"Arch-Mechanic Tenora?"

Tenora turned. Karis strode across the floor, sunglasses perched atop her head. She'd arrived a little while ago and taken charge of the town guard outside.

"Veritor Karis, welcome to my workshop. I wish it were under better circumstances."

"Indeed."

Karis stopped. Those steel-grey eyes flicked down towards Tenora's ear. Her brow furrowed.

"It's just a minor wound. Healer Omas saw to it earlier."

From a bag slung over her shoulder, Karis drew a notepad and pencil. She flipped it to a blank page. Her frown disappeared. Again, Tenora received a look that could cut crops.

"I have spoken to the witnesses," Karis said. "They stated you and Mechanic Somath tried to stop the explosion."

Tenora nodded.

"Tell me exactly what happened," Karis ordered. Tenora had no doubt many a crook had withered under that stare. But this time, she had done nothing wrong. Such bluntness was uncalled for. Especially here, in her own workshop. A smile crossed her lips, one that didn't reach her eyes. She reserved it for upset clients. When she spoke, her words came evenly, with just a hint of annoyance.

"I know you have a job to do, Veritor Karis. But I'd like you to understand something. I'm also worried about another explosion. I too want to stop whoever's interfering with these runes. And this is **my** workshop, not the town guard barracks. While you may address your subordinates in such a manner, I am not one of them."

Despite the smile, Tenora's heart raced. But no words came from Karis. Instead, the veritor met Tenora's gaze again, this time with a more reserved look.

"My apologies, Arch-Mechanic Tenora. Can you please tell me what happened?"

Tenora did so, disclosing as many details as she could. Karis took notes and asked questions.

"This panel is the only strange thing I've found," Tenora finished. She handed it to Karis. While the latter examined it, Tenora retrieved a sheet of paper she'd left atop the bonnet of the car in the next repair bay. She held it out.

"As far as I can tell," Tenora began, "that middle engraving has lines for several runes. They're inscribed over each other. These are the ones I've identified."

Karis looked from the panel to the list in Tenora's hand. Seconds later, a slight shift in those grey eyes signalled a new understanding. Tenora peered at the other woman. Karis appeared to be about in her mid-thirties, a good six or seven years older than Tenora.

"Are you familiar with the rune capacity problem, Veritor Karis? I think you may not have learned about it in school. My brother didn't, and you appear to be of similar age."

Steel-grey eyes met Tenora's. Karis' left hand reached up and fiddled with her brooch.

"You are right, Arch-Mechanic Tenora. This rune capacity question, I imagine it has to do with the minimum size required for runes and the limitations of space for them. Is that correct?" Karis asked. Tenora nodded, recalling how Mage Banoth had taught it during runology lessons in school.

"More or less. I suspect someone's tried to solve it by overlaying runes in the same spot."

Karis frowned.

"That would negate the order of operations."

"Exactly. I think that would account for all malfunctions we've heard of."

Karis put down the rune panel. She picked up her notebook and pencil.

"Please proceed," she said. Tenora pulled the cigarette butt out of her mouth. A spell extinguished it. Without looking, she flicked it over her shoulder. A soft but satisfying clink came as it landed in the bin by her office door. With her now-empty hand, she pointed to the wreckage before them.

"I suspect this sedan and the tractor I examined experienced a burst of fire, which would have created a surge of steam. That would account for the damage I saw in the tractor's firebox, too. Runes feeding back into themselves, out of order, would explain how the flames in that car I chased down re-ignited, too."

"Were there any other malfunctions?"

Tenora pointed to the panel.

"Those are firekind. Their shape makes that clear. But a lorry also lost power without warning. A surge of unheated water would drop the boiler temperature and steam along with it. A waterkind rune stacked in this manner could cause that."

Karis made another note. Tenora cleared her throat.

"Please don't take this as fact, Veritor Karis. I'm just deducing based on my knowledge."

"I understand, Arch-Mechanic Tenora. Yet I cannot see the purpose of such a panel. Do you have any ideas?"

Tenora pinched the bridge of her nose. A sigh escaped her, and she drew her cigarette case. Within moments, she had another cigarette lit in her mouth.

"Farmers ask what we can do to make their vehicles stronger," Tenora replied. "We hear that question at least twice a week. Fewer trips to deliver produce means more time to tend to crops or spend with their families. Luxanke knows, they don't get enough of that."

Karis' expression darkened for a moment. But she said nothing. Tenora took a drag on her cigarette.

"I'm working on that myself, but my focus is improving mechanical output."

"That would be the gearbox you were testing yesterday?"

Tenora nodded. Karis made another note.

"That provides motive. Now for means and opportunity."

Tenora frowned.

"Means and opportunity?"

"We search for those three elements in every crime."

Karis lay aside her notepad and picked up the rune panel. She traced a finger over the lines.

"Means may not tell us much. These are not smooth, they appear to be hand-carved. Everyone learns runology in school, so anyone with a chisel could have made these. Who were these farmers you mentioned? We should start by determining if they noticed anything strange around their barns."

Tenora chuckled.

"You didn't grow up on a farm, did you?"

"No. What told you that?"

"My parents run one just north of town."

Fond memories came back, and a smile crossed Tenora's lips.

"There's a lot that can happen unnoticed in a barn. Meetings, trysts, that sort of thing. Farmers spend most of their day working in their fields and paddocks. You should ask who swapped them out before those engines were examined."

"You are assuming it was not the mechanics themselves."

Tenora stopped, her next sentence dead on her lips. Her gaze dropped, landing on the very first mark of her terax. All Rychillans had it, it marked them as rynil. Trustworthy unless evidence said otherwise. Neither Jotol nor Warrett bore the symbol of a change of class.

"Are you about to tell me they are both rynil?" Karis asked. A familiar warmth blossomed in Tenora's cheeks. Her gaze landed on Karis' terax marks. One mark was repeated multiple times, and it showed the bearer had been of service to the kingdom. Given Karis' line of work, Tenora could guess why.

"I imagine you've seen your share of ex-rynil, Veritor Karis. But I haven't discovered evidence against Jotol and Warrett, unlike last time."

"Last time?"

"Oh, it wasn't those two. Some junior mechanics were embezzling from here when I took over as Arch-Mechanic. I soon put a stop to that."

Karis frowned.

"I found no mention of such a case when I checked your record."

"They were forging documents. Changing numbers here and there on invoices. Subtle, but I noticed the inconsistent handwriting. So I kept a close watch, then fired them after catching them in the act."

"You didn't report it to us?"

"No. But I refused to give references for either of them."

"I see. You still should have reported it."

Tenora nodded and glanced down.

"Understood, Veritor Karis."

"Now it is clear this investigation will require the knowledge of an expert mechanic. Would you be willing to provide such support?"

"Of course. What do you need me to do?"

"I shall send a guard sergeant to discuss this with Mechanic Jotol and Arch-Mechanic Warrett. It would be helpful if they had you with them, should the discussion turn technical. Furthermore, you are acquainted with both of them."

Tenora frowned.

"You're not going to talk to them yourself?"

Karis flipped her notebook closed and slipped it into the bag from whence it came. With the toe of her boot, she tapped the rune panel.

"There is the question of how many of these panels are installed. Would you agree these present a threat to the peace of the kingdom?"

Tenora scoffed. The cigarette fell from her mouth. She caught it and used it to point to the wreckage before her.

"Do you really need me to answer that, Veritor Karis?"

"Yes, in writing. There are steps I must take to minimise this hazard. The testimony of an arch-mechanic will carry weight."

Tenora nodded. That made sense.

A few minutes thereafter, she'd written a formal statement to that effect. With that sorted, Karis introduced her to Guard Sergeant Palron, a man with hair the shade of varnished wood and pale, dried-hay skin. The sign of someone who'd grown up in town. After a brief discussion, Karis left.

* * *

One busy hour later, Tenora found herself on the verge of lighting another cigarette. Multiple worries prickled her thoughts. First, this town guard car needed repairs. A faint hiss escaped after every exhaust beat. The urge to repair it gnawed at her. But of more concern, Jotol hadn't arrived at Thirer's workshop.

Tenora and Palron had traced Jotol's movements from his appointments this morning. After meeting Tenora, Jotol had visited another farm to perform regular maintenance on their equipment. He had finished there and mentioned he'd be stopping for breakfast before coming in. Thirer had given them Jotol's home address.

A few minutes later, they reached Jotol's house. It stood amongst others, on the mountain side of town. Unlike Tenora's own, it had wooden gates on both sides leading to the backyard. Above the verandah, a crop-green corrugated iron roof met the bricks. Palron parked the car outside. With one last hiss, the car's engine shut down.

Tenora let Palron get ahead of her on the short walk to the door. This was his area of expertise. She'd offer her own when needed. They reached it and Palron knocked.

"This is Guard Sergeant Palron. Mechanic Jotol, we'd like to talk to you."

Inside, glass shattered.

"Mechanic Jotol?" Palron called.

A slam came from behind the house. Tenora jumped back. Palron dived left. One hand grabbed the florakind crystal on his necklace. His other fingers flicked out. The gate slammed against the wall. Palron dashed through it. Tenora followed, then stopped. Realisation struck her. Jotol was trying to escape, and his home had two gates. She spun on her heel.

Someone ran out from the right. Not Jotol. Too tall and they wore the hood of an atoning connil.

"Stop!" Tenora called. They didn't. She broke into a run. Her hand shot forward. Magic crackled over her skin. Flames flicked up ahead of the running Rychillan. Their fingers flung out. A dull boom sounded. Sudden wind extinguished the fire. Tenora uttered a few choice words.

The fleeing connil glanced back. They raised their palm. A haze appeared between them and Tenora. She skidded to a halt. One elbow banged against solid air. It went numb save for that uncomfortable tingle which came from such a bump. Tenora shook her arm and looked around. The airkind wall blocked the footpath and a third of the road. Another flurry of profanity escaped her.

From behind, a whistle sounded out. A car swerved to miss the barrier. Its tyres skidded on the cobbles. Instinct took over and Tenora jumped aside. She landed and staggered. With one hand, she steadied herself against a house. Her head whipped around. Left to right to left again. Of the running connil, she saw no sign.

Her breath came shallow, and sweat rolled down from her brow. Normally, the use of spells wouldn't faze her. But as convicted criminals, connil were prohibited from using magic. Tenora let out a sigh.

She returned to Jotol's house a minute later and knocked on the door. Palron answered it, a frown on his face. A faint odour drifted out from the room behind him. Tenora couldn't quite place it, but it stirred vague memories of the barn on her parents' farm. She gestured down the street.

"Someone tried to run away. They stopped me with an airkind wall. That's when I lost them."

Palron folded his arms.

"You're not a constable. You shouldn't risk your life to catch crooks."

"Don't worry, I didn't. But it wasn't Mechanic Jotol. I couldn't get a good look at their terax."

Palron glanced at his feet. His skin appeared paler than before, almost the shade of paper.

"You are right," he said softly, "that was not Mechanic Jotol. Did you know him closely?"

Tenora blinked. Her stomach turned. Palron's manner and words did not bode well.

"I only met him this morning. Why-"

She broke off. A mess occupied the living room behind Palron. Books lay scattered across the floor. One chair and the sofa rested at an odd angle, their undersides exposed. The other armchair still stood upright, with Jotol slumped in it. A pallor discoloured his skin. No movement came from him, save for the slow creep of the red stain spreading over his shirt. Her eyes widened.

"Is he, um...?"

Palron nodded.

"I'm afraid so. Stabbed, at least a few minutes ago."

Palron gestured towards the messenger light on the roof.

"I've already sent word. We need to process the scene."

Tenora nodded. Only now did it sink in. As a farmer's daughter, she had seen injury and death before. Working amongst tractors and ploughs carried that risk. But this was a person. A mechanic just a few years her junior, with whom she'd worked only a few hours ago. That fleeing connil must have killed him. She blinked. Palron was asking her something.

"What did you say, sorry?"

"Are you alright?"

Tenora took a deep breath, but her heart still raced. She drew a cigarette. A disapproving frown crossed Palron's face. She stopped, with it halfway to her lips.

"Thank you," Palron said. "We don't want to disturb anything until we've looked at it."

"This is enough to do that?"

"If it drops ash, yes. Even touching something could obscure the fingerprints on it."

That made sense. Tenora returned the cigarette to the case, then slid the latter back into her pocket. After two deep breaths, she gestured over Palron's shoulder. Practical action would help steady her nerves.

"You brought me here for a reason. I may as well have a look. See if I can spot anything relating to these rune panels. I'll be careful."

Palron nodded and moved aside. Tenora stepped into the living room. Only a few square feet of the floor remained clear of mess. At the entry to the kitchen lay the remains of two drinking glasses.

"The killer was searching for something," Palron said.

"Those stacked runes?"

"I'd be surprised if it were anything else."

Tenora cast her eyes over the chaos. Nothing resembling a rune panel sat amongst it. She stepped into the back garden. Fresh air washed over her. Beyond the verandah lay an overgrown yard. A shed stood beside the rear fence, with a path of trodden grass leading to it. A padlock dangled from its door.

Tenora stepped inside and caught Palron's attention.

"Whoever did this wasn't a mechanic," she said.

"How do you know?"

"They'd have thought to check the shed out back. The key for it may be in here somewhere."

Palron glanced over at the mess.

"I can try the lock without it, if that would disturb the, um, scene," Tenora added. Palron nodded.

"That would be best."

Tenora strode out to the shed and drew a set of miniature screwdrivers from her overalls. Narrower than fairy fingernails, they were the perfect size for working on watches or other intricate mechanisms. She opened their wooden case and got to work on the padlock. 'Twas identical to the ones she'd tinkered with on her family farm during her youth. After half a minute, she had it unlocked. After returning the tools to her pocket, she pushed on the door.

It swung open without hesitation or creaking. For a moment, Tenora hesitated. Most mechanics were tinkerers at heart, with their private workshops in their sheds. Places of tinkering and experimentation, full of personal projects. To enter uninvited was to pry.

Tenora took a deep breath. Someone had murdered Jotol. Unlike the chaotic house, she could reap answers here. She stepped inside. From the two windows at the front, light flowed in and illuminated the shed's interior.

A large tool chest stood against the rear wall, an elegant design built from varnished ironwood with brass trim. Tenora ran her hand over it, an appreciative glint in her eye. She'd considered buying such a chest herself, but the cost made it an indulgence. She would stick with her pine-and-steel one.

Tenora turned her attention to the rest of the shed. Shelves hung off the front and left walls. A well-stocked assortment of gears, springs and sprockets rested upon them. A desk stood against the right wall. It had seen some use, as had the chair before it.

Tenora walked up to the desk. A grid of papers covered half of it. Behind them sat a book, open at a certain page. 'Twas a volume Tenora knew well, *The Machines of Firan Leinad*. Unlike her own copy, this one showed barely a tatter or blemish. Tenora leaned in for a close look.

"A hovering rivercraft?" she said to herself. She shook her head. Nobody would kill over that. Firan Leinad had lived over a century ago. Many had tried to build his designs, few had succeeded.

She went to sit on the chair, but stopped. Two neat, vertical cuts broke the wood frame at the front of the desk. Tenora frowned. She'd used a few desks in her time. Never had she seen marks like that. They'd be weak points. She ran her thumb along the front. Nothing stuck out. 'Twas a different story underneath. Her fingers struck something about an inch in.

Tenora crouched down and peered at the desk's underside. Now she understood those cuts in the frame. A drawer hung below the desk, with just a latch holding it closed. Tenora glanced towards the door. Perhaps Palron should open this. He had been rather firm about disturbing evidence. But on the other hand, she didn't know what it contained.

She flicked the latch. The drawer opened. Three pieces of wood lay along the left side of it. Despite being the size and shape of large printers' blocks, they lacked the rounded edges and varnish of those she'd seen in printing presses. Nor did they have the cast-iron stamps used to put ink onto paper. Instead, they bore stacked runes, smoothly carved into the wood itself. Just like on a genuine rune panel.

Tenora turned her attention back to the drawer. Beside the blocks sat a bundle of letters. A single loop of twine held them together, save for one slipped down next to them. Tenora reached for it, but hesitated. These were Jotol's private communications. But he'd been murdered, and this could lead to his killer. A lot of effort had gone towards concealing it, after all. With that in mind, she opened and read it.

No salutation started it, but it was dated two days before. That was strange enough. It wasn't correct correspondence writing at all. As she went through it, Tenora grew more and more horrified. Its author expressed disappointment with how many 'compressed' panels remained uninstalled for trial runs and threatened to withhold payment. Tenora put the letter back. They'd have to examine all these letters. She should leave that to Palron or Karis. This was their area of expertise.

She pulled out the blocks and placed them side-by-side on the desk. All three bore compacted runes. One matched the panel she'd shown to Karis. The others, whilst unfamiliar, were just as complex.

Tenora ran a finger over the engravings. They equalled the quality of a genuine rune panel, down to the smoothness and consistency of the engraving. No chisel had made these marks. But only a few places in town had engraving machines. Tenora put the block down carefully, almost as if she expected it to bite her. She had found what Jotol's killer sought.

7

Connections

The taxi bumped over the cobblestones, a steady beat coming from its engine. Inside, Yaetherim's satchel bounced against his stomach. He lifted its strap over his head and tossed it backwards. With a spell, he caught it and guided it onto the rear cushion. It held all the evidence from Cerrane and that morning. It wouldn't do to damage it.

That done, Yaetherim grabbed both sides of the fairy notch in the top of the front bench seat. To his right, Kaetarpen did the same. Both he and Naeliya had been waiting when Yaetherim returned to Cropper's Crony. He'd filled them in. Naeliya needed to rush off afterwards, to report for duty on east mail tower three. But she'd told Yaetherim to find her if he required more help. She had been rather insistent about that.

Yaetherim glanced at Kaetarpen. The protector captain hadn't spoken since seeing the belt found in the boat. He'd just shed a single tear and confirmed it was Paetobim's. Kaetarpen cleared his throat.

"You mentioned some thefts, Yaetherim? I am curious about how these took priority over attempted murder."

Yaetherim rolled his eyes and cracked his knuckles.

"It's the merchants' guild. Some of their shipments arrived one or two items short. Yet the paperwork says they weren't sent that way."

Kaetarpen stared as though Yaetherim had sprouted a third wing.

"Is that all?"

"Apparently, they've been leaning on him like a fallen ironwood."

Before Kaetarpen could reply, a soft clunk came from the front of the taxi. The beat of the engine dropped off. Yaetherim's head snapped forward. His right hand closed around his stinger. Ahead, two cars stood stopped on the road.

"What is happening?" Kaetarpen asked. He'd spoken in Rychillan. But his Fairic accent made his words as clear as a coughing fit. The driver glanced back.

"Don't worry, just the town guard having a search. Shouldn't take too long."

As the taxi braked, Yaetherim pushed himself off the seat. He shot forward and flared his wings. His feet slapped onto the dashboard. For a moment he staggered, then steadied himself. His hair brushed the windscreen.

"Is this common?" Yaetherim asked.

"When they're trying to make an arrest, yes."

A guard constable stepped around behind the car ahead of them. He crouched and opened a panel on the side of the engine. After a quick examination, he closed it and returned to the front of the other vehicle.

"Seems a strange place to seek someone," Yaetherim commented. The taxi driver chuckled. He gestured to another constable striding towards them.

"I think we're about to hear why," he said, and wound down the window.

"Please drop the fire in your engine. We need to examine it on orders from Veritor Karis."

The driver nodded and pulled two of the control levers to their lowest positions.

"What do you expect to find there?" Yaetherim asked. That earned him a glance.

"Illegal runes."

Before Yaetherim could reply, the guard walked behind the car. Yaetherim frowned. To most, that would be meaningless. But he'd heard such a thing suggested earlier. Naeliya had mentioned the possibility upon seeing the page from the clearing.

Yaetherim flew over to the back seat and landed next to his satchel. With two quick movements, he flicked it open and pulled out the paper from Cerrane. This rune's outline was hexagonal, going by the angles. If he recalled correctly, that signified a firekind rune.

A clunk sounded from the rear of the car. It rocked for a couple of heartbeats. The constable walked around to the front and marked it with chalk. He returned to the driver's window.

"You're clear to leave."

"May I ask something?" Yaetherim said.

"Go ahead."

"You mentioned Veritor Karis was looking for illegal runes?"

"Correct."

"Why?"

"You hear about that explosion this morning? Someone's been experimenting with them."

"Thank you."

As the taxi moved off, suspicion sprouted in Yaetherim's mind. So that's what had woken him earlier. Of course, those performing these experiments would want to avoid discovery. He held the page out towards Kaetarpen.

"Remember the scorched walls in the hut where we found this? I think they were carrying out some of their tests there."

Kaetarpen nodded.

"Away from any Rychillans who'd notice what they were doing," he said. "It makes sense. Would explain the cache of crystals too."

Yaetherim's wings twitched. He almost smiled. Now he knew what they'd been doing in Oato Clearing. That hole found next to him had probably held a similar stash. So, after eight months, he had one answer. Yet he still lacked two crucial ingredients, the who and why. But it was a start.

They arrived at the town hall. The driver parked in front of the building. After paying, Yaetherim and Kaetarpen headed inside. They flew a couple of arms' lengths above the Rychillans milling around in the lobby and soon reached the reception desk. Veritor Jorryn was expecting them, and they were sent straight up.

Yaetherim led Kaetarpen up the spiral stairs to the third floor. Several doors lined the wood-panelled corridor. Yaetherim stopped halfway along, just before the staircase up to the governor's office. To their left, the door bore three brass plates. From top to bottom, they displayed the names of the town's veritors: Rakin Belvar, Karis Relinda, and Jorryn Lorem. Yaetherim murmured a quick prayer and knocked.

"Come in," called a voice from within. That precise pronunciation, with the soft vowels of a northern accent, was the voice of Karis Relinda. Just who he needed.

With a blast of magic, Yaetherim pushed the door handle down and forward. Once half-open, he flew around it. For once, pages covered Karis' desk directly opposite. She sat bent over them. After shooting the two fairies a glance, she returned to her work.

As per usual, Jorryn's desk, to the left, resembled a forest floor. Papers lay scattered about, atop notepads, books, and a wood case with a lens on the front. An inkwell perched on the edge, with three fountain pens sprouting from it. It was a wonder it hadn't tumbled off. In a clearing in the middle stood an evidence box, wooden with a padlocked lid. A brass frame on it displayed a single slip of paper. It bore Yaetherim's name in Jorryn's spiky handwriting.

Yaetherim landed just in front of the inkwell, atop a semi-straight stack of papers. While Kaetarpen touched down, Yaetherim stepped around the box. He glared at the Rychillan sitting behind the desk.

"Hello, Veritor Jorryn."

Jorryn leaned back in his chair. When he spoke, he couldn't meet Yaetherim's gaze.

"Good morning, Yaetherim. I think I know why you're here."

"To give you an update on your investigation, aye," Yaetherim snapped. "It should be the other way around!"

Yaetherim pulled the three spent waterkind crystals from his satchel. He tossed them down onto the papers.

"Do these look familiar? Paetobim was holding one when he died," he said. Jorryn picked up a crystal and examined it. He then checked the other two. Yaetherim frowned.

"So what excuse is it this time? Those thefts again?"

Jorryn put the crystal down. He leaned forward, rested his wrists on the side of the desk and lowered his hands so his fingers lay flat across the top. Just like a fairy lowering their wings. Yaetherim had never seen such a gesture of sincerity from him.

"No," Jorryn replied. "Not this time. I acknowledge I've been a bit, ah, distracted from your case. I offer nothing but my sincerest apology."

Yaetherim blinked. That wasn't what he'd expected at all.

"Before I accept that, there's something I want you to understand," he said. "I comforted Paetobim's sister last night."

Kaetarpen's head snapped around. Yaetherim's gaze didn't shift.

"She was trying to work out the purpose of her brother's death. He died protecting Verbore Island. That was his duty. But he would still be alive today, had you carried out yours. Instead, you gave excuses about thefts from merchants. What have they lost now?"

"Goods worth 1,242 kerlum, 3 kerlar and 2 kerlo."

Yaetherim folded his arms and glowered.

"So that's how much you value a life, then?"

Jorryn sighed. He ran his hands through his hair. Somehow, this left the brown strands even more unkempt.

"Alright, you've made your point," he said. He glanced at Kaetarpen, who'd landed next to Yaetherim.

"You must be Protector Captain Kaetarpen?" he asked in Fairic. Kaetarpen nodded. Jorryn drew a key from his pocket and unlocked the box. Yaetherim stepped over and peered inside. Only a single notebook and some loose pages lay within.

"Correct me if I'm wrong," Yaetherim said, "but shouldn't that actually contain evidence? Not much for eight months, is it?"

"No," Jorryn mumbled. He pulled out the notepad and opened it to a new page. With a pen, he pointed to the crystals.

"You mentioned Paetobim had one of these when he died. Another is from Oato Clearing. Where did you find the third?"

"In the boat they used to get to Cerrane. There's more."

Yaetherim turned. Habit brought his fingers to his mouth. He stopped. No need to whistle for attention here.

"Excuse me, Veritor Karis, but I think I've got two of those strange runes you're searching for."

Karis stood up. She picked up a notepad and pen.

"Where did you find the panels?"

"Nay, not panels, papers. They were experimenting in the forest."

With a few quick strides, Karis joined them. Yaetherim pulled the torn pages out and held them up. Karis leaned down. Her eyes flicked between them. She straightened up and spun on her heel.

"Please put those on my desk."

Yaetherim did so. Karis stepped behind it and reached down. She placed a wood board next to the drawn runes and glanced at Jorryn.

"Veritor Jorryn, Protector Captain Kaetarpen, you should see this."

The other two joined them. Yaetherim hovered above the panel for a better view. The marks chiselled on it formed a complex pattern. Splinters across the middle showed where it had been reconstructed by a florakind. Karis took the page from Cerrane and placed it atop the engraving. After moving it around for a few heartbeats, she lined it up. The lines matched perfectly.

"Where did you find this?" Karis asked.

"Cerrane," Yaetherim replied, "did that panel come from the car that exploded this morning?"

Karis nodded. Her eyes met Yaetherim's.

"You mentioned you had more?"

Yaetherim and Kaetarpen recounted yesterday's events. Both veritors made notes.

"So I took a room at Cropper's Crony. I'll be staying there until one of you catches these killers," Yaetherim finished. He shot a glare at Jorryn. The latter opened his mouth to speak, then stopped as Karis looked over at him. His shoulders slumped, and he turned to the fairies.

"Could you please excuse us for a few moments? I think Veritor Karis would like a word with me."

Yaetherim and Kaetarpen nodded and flew out into the corridor. They landed on the floor and moved aside so Rychillans wouldn't step on them by accident.

"I'll need to talk to Yaemetan," Kaetarpen said. "You didn't mention where I could find him."

"That would break my promise of silence. I can arrange for him to meet you, though. Maybe at Cropper's Crony?"

"That would be suitable. Perhaps over lunch, I enjoyed breakfast there."

A smirk flicked across Yaetherim's lips. Kaetarpen did not seem to notice. Instead, he stared down the corridor. Several dozen heartbeats later, Jorryn stepped out and beckoned them back in.

"Veritor Karis wants to see you."

They re-entered the office. Jorryn exited and closed the door behind him. Yaetherim wondered where the young veritor was going.

He landed on Karis' desk, beside the evidence box. Kaetarpen touched down next to him. Karis leaned down, bringing her eyes level with the fairies.

"Veritor Jorryn is no longer investigating this matter," she said. "I have taken it over, as it is connected to my case."

"So you'll actually investigate it, then?" Yaetherim asked, not bothering to hide his disbelief.

"'Tis an obvious threat to the peace of the kingdom. As a veritor, it is my duty to see it stopped. As a tenil, I give you my promise it will be."

Yaetherim scoffed. He stepped forward. His wings flicked out as wide as they'd go. She didn't lean further back, but kept her gaze on him. Yaetherim jabbed his hand towards the door.

"Veritor Jorryn has shown the value of a tenil's word. I've seen rotted logs less hollow."

Kaetarpen gasped. Karis sat up straight. She lay her left arm across the desk between her and Yaetherim and leaned over it. Yaetherim ignored the terax marks tattooed along it. Instead, he folded his arms. Karis needed to understand he would not settle for excuses and evasions again. But it was Kaetarpen who broke the silence.

"With all due respect, Veritor Karis," he began, "my village council also has concerns regarding the way the town guard has handled this investigation."

"I see," Karis replied, "but whilst your concern is understandable, I am not Veritor Jorryn Lorem. You would do well to remember that, Protector Yaetherim-"

"Ex-protector," Yaetherim corrected. "Two of your fellow Rychillans saw to that."

"My apologies. You said you would stay at Cropper's Crony until we completed this. Is that correct?"

"Aye."

"Then I shall report to you there, daily, until this is resolved. Would that sate your concerns?"

Yaetherim's wings drooped.

"I suppose so."

Karis put her pen to the page once more.

"You have covered yesterday. Did you find anything more this morning?"

"Aye, I spoke to Yaemetan and his beloved. Did some looking around based on that. I think the College of Mages-"

A series of sharp knocks from the window interrupted him. Outside hovered a town fairy, clad in their typical garb: a cotton shirt, trousers, and goatskin boots. A maroon satchel hung over his shoulder. Only messengers carried bags that colour.

Karis quickly opened the glass and beckoned the messenger in. The moment he was inside, she stepped back and spun on her heel. Two quick steps brought her to her desk. She slid into her chair. He landed in front of her and glanced at Kaetarpen and Yaetherim.

"I've got a message for Veritor Karis from Guard Sergeant Palron," he said in Fairic, his words accompanied by a shooing gesture. Karis nodded.

"They can hear it. Sergeant Palron is working on this case," she replied in Rychillan. The messenger cleared his throat and spoke in the same language.

"He and Arch-Mechanic Tenora have found Mechanic Jotol fatally stabbed at his house. They requested your presence."

Yaetherim's wings twitched. His blood ran cold. They were killing Rychillans too.

Karis tore a clean page from her notepad. With quick movements, she scrawled several sentences on it.

"Please give this to the duty captain at the guard barracks."

The messenger departed with the note. Karis stood and glanced back at the fairies.

"My apologies, but I must take my leave."

As if to underline her words, she pulled a pair of sunglasses from a desk drawer. Kaetarpen nodded. Yaetherim took off and hovered in front of Karis.

"Shall I come with you? You still haven't heard what I found this morning. I could help. There may be something at this Jotol's house familiar to me."

"It would also mean you will not need to rely on my reports," Karis observed. Yaetherim smirked.

"There is that."

Karis gestured for Yaetherim to follow her and headed for the door. He caught up. She moved like a lizard fleeing an eagle.

"I'll wait for you at Cropper's Crony," Kaetarpen called.

Karis turned towards the staircase and slowed. Yaetherim overshot, then corrected himself. He wouldn't have minded a warning.

"What did you discover this morning?" Karis asked. Yaetherim started with his visit to Dinsec's workshop, leaving out the armourer's name. He'd only just mentioned the map when they reached the ground floor. Karis weaved her way through the handful of people in the lobby. Yaetherim flew over them. He wouldn't lose her. She stood taller than everyone else in the room.

"So you took it upon yourself to investigate this boat?"

"Aye. I found Paetobim's belt there, along with that third crystal I showed Veritor Jorryn. Can't see how they'd have ended up in it otherwise."

"You didn't consider getting him to accompany you? Rychillans used that craft, not fairies."

"What, and give the killers time to remove the evidence?"

Karis pulled a set of keys from her pocket. She led Yaetherim to an unmarked door opposite the staircase, unlocked it, and held it for him to enter. He found himself in a large room, which outdid most forest clearings. But instead of flowers, the odours of oil and grease hung in the air. Six cars sat before him, three parked on each side. At the far end, a wide gap in the wall opened onto the street beside the building. Karis strode towards a dark grey car, halfway down to the left. She paused next to it and donned the sunglasses.

"You mentioned the College of Mages?"

Yaetherim explained how he'd checked the road and forest.

"Did you speak to anyone there?"

"Nay, the only Rychillan I spoke to was Yaemetan's lover. Before you bring up the Accord of Reiksoft, let me ask something. Would a veritor like you have got the same answers? Or any at all?"

Karis climbed into the car. Yaetherim flew in and settled into the fairy notch beside her. The control levers clunked into position. Yaetherim glanced back at the engine.

"It will be ready in a minute," Karis said, "and your conclusions make sense. But murder is a serious accusation, as are assault and trespass. You know we hold mages in high regard, do you not?"

"Aye."

"Then if the College of Mages is to be investigated, we need more justification than one person's deductions."

Yaetherim pursed his lips. His wings flared. These killers had struck thrice, now. Surely that would be enough to lay aside political concerns. A sigh escaped him. At least Karis hadn't completely pruned that branch.

"You said this Arch-Mechanic Tenora was helping investigate?"

A hiss came from the engine. Karis shifted another of the control levers. She guided the car out onto the street. The wheels bumped on the cobblestones. While Karis drove towards the north side of town, she filled Yaetherim in on all that had happened. By the time she'd finished, one thing was obvious. Those experiments in Oato Clearing and Cerrane had only been the start.

"Why would someone go to such an effort?" Yaetherim asked.

"Arch-Mechanic Tenora suspects they are trying to solve the rune capacity problem. A question of getting more work from crystals within engines. She is working on a mechanical solution to that challenge herself."

Yaetherim barely heard that last sentence. Eight months of stress and pain. That dull ache in his right wing that never quite went away. Those several weeks he'd spent confined to a bed and two murders. All just for that. His fists clenched, fingernails scraping against his palms. He let loose a few choice words in Fairic, in a tone harsh enough to wilt a flower.

"Are you telling me," he growled, "that this is all about making faster engines?"

"Stronger. To increase the load lorries and other vehicles can carry."

That made sense. Presumably, whoever solved this problem would gain prestige, along with whatever money they could make. The latter came as no surprise. Gluttony of coin seemed a common affliction amongst Rychillans. Well, he'd see about that. Yaetherim cracked his knuckles, his anger dissipating with each pop. He had the what, and the why. Now he just needed the who.

A hiss interrupted Yaetherim's thoughts. He blinked. The car slowed and the beat of the engine trailed off. Karis steered it to the side of the street and parked. Yaetherim followed her out. After pocketing her sunglasses, Karis led him into a nearby house.

Several town guards stood in the first room. Some picked up items from the floor, others examined and took notes on them. Amidst all this sat an armchair with a Rychillan man slumped in it. Judging by the pallor of his skin and the bloodstained shirt, he must have been Jotol.

"Sergeant Palron's over there, ma'am. They found some evidence in the shed," said one of the guard constables. He pointed to a writing desk in the corner of the living room.

"I see. As you were," Karis replied. She stepped over to what remained of Jotol, but Yaetherim hung back. Too close and he'd be seeing his breakfast again. It did not seem to bother Karis. She leaned down and performed a careful examination. When done, she straightened up. For a few moments, she stood with her head bowed, mouthing words. Yaetherim didn't try to lip read. This conversation was probably between her and Luxanke.

"Learn anything?" Yaetherim asked when Karis finished. She headed for the kitchen. Yaetherim followed her.

"They stabbed him underarm, through the heart. He died instantly."

She'd spoken as though describing a tree branch.

"Underarm?"

"It's how the Druhlac do it when hunting. A stab from beneath puts the weight of the animal onto the blade."

Yaetherim shuddered.

"Don't tell me this involves a Druhlac too," he said. Dealing with the Rychillans was stressful enough. Last thing he needed was another complication.

"I doubt that. These killers are trying to conceal themselves."

"Makes sense," Yaetherim replied. They headed over to the desk, and Yaetherim landed on it. A Rychillan man in a guard sergeant's uniform and a young woman in overalls stood behind it. A lit cigarette dangled from the latter's mouth. Calluses on her grease-stained fingers spoke of hard work. Yaetherim did not need to check their teraxes to realise who they were. Palron looked up and saluted. Karis nodded.

"As you were, Guard Sergeant."

Even this didn't draw Arch-Mechanic Tenora's gaze away from the letter in her hands. Several others sat on the desk before her in a semi-organised pile. Three wood blocks stood on the far side of it. Yaetherim landed next to the letters.

"Interesting reading?" he asked. He'd spoken in Rychillan, but she replied in Fairic.

"More like frustrating. He was corresponding with someone to coordinate these experiments. But none of these mentions who."

"I know a messenger who could help with that," Yaetherim offered.

"That would be-"

Tenora broke off and moved the letter to the side. Violet eyes stared down at Yaetherim for a couple of heartbeats. She reached for her cigarette.

"Don't worry," Yaetherim said, "stray smoke isn't the worst a Rychillan's done to me."

Tenora dropped her hand. Her gaze flicked over to his wing.

"Have we met before? You seem familiar," she asked. Yaetherim peered at her. She'd broken her nose in the past, going by the slight bulge in it. A half-depleted firekind crystal sat in a ring on one finger. For some reason, she had a rag tied around her left ear, marred by a red stain. A memory percolated in Yaetherim's mind, blurred by what he'd been drinking at the time.

"We may have crossed paths at Cropper's Crony."

"I think that's it. What brings a countryside fairy like you into town, Yae-?"

"I'm Yaetherim of Riala Village, South Alken Forest."

Yaetherim paused. Not only did Tenora speak Fairic with barely an accent, but she'd noticed his clothes. Most others only saw his scars. But this was the one time he wanted them acknowledged. He held out his right arm, at the same angle the Rychillans used to show their terax.

"Did these help you recognise me? They're not tattooed marks, but people notice them first."

Tenora glanced down, then nodded.

"Yes, and your wings."

Yaetherim flexed his wing patch.

"You mean this?"

"I must admit, it caught my eye. It is a brilliant piece of engineering. A simple design with clever use of a distributed load. Airship skin, isn't it? Do you-"

Tenora broke off. Her cheeks flushed red beneath smudges of oil.

"Sorry," she said. Yaetherim shrugged.

"It's better than pity."

He glanced through the kitchen door, towards the body.

"Anyway, my wounds are from the Rychillans who did this. They killed a protector in Cerrane to hide their experiments, too."

The letter fell from Tenora's hand. Yaetherim took off to avoid it. Even Palron gasped.

"Verbore Island," he said, "but that's trespassing under the Accord of Reiksoft."

"They're willing to murder to cover their tracks," replied Yaetherim. "Do you think they'd care about a treaty?"

"But you're from South Alken Forest," Tenora said. "Did they trespass there too?"

"Aye. It's a bit of a long story."

He landed again and gestured to the pile of letters.

"And I understand you've got one to tell us, too. Would you like to start, or shall I?"

Tenora glanced at Karis, who'd been watching the conversation.

"Perhaps you should go first, Arch-Mechanic Tenora."

Tenora nodded and did so. Both Yaetherim and Karis paid attention. Yaetherim's wings twitched at the mention of the hooded connil. When Tenora showed them the printer's blocks, he couldn't help smirking. After she'd finished, Yaetherim cleared his throat.

"So there's nothing to identify who sent these letters?"

Tenora shook her head.

"Just the return address. A tower letterbox, not a building."

"Would the College of Mages have one of these engraving machines?"

Tenora moved the printer's blocks next to Yaetherim. Both he and Karis leaned in. The engravings on them matched what he'd seen at the town hall, but were much neater.

"This is how the rune panels appear when we get them from the College of Mages," Tenora said, "smooth lines with consistent depth on the engraving. But a newspaper office or printing press would also have them. You know, for images or logos as needed."

Yaetherim smirked.

"Does that sound like more than one person's deduction to you, Veritor Karis?"

He ignored the looks from Tenora and Palron. Instead, he set his own steely stare upon Karis. After a few heartbeats, she nodded and turned to Palron.

"Beside these letters and the panel, have you found anything else of interest?"

"Not much, ma'am. I had a constable check at both temples. They can account for all their connil. But we got some fingerprints from the drinking glasses. Some matched Jotol, the others didn't."

Tenora tucked her hair behind her ear.

"You mentioned these fingerprints before," she said. "What are they?"

"Have you noticed those little lines on your fingers?" Palron replied. Yaetherim peered down at his hands. He'd seen them before, but had given them as much thought as a bird gives a blade of grass.

"Yes, when wiping grease off them," Tenora replied.

"They leave marks behind on touch, and we can bring these out with powdered pigment. They're unique for everyone, just like the patterns on fairy wings."

"So you still need to identify their owner?" Yaetherim asked. Palron nodded.

"It's more of a confirmation thing," he replied. Karis looked up from her notebook.

"There are three angles we must consider. Yaetherim, is this messenger friend of yours trustworthy?"

"I'd say so. Naeliya's eager to help."

Something shifted in Karis' expression.

"I know Messenger Naeliya," she said, "and she is reliable when sober. Please ask her to investigate this tower letterbox on my behalf."

Yaetherim nodded.

"That still leaves this panel," Karis continued, "and the hood worn by the killer."

"Would they only have one?" Yaetherim asked. All three humans shot him curious looks.

"We already know this involves two of your lot. They won't want to be noticed, will they? A connil hood is just like a stick insect, hidden in plain sight. I mean, connil are convicted criminals. I've seen you Rychillans passing them in the street. You barely glance at them."

Yaetherim scoffed.

"They may as well not exist," he finished. Palron and Tenora exchanged a look. Karis made a note in her notepad.

"Yaetherim, do you recall seeing a hooded person around Oato Clearing?" she said. Yaetherim shook his head.

"Oato Clearing?" Tenora asked.

"That's where they attacked me," Yaetherim replied. He explained what had happened since, speaking Fairic to ensure he missed nothing.

"Based on that, I think it may involve the College of Mages," Yaetherim finished. Tenora blinked twice and wiped a tear from her eye. She turned to Karis.

"I've worked with the mages before, Veritor Karis. Usually via correspondence, in relation to rune panel replacements."

She shot an uncomfortable look towards the living room.

"I can't do much more here. But I don't want to see anyone else killed."

"Then would you accompany me to the College of Mages? Your practical knowledge of runes may be useful," Karis asked.

Tenora nodded without a moment's hesitation. A brief discussion ensued, during which Yaetherim found himself preoccupied. After months of nothing, he had Rychillans volunteering to look into this. They'd made quite a bit of headway, as well. It was nearly too good to be true. Perhaps there was a reason for that. After all, this progress had only come once a different veritor had taken the case.

But that suspicion could wait. Right now, he needed to find Naeliya. He agreed with Tenora; he didn't want to see anyone else killed either.

8

Major Questions

Tenora stepped backwards. That look on Arch-Mage Darnith Sekan's face usually preceded a tongue-lashing harsh enough to strip the thread off a screw. She'd never received such a scolding herself, but had seen them unleashed upon her classmates. Sweat formed on her brow, and not just from the humidity.

Darnith got to his feet. He leaned forward and placed both hands on the desk. His eyes flicked down to the printer's block resting amongst the papers before him.

"I hope you don't mean to suggest, Veritor Karis, that this business involves one of my mages."

He'd spoken with a note of anger. That would build as he went on. Karis just picked up the wood. She turned it so the engraving faced Darnith and held it out.

"Could this have been made here? Using the machine you have in this building?"

"Yes, but that's no reason to suspect us."

There it was, a hint of heat in his voice. Yet Karis didn't even blink.

"Not on its own," Karis replied, "but it is sufficient to justify checking all such machines in town. Do not forget, those responsible have murdered and maimed. We have indications they are familiar with this part of the forest."

Darnith did not reply. Instead, he turned his attention to Tenora. A reflex brought her left arm forward, her terax up. By the time he made eye contact, a smile curved her lips. The same one she'd used on Karis in her workshop just a couple of hours ago. Words rolled off her lips like a newly greased bearing.

"I understand this is inconvenient. But the sooner we inspect your engraving machine, the quicker you can be on your way. I mean, ah, get on with your work."

Darnith frowned.

"You learned magic here, didn't you? Your face is familiar."

"Yes, you taught me runology for three years. I completed my schooling a decade ago."

"Very well."

Darnith strode across the office to a small steel cabinet mounted on the wall. No bigger than two closed fists, only a single key could fit within it. But it was the rectangular cutout next to the keyhole that caught Tenora's eye. Behind it, a pair of metal plates each bore an engraved number. Darnith unlocked the door and the rightmost digit rotated around. With a soft click, it locked into position, showing an increment of one.

"A counter lock?" Tenora asked.

"Yes," Darnith replied. "We record each use of this key."

He returned to the desk. From the top drawer, he pulled out a large, leather-bound tome. A ribbon bookmark stuck out about three-quarters of the way through its pages. Coffee and ink stains marred the cover. Darnith lay the book on the table and opened it to the page bookmarked.

"Is that all you keep recorded?" Karis asked.

"No," Darnith replied. He ran his finger across the bottom line of handwriting. His gaze jumped from one column to the next.

"Mage Kepan was the last to use the engraver yesterday. He produced two sequences for the airship *Maetaril*. After that, there are twelve blank panels left in storage."

"I see. Does the tally on the lock match that recorded?"

"It does, Veritor Karis."

Karis jotted a note in her notepad. Darnith made his own record, filling out the next line of the book with precise strokes. When done, he handed the key to Tenora.

"Return this to me when you're finished," he said. "I will need to sign it back in. Engraving room's up the corridor. On this side."

"Thank you," Tenora replied. She and Karis stepped out of Darnith's office. Upon reaching the room he'd mentioned, Tenora inserted the key. It shifted before engaging, and it took a moment of jiggling to move. Such wear told a tale of frequent use.

Tenora flicked the door open, to be greeted by an aroma of pine. Specks of dust danced in the sunlight streaming through the window. Tenora entered, with Karis just behind her. Once inside, Tenora turned and examined the lock. 'Twas nothing special. Sawdust coated it. Even the slots in the screws holding it together were full of the stuff. Seemed they did use this room often.

Tenora paused and leaned in. The screwheads were indeed covered in sawdust. She glanced back at Karis.

"Doesn't look like anyone's tampered with the lock. It could probably use some oil."

Karis nodded, and the two women turned their attention to the rest of the room. Wood shavings lay in the gaps between floorboards and upon the cupboard by the right-hand wall. But the engraving machine, in front of the window, showed no signs of dirt or dust. Neither did the three pedestal tables before it, or the fourth one to the left. Above the latter, a rod tapered to a point hung from a control arm. Drill bits waited, suspended, in identical positions above the others. Despite the complex arrangement of gears and other parts, using it was quite simple. The drill bits would mimic the movement of the pointed rod, thus allowing rune sequences to be traced from paper into wood. Metal clips at the top of each table held the work firmly.

That last thought brought a frown to Tenora's brow. She turned to Karis.

"Veritor Karis, may I please have that page Yaetherim found in Cerrane?"

Karis handed it over. Tenora strode over to the control rod and clipped the sheet in place below it. Both indentations on the paper, above the rune, lined up perfectly with the table's clips.

From one pocket, Tenora drew another of the printer's blocks from Jotol's shed. She performed the same check at the nearest engraving table. Everything aligned precisely. Even the drill bit matched the width of the engraved lines.

Tenora thought back. While she hadn't worked on this machine, she had maintained a similar one in a local newspaper office. Her thoughts returned to the last time she'd serviced it. A profanity shot from her lips. Karis stepped away from the cupboard.

"Are you injured?"

"No," Tenora replied. She took a couple of deep breaths and arranged her ideas. Her free hand reached for the cigarette case, but she stopped herself. A spark would surely ignite the sawdust lying around.

"These indentations on the page and the blocks match the clips exactly, Veritor Karis."

Karis frowned.

"Are all these engraving machines built to the same design?"

"The gearing and control arms, yes. Not the tables that hold the work."

Tenora tapped the printer's block and gestured to the nearest table.

"I've serviced the engraver at the newspaper office near my workshop. Their setup grabs these blocks around the edges, to avoid marring the printing surface. Besides, 'tis a rare cabinetmaker who can make two pieces identical to within a fraction of an inch."

Tenora put the block on the table, just below the clips. Karis leaned in. Her eyes flicked back and forth a few times, then she straightened up.

"I must have a word with Arch-Mage Darnith."

Tenora pinched her nose. A familiar pressure pushed against her brow, as though 'twere being squeezed in a clamp. For the second time in as many minutes, she reached for her cigarette case and stopped herself.

"May I step outside for a moment first? Just have to clear my head."

"Of course. To keep one's wits about oneself is essential. I only need Arch-Mage Darnith to arrange a meeting."

Tenora nodded and returned the printer's block to her overalls. She strode out onto the balcony. Beneath her boots, the floorboards creaked. She headed to the rear of the building. About halfway along, she stopped and leaned on the railing. She drew a cigarette, lit it and placed it between her lips.

During her school days, this upper level had been off-limits to her and her classmates. She had often wondered about the view from here. But she'd have preferred to see it under more pleasant circumstances. It wasn't bad, though. She had an unobstructed view of the clearing behind the college. Two mages stood at the far end, teaching on the banks of a stream. A class of schoolchildren watched them. Movement between the trees, further back, could have been birds, fairies or something else.

Tenora took a drag on her cigarette. One particular fairy came to mind. She had seen Yaetherim at Cropper's Crony some time ago. As she'd said, that airship skin patch had caught her eye. But his manner spoke of a person tired of pity, more so than his words. So she had talked of technicalities. Yet someone had given him those scars and mutilated his wing. Then they'd killed two more people. Stolen the life provided to them.

Even now, the thought of it turned Tenora's stomach. Karis had briefed Tenora on the drive out of town. Yaetherim had been on the receiving end of a water lance whilst simply doing his duty as a forest protector. Tenora had seen that spell performed. Machinists used it to cut steel, and it required concentration. Yet someone had cast it twice in panic. Such action spoke of experience or natural talent. Combined with her findings in the engraving room, it led to a single conclusion.

Tenora's gaze fell upon the two mages in the clearing below. Neither had taught her. They were too young for that. But both had used waterkind magic since she'd lit her cigarette. Tenora's hand clenched, her fingers digging into the wooden balustrade. At least one of them must be a murderer. That thought lingered like steam from a funnel.

Tenora leaned upon the railing. After a while, the lesson below drew to a close. A comforting beat drifted through the air, growing louder. Too deep for a car engine, it was likely a bus arriving to collect the students.

Behind Tenora, a floorboard creaked. Karis stopped a few paces back from the edge of the balcony. Her left hand fidgeted with her brooch.

"Arch-Mage Darnith has arranged an immediate meeting, for all college staff. We are to attend."

Tenora put out the remains of her cigarette. She tucked it into a small pocket of her overalls and followed Karis. She led Tenora into the room between Darnith's office and the one with the engraving machine. A table ran along most of its length, with Darnith at the head. Tenora nodded to the brown-haired man in the seat next to him, Mage Banoth. A puzzled frown joined the wrinkles on his brow.

"It's Tenora, isn't it? Tenora Perskel?"

She showed her terax.

"That's right, sir."

He checked the tattooed marks and chuckled.

"So you're here to ask more questions, are you? You always had good ones."

Tenora found it difficult to return his smile. While none of the mages seated before her were waterkinds, two Rychillans were involved. Anyone could wear a connil hood as a disguise. Even another mage.

"Are you alright, Arch-Mechanic Tenora?"

That question came from the attractive woman sitting to Darnith's left. Brown eyes and soft features poked out from beneath curly, ash-grey hair. Tenora caught herself staring, blushed, and glanced down.

"Yes, just lost in thought, Mage, ah…"

"Endra, Endra Lotal."

Tenora nodded. Endra wore a bracelet on each wrist. Both were of the same ornate design, silver with gold inlay. Only the crystals clasped within them set them apart. Florakind on the left, a half-used airkind crystal on the right.

Tenora frowned. She ran her gaze over Endra, ignoring the mage's terax. Judging by those bracelets and lace trim on her dress, she enjoyed the finer things in life. A solution to the rune capacity problem would bring plenty of kerlum along with the glory. Endra's slender build matched the person under the hood. But that could apply to the others, including the two she'd observed outside.

The door creaked open, and both waterkind mages strode in. As they crossed the room, Tenora sized them up. Either could have been the false connil. But only one of them wore both an airkind and a waterkind crystal in their jewellery, and his appearance sparked a twinge of familiarity. He could've been the person under that hood, too.

That last thought brought a flush to her cheeks. Her eyes flicked down and her fingers twitched. Such suspicions would lead nowhere. They were here to obtain facts. Setting one's nerves on edge would only distract from that.

Tenora shoved her thoughts aside and turned her attention to the young man who'd followed the two mages in. Barely old enough to have finished school, his terax indicated he'd only reached the rank of apprentice. His brown eyes met hers for a moment, then turned to Karis. He paused, then took a seat at the foot of the table. Karis glanced at him, then turned to Darnith.

"Do you not have two apprentices here?"

"Apprentice Kelnoss is applying at the Poloft College of Mages. We expect her back in a day or so. This is Apprentice Yerom."

Tenora frowned. Poloft was well off to the north-west, at least a couple of days by river boat. If this Kelnoss did know anything about this, they'd have to wait. As for Yerom, he may not be involved. Florakind and firekind crystals, both mostly spent, hung side-by-side in his necklace. Neither of those elements were involved in this.

Tenora took a seat beside Karis at the end of the table. She'd put names to three of the five mages. Based on her letters regarding replacement panels, the two waterkinds must be Peran Oaklon and Kepan Ardmoor. The first name ignited memories, and she looked at the familiar one. Recognition dawned. He was Mage Peran. Tenora had known him in school, just in passing. He'd been a couple of years ahead of her. Which made the other, sitting next to Endra, Mage Kepan.

Silence fell for a moment, then all eyes turned to Karis and Tenora. The former rose to her feet and stood straight.

"Several crimes have been committed in the past eight months, concerning rune tampering and concealment of it. These include the murders of Protector Paetobim and Mechanic Jotol, an assault on Protector Yaetherim, and sabotage. This latter caused wounding to Arch-Mechanic Tenora."

Tenora blinked. Between the healer's poultice on her ear and the events of the day, she'd almost forgotten about her injury.

"We have found firm evidence," Karis continued, "that a mage from this college is connected to these crimes, if not responsible themselves."

A range of reactions greeted her words. A few of the mages gasped. Most of them sat straighter in their chairs. Kepan folded his arms and leaned forward.

"These are significant accusations, Veritor Karis," he said, "and you seriously think we're involved?"

He broke off as Karis got to her feet. With a smooth movement, she reached up and hooked her hair up over two bone nubs, behind and a half-inch above each ear. Tenora's eyes widened. Until that moment, she hadn't noticed them, concealed as they were. So those rumours, at least, were true. Karis did have some Druhlashi blood in her. Some gasps came from around the table. Darnith and Peran both sat up even straighter in their chairs.

"I am serious," Karis said, "and I can show you this evidence right now."

Karis had just spoken with authority, without raising her voice. She'd already got their attention. Their expressions made that clear. Tenora leaned in.

"Could you please?" Peran asked. Karis nodded. She recounted Yaetherim's testimony, and his observations of the college. When she finished, the mages exchanged a look.

"So you're making this accusation based on the guesses of a flutterby?" Kepan asked. Reproving looks shot at him from all around the table. One came from Tenora. No legitimate excuse existed for describing a fairy that way.

"They may just be a fairy's observations," Banoth said, "but I can see the logic behind them."

"That is not all," Karis replied. She gestured to Tenora, who stood up. Her right fingers clasped empty air. Normally, she'd have a spanner or some such tool in hand when instructing. A deep breath steadied her nerves.

"There have been several cases of steam engines malfunctioning," she began. As she continued to talk, the words came easier and smoother, like the exhaust of an accelerating engine. Just the facts. That's all she needed to say. So say them she did. She recounted everything, from the runaway car to finding Jotol's body.

"I searched Jotol's shed, and found these," she finished. From her overalls, she drew the printer's blocks. She lay them on the table between the mages, then placed the page from Cerrane beside them.

"Please check the impressions on the top edges."

Peran leaned in and picked up one block. He examined it, then passed it to Banoth. Tenora flicked her left thumb out.

"Those marks perfectly align with the clamps on your engraving tables." That sentence earned her a few looks.

"Furthermore," Tenora continued, "I inspected the door to that room. I didn't find any signs of tampering on the lock. No scratches, and it's covered in sawdust. Even the slots of the screws were full of it."

Darnith leaned forward.

"What are you getting at, Arch-Mechanic Tenora?"

Tenora pursed her lips. She'd thought the implications of that were evident. But as she recalled from her school classes, Darnith couldn't stand ambiguity.

"Anyone tampering with the lock would've disturbed the sawdust. At least, the screws would be clear of it. Hence, only someone with a key to that room could've engraved those blocks using that machine," Tenora explained. In the corner of her eye, Karis nodded.

"I concur," Karis said, "and we know two Rychillans are involved. From this evidence and Yaetherim's testimony, one is a waterkind mage. Their accomplice is an airkind."

Darnith leaned forward.

"Alright, you've made your points. We should resolve this as soon as possible. What do you require from us?"

"Your car keys," Karis replied, "as we shall conduct a full search of this college, the grounds and all vehicles on it. Arch-Mechanic Tenora will perform the latter. I shall also question each of you."

"Surely that's not needed," Kepan said. "We have been here all morning, teaching classes and doing our work. We barely have time for a coffee, most days, let alone murder."

That statement earned him a stern look from Karis.

"Can you say that with absolute certainty, Mage Kepan? Do not forget, two Rychillans are involved. One could provide false testimony for another."

Kepan sat back, but Karis had more to ask.

"Where were you last night between the nineteenth and twenty-first hours?"

"Dining at Shipwright's Tavern, down at the harbour."

He shot a look at Darnith.

"It was a rare evening. I was actually able to finish here on time," he added. Darnith didn't reply, but Endra spoke up.

"We all have to work late occasionally, Mage Kepan," she said soothingly. Karis cleared her throat.

"Do you have a witness for that?"

Kepan closed his eyes.

"I think the waiter's name was Otrai. If you must know, I had roasted nistyr root in cheese sauce with potatoes and carrots. I hope that is enough information."

Karis made a note and turned her gaze onto Peran. He shoved himself back from the table and fiddled with the two crystals dangling from his necklace. When he spoke, Tenora had to strain to hear his voice.

"Could we please discuss it in private, Veritor Karis?"

Karis' eyes narrowed.

"Do not expect to return to your office until after I have searched it. I trust the corridor shall provide sufficient privacy?"

"That'll do."

Peran stood up. He followed Karis out of the room, handing Tenora a bundle of keys as he passed. The door closed with a soft thud. Tenora found herself on the end of several curious looks.

121

"While we're waiting," she said, "can you pass me your car keys?"

"Is that necessary?" Darnith asked.

"No," Tenora replied. She pulled a miniature screwdriver from her overalls.

"Some of you used to teach me. But there are some skills I didn't learn in school. I got my start in tinkering by experimenting with locks on my family's farm. I've played with them for years."

She held up the screwdriver so they could see it.

"I could open your cars with this. But it would go quicker if I had the keys."

Silence hung in the air for a few seconds. Kepan turned to Banoth.

"Was she this cavalier when you taught her?"

Tenora sprung to her feet. Her hand flicked out, the gesture taking in the seated mages. Only a flick of her finger prevented the screwdriver from flinging out.

"You want to talk about being cavalier, Mage Kepan? We share a responsibility, to every person who climbs into a car, bus, truck, boat or airship. An implicit promise that those vehicles and vessels are safe. At least one of you has flaunted that duty. Not to mention murder and wounding in a shabby attempt at concealment. Just for the glory and money from solving the rune capacity problem."

Her hand shot towards the door, a finger pointing straight out.

"If you are going to say this isn't my area of expertise, you're absolutely correct. It's Veritor Karis'. If she deems this search necessary, I will conduct it by any means available to me."

Tenora locked eyes with Darnith. A favourite phrase of his crossed her lips.

"I trust that's clear?"

The room went quiet. A familiar warmth spread across Tenora's cheeks. Realisation came with it. In her outrage, she had reprimanded two of her former teachers. But she had meant every word she'd said. With one hand, she tucked a lock of hair behind her ear.

A metallic jingle broke through the silence. Banoth wriggled in his chair. After a few moments, he extricated his car keys and slid them along the table. They stopped in front of Tenora. She nodded.

"Thank you."

Darnith's arrived next, followed by those of Kepan and Endra. Tenora picked them up and sorted through them. She paused and looked at Yerom.

"Um, I ride a bicycle," he said, "it's chained up outside. Just with a padlock, will you need the key for that?"

Tenora shook her head. A floorboard creaked, heralding Peran's return. He took his seat, and Tenora joined Karis in the corridor. The latter leaned into the meeting room.

"Wait here," she ordered, "I will let you know when we have finished."

"But-"

"This is not up for discussion."

With that, Karis closed the door. She glanced down at Tenora's hands.

"Did they give you too much difficulty?"

"No. Just needed to make a point."

Tenora fiddled with the keys. Her fingers stopped on one particular set.

"Do we need to search Mage Banoth's car? He's neither a waterkind nor an airkind. I mean, there aren't any known cases of trikind mages."

"Are there any places in a vehicle where something could be concealed without the driver's knowledge?"

Three such spots came to mind.

"I take your point."

"I shall meet you in the carpark once I have completed my search."

Tenora nodded, and Karis strode off. Tenora headed downstairs. She couldn't help but wonder how it had come to this. Mages should be paragons, their conduct above reproach. Yet here she was, searching their cars to determine which of them had lied and murdered. Hopefully, she'd find something. The sooner they ended this, the better.

9

A Pinch of Distrust

Wind whistled past Yaetherim as he swooped down from the mail tower. Below him, the rooftops of Alkentoft spread out, each bearing a message lamp. In three directions, they gave way to farmland and forest. To the east, they met the ocean.

Naeliya flew beside him for a few heartbeats. She banked southwest, towards the College of Mages. Yaetherim shot her a parting glance. He had asked her to deliver an update to Karis or Tenora, and she'd perked up. This wasn't the Naeliya he'd seen on his last two visits. More of a fresh sapling than a broken branch. That almost brought a smile to his lips. But other thoughts forestalled it.

After a bit of convincing, the tower director had told them who'd leased the letterbox used to send that correspondence to Jotol. Not a person, but the merchants' guild. They'd hired three there. Yet none of the messengers had seen anyone use it. Nothing suspicious there, for once. They didn't need to watch the base of the tower. The letter boxes within were checked regularly.

The more Yaetherim thought about it, the more a merchant's involvement made sense. As he'd noted in Cerrane, that cache of crystals would cost rather a bit, if not stolen. And those were the ones left behind. Months of experiments would run up quite a bill. That sum could be 1,242 kerlum, 3 kerlar and 2 kerlo.

A familiar tickle stirred Yaetherim's stomach. Nothing unpleasant. Just that feeling of something awry. Pressure from the merchants had distracted Jorryn from investigating his case. Now it appeared it may involve them.

Yaetherim reached the market hall a few heartbeats later. It occupied all of what Rychillans called a block, being bordered by streets on all sides. From outside, it could be mistaken for a warehouse. But the voices and aromas spilling from the large door halfway along belied this. Memories of grocery shopping with Tarlon Emgar flowed back. Then, they'd come in search of ingredients for Fairic food to serve at Cropper's Crony. But this time, Yaetherim sought a certain veritor.

After pausing for a couple of Rychillans to exit, Yaetherim flew in. A pair of perpendicular paths divided the lower floor into quarters. Smaller walkways branched off and ran between stalls. To the left, both areas had stands displaying meats and produce from surrounding farms. A few showed an array of spices, the aromas of which filled the air. On the right, those in the nearest section sold other local goods. Clothes, jewellery, weapons and candies amongst them. Behind each stall stood a Rychillan wearing a wheat-yellow sash. More obvious than terax marks alone, these served to identify merchants from a distance.

Yaetherim flew to the far-right quarter. Unlike the others, the wares here came from beyond the borders of the region. Some even from outside the kingdom itself. All of those thefts had been from shipments leaving Alkentoft. Jorryn would be amongst these merchants if he were here. But of all the Rychillans milling about, Jorryn was not among them.

Four stalls stood at the intersection of the main walkways. Here, they'd see almost everyone who entered the market hall. Yet one remained clear of customers. A merchant sat behind it, an arm resting on small wooden boxes of wares. He looked up with hope each time someone passed by. But of the half-dozen people Yaetherim observed, none showed an interest.

Yaetherim flew down and hovered in front of that stall. He inquired about Jorryn. A brief conversation followed. The merchant agreed to tell Yaetherim where Jorryn was. In exchange, he asked Yaetherim to sample some of the Druhlac food he was selling. One item, a dried vegetable called brookweed, caught Yaetherim's interest. It brought a few culinary possibilities to mind. Yaetherim got the merchant's name. He'd be back after sorting out these murders.

As it turned out, Jorryn had gone upstairs to meet with Arch-Merchant Naltan and Merchant Rynach. A spiral staircase in the corner led to the top floor. Yaetherim flew over to it. Halfway up, a familiar voice drifted down from the landing above.

"You'll have any update as soon as it happens."

Yaetherim perched on the handrail and waited. He didn't have to wait long.

"Speaking of updates, Veritor Jorryn, I've got another one for you," he said, as Jorryn reached the step above him. The latter stopped and stared. He folded his arms.

"How did that come about? We're not even investigating the same case anymore."

"They stabbed Mechanic Jotol to death in his house earlier today. He was corresponding with someone about these compacted runes."

Jorryn pinched the bridge of his nose.

"How's that related to the thefts?"

"I traced the letters. They were being sent from a tower box hired by the guild of merchants. Tell me, how many crystals can 1,242 kerlum, 3 kerlar and 2 kerlo buy?"

Jorryn leaned against the staircase column. From his pocket, he pulled out his notepad and pencil. The latter flicked over the paper, leaving twig-like scratches across the page. Upon closer inspection, they formed Rychillan numbers. Jorryn looked up, his face pale.

"At least 157 crystals, maybe more, depending on prices at the time. It could be a coincidence, but I..."

Jorryn trailed off and tapped a finger against his free thumb.

"I need a coffee for this. Come on."

Jorryn waited for Yaetherim to do his pre-flight checks and take off. They headed down through the crowd of merchants and customers. Neither spoke until they reached a four-wheeled cart parked between two stalls. Several

Rychillans and Fairies queued before it.

"Would you like one too?" Jorryn asked. Yaetherim went to answer, but stopped. His wings ached, and the sleep he'd missed last night weighed upon his eyelids. Not that he usually slept well, anyway. He reached into his pouch and felt about for his few kerlum coins.

"Don't worry about that. I'll pay. Least I can do," Jorryn said. Yaetherim looked up, and Jorryn nodded. Silence fell between the two of them.

Before long, they arrived at the head of the queue and bought their coffee. Jorryn handed Yaetherim a fairy-sized paper cup. The latter sniffed at it. An earthy, acidic aroma wafted up. No scent of the needless extras that Rychillans insisted on adding. Even as Yaetherim took a mouthful, Jorryn grabbed a jar from atop the cart. He poured a dash of the pale orange liquid within into his drink. Yaetherim frowned.

"Nistyr nectar? How can you taste any of it?"

Jorryn shrugged.

"It's not that. It adds a bit of sweetness."

He punctuated his words with a sip. After returning the sweetener, Jorryn led Yaetherim away.

"Now what's this about Mechanic Jotol?" Jorryn asked. Yaetherim recounted that morning's events. Gulps of coffee accompanied his sentences. With each word, Jorryn's frown deepened.

"So I thought there could be a connection," Yaetherim finished. Jorryn took a mouthful of his drink and swished it around before swallowing.

"You said this was just a hunch," he replied. Yaetherim frowned.

"As you calculated, it's an amount that can buy a substantial number of crystals. You mightn't have done much about this, but it would surprise me if those rune experiments stopped. Those experimenting would need a steady supply."

Jorryn met his gaze for a moment, then developed a sudden interest in his coffee.

"It couldn't hurt to check. Luxanke knows, I've been hoping for a break in this case."

He finished his drink in a single swig and took the now-empty cup in Yaetherim's hand. After tossing the cups in a nearby bin, he rejoined Yaetherim.

"I'm puzzled by that hood you mentioned," he said. "They're only issued to sincere repentant connil."

Yaetherim scoffed, and Jorryn nodded.

"Exactly," he added, "murder is not an action of repentance. But I've not had reports of any hoods being stolen."

Now it was Yaetherim's turn to stare. He flew back, and his heart raced.

"Are you serious? They haven't reported the one item that has shown up?"

Jorryn's left hand reached up and fiddled with the crystal hanging from his necklace.

"No, it hasn't. Perhaps we should start there. Maybe they weren't stolen from here. Merchant Celys looks after those. Didn't see her upstairs, so she should be in the import quarter."

"There are a few merchants over there. Could you be more specific?"

"I've interviewed her about some of these other thefts. Curly blue hair, soft grey eyes. Like a storm cloud rolling in. Has a rather charming smile."

"You're reciting a love poem. Got something not in the eye of the beholder?"

Jorryn blushed and glanced towards the stands.

"She's about my height and has a small mole on her left cheek. Wears her crystal, florakind, in a ring on her right hand. She specialises in garments and fabrics."

Yaetherim nodded and took off. Again, he flew over the crowd, his eyes flicking from one stall to the next. He skipped those not selling clothes. He soon spotted someone fitting Jorryn's description. She stood behind her stand, talking to a Brial with distinct yellow crest feathers on his head.

Yaetherim waved to get Jorryn's attention. Without thinking, he signed two words.

"Over here!"

"Okay," Jorryn gestured back. Yaetherim blinked. Most Rychillans only knew spoken Fairic. He swooped down and landed on that stall, in a clear spot beside a stack of shirts, sized to fit Fairies. Well-crafted, but not what he'd choose. The seller glanced over.

"Merchant Celys?" Yaetherim asked.

"Yes, I'll be with you in a moment."

Yaetherim nodded, and Celys returned her attention to the Brial man. Yaetherim turned aside. There wasn't much point in listening. He didn't understand a note of Brialish. Jorryn shouldn't be too far behind. He spotted the veritor a short distance away, trying to get around two Druhlac built like tree trunks and carrying bananas. A movement caught Yaetherim's eye. Turning back, he found Celys had finished with her customer. Her gaze fell not upon his scars, but his clothes instead.

"That's well tailored," she said. "I have a few garments of similar quality."

Yaetherim pursed his lips. No doubt she used that spiel on most customers.

"I'll pass the compliment onto Paechalor," he replied, "but I'm here with-"

A shout sounded out. Yaetherim's head whipped over. Jorryn got to his feet, his hands clasped around some bananas. A giggle came from Yaetherim's left. He turned back. The last vestiges of a smile vanished from Celys' lips. Yaetherim shrugged and flicked his hand towards Jorryn.

"With Veritor Jorryn?" Celys asked. Yaetherim nodded.

"Is it about those thefts?"

"Aye. We suspect a connil hood or two were stolen."

"Let me think," Celys replied. She picked up a notebook from beneath the stall. Jorryn reached them, his cheeks rosy. Celys looked up, glanced at Jorryn, then turned to Yaetherim.

"Yes, you're right. We sent them up to Tolenoft with riverfarers. Part of a shipment up there. A couple of crates fell into the river while being put aboard, but the salvage crew recovered them."

Yaetherim frowned.

"Salvage crew?" he asked. Celys nodded.

"We have two or three of them help whenever we're loading or unloading a boat. Standard procedure, just in case. The less time our goods spend in water, the better."

"Makes sense," Yaetherim commented.

"We pack the hoods six to a crate," Celys continued, "but when they opened these crates to check for damage, two were missing."

"One for each Rychillan involved," Yaetherim said, "so that confirms it. These thefts are connected."

Jorryn shook his head.

"The thieves could have just sold them. Did you report this, Merchant Celys?"

She blinked and stood straight.

"Of course I did!"

"When did it happen?" Yaetherim asked.

"Around day 63 of this year. A couple of days after Luxanke's tears finished."

Yaetherim blinked. He hadn't heard that term before. Based on the date, it must be what Rychillans called the Rains.

Jorryn made a note in his notebook.

"Yet I was not told of this."

Celys folded her arms.

"What are you getting at, Veritor Jorryn Lorem?"

"I, ah…"

Yaetherim took flight and hovered between the two Rychillans. He faced Celys.

"We're trying to get at facts. Someone stole these hoods. It is a fact that Jorryn wasn't made aware of this theft. Who did you report this to?"

"One of the other merchants. Can't quite recall who. It was a while ago."

Before either investigator could reply, a Rychillan woman strode up. A few strands of white amongst her grey hair marked her age. She stood next to the stall and shot a look at Celys. The merchant glanced over.

"Can you tell us anything else?" Jorryn asked. Celys shook her head.

"Nothing else comes to mind. I'd better go."

Jorryn nodded, and Celys turned to her customer. After jotting down a few sentences, Jorryn pointed to the far exit.

"I'm going to need to check my notes. We'll talk on the way."

Yaetherim followed Jorryn out, lost in thought. News of this particular theft had died within the merchant's guild. His earlier suspicions had indeed borne fruit.

Jorryn stopped next to a grey four-door car with a solid roof. Yaetherim landed on top of it.

"It doesn't exactly match the others," Jorryn stated. "They reported those to me, and we know when these hoods went missing. Sometime between the warehouse and the riverfarer docks."

Yaetherim frowned.

"Are you sure about that? It was only by accident they discovered this theft then. Nothing to say it didn't happen earlier."

"What, you mean before it was dispatched? But that implies a merchant, or one of their workers. That's a pretty big accusation, Protector Yaetherim."

"That isn't my title anymore. But do you know how protectors spot poachers?"

Jorryn frowned. Of course he wouldn't. Town guards only arrested poachers once they'd been identified.

"I'm not sure," he replied, "footprints?"

"By looking for what's gone. A hole between two tasal plants, with overturned earth. They only grow in threes. Or a gap between eggs in a bird's nest."

Jorryn tilted his head.

"I think I see what you're getting at. The report of this theft is missing. But that doesn't mean the thieves are your attackers. This hood is the only stolen item that's shown up again. So they've just sold it here instead of wherever they usually do."

Yaetherim raised an eyebrow.

"There's something else. Mechanic Jotol wasn't sliced up with a lance of water, like me and Paetobim. They stabbed him underarm. Veritor Karis said that is how the Druhlac do their hunting."

"Are you saying there are Druhlac involved in this?"

"Nay, but who spends more time working with them than a merchant? Consider it. Two murderers, two hoods, two methods of killing," Yaetherim replied. Jorryn slumped against the car. He pinched the bridge of his nose.

"That makes sense. They'd be able to suppress news of that theft, too," he said.

"I mean, you'd have investigated it, wouldn't you?"

Jorryn frowned.

"Of course I would. I'm sorry for dillydallying on your case, Yaetherim. Truly, I am. But that doesn't make me lazy."

Once again, he'd spoken sincerely.

"That isn't what I meant. Whoever suppressed this didn't want you to link it back to them," Yaetherim clarified. Jorryn's frown deepened.

"But they let me investigate the others."

"Perhaps they could only suppress some of them."

Jorryn scoffed.

"I've barely had time to look into anything else. If these robberies aren't all of them, then the merchants are shedding money."

He continued to speak, but his words flowed past Yaetherim like river water.

"They've been keeping you occupied," Yaetherim said, "but what evidence do you have that these thefts actually happened?"

Jorryn blinked and broke off.

"What do you mean? They were reported to me. Invoices show more items sent than received."

"Is that it? No broken locks, damaged crates, anything like that?"

"Well, no," Jorryn replied.

"Doesn't it take just a few pen strokes to alter an invoice?"

Jorryn took a deep breath. Yaetherim watched him. If Jorryn were worthy of his title, he should infer the same possibility.

"They could be fake," Jorryn said, "but that's a bit of a leap."

Yaetherim folded his arms.

"I may be taking this with a pinch of distrust, but isn't that worth considering? It seems all these thieves have actually accomplished is distracting you and stealing two hoods. Then there's the money the guild has lost. Enough to cover how many crystals?"

"At least 157," Jorryn replied. He tapped his fingers on the roof of the car. For a few dozen heartbeats, he remained silent and stared off into the distance. Yaetherim didn't speak. He'd made his point. Several swear words shot from Jorryn's lips. He sagged and leaned against the vehicle.

"That would explain why I did not get anywhere," he finished, "there wasn't anywhere to go."

"So what do you have on these? I mean, you took action on this case."

Jorryn shrugged.

"Notes, back at my desk. I suppose there may be some sort of pattern to them."

"Mind if I join you? Two pairs of eyes can watch more of the forest."

Jorryn nodded and opened the door of the car. They climbed in and drove off.

* * *

A short while later, Jorryn led Yaetherim into the veritors' office. They'd gone via Cropper's Crony. As Yaetherim had hoped, a message from Charlys had been waiting. It only said that patrols had seen a pair of connil walking to and from Dinsec's boat.

Yaetherim flew over to Jorryn's desk. By some stroke of luck, a clearing lay amongst the mess scattered upon it. Yaetherim landed beside a stack of notepads. Jorryn took a seat and pulled a notebook from another pile.

Yaetherim leaned in. Now he'd see what facts Jorryn had foraged over these last few months. Despite the mark of a tenil on the veritor's terax, Yaetherim found it hard to believe these thefts required so much time.

Jorryn lay the notepad on the desk so Yaetherim could read it. He flicked through the pages. Text and sketches flew past and blurred together. Jorryn stopped on a page near the end. Yaetherim stepped in for a better look. Despite his experience with reading Rychillan, he struggled to make out the words before him. He'd seen more comprehensible piles of twigs. But the numbers that started each entry showed the date.

Yaetherim ran his finger over the lines, tracing out the so-called handwriting. One note, dated day 61 of year 107, age of magic, covered the theft of three bushels of sugarcane. The next, four days later, recorded the robbery of a half-dozen bottles of wine. Both cases had unfolded, as Jorryn had described. After leaving the guild's warehouse, they'd not arrived at their destination. Not a word about missing garments.

"Are these notes complete?"

Jorryn gestured to a stack of notepads.

"That's all of them. As I said, I've not heard of hoods being stolen before today. Jewellery, sugarcane, wine, candies, weapons, almost anything you can think of is in there except meat and clothes. I'd remember something like a connil hood."

Yaetherim smirked. The more he learned, the more his suspicions blossomed.

"These reports are exactly two days on either side of that hood theft. That's suspiciously precise. And the hoods were spotted on Rychillans walking to the boat the killers used. Bit silly of them to use a guild letterbox to send letters about the runes."

"Doesn't narrow it down that much. There's over 60 merchants in Alkentoft."

"It's less than the entire town."

Jorryn looked up.

"Fair point," he muttered.

"So, where has your investigation led?"

Jorryn sighed.

"Nowhere. I've spoken to aircrew, riverfarers, lorry drivers, and everyone else involved. Whenever I think I have something, another theft happens which points in a different direction."

"Yes, they did a good job of distracting you. Are there any merchants whose names seem to keep cropping up?"

Jorryn stood up and pulled two evidence boxes off the shelf behind him. He placed them atop a nearby pile of notebooks, this one coming up to Yaetherim's chest.

"These are all the documents I have. Copies of invoices, victim statements, letters. Everything I've got. Perhaps reviewing them with a, um, pinch of distrust will turn up something."

Yaetherim's wings twitched. He shot a look at the mess surrounding him. "Do you expect to lay them out here?"

"Arch-Veritor Rakin won't mind if we use his desk. Provided it's clear by the time he arrives for night duty."

That wouldn't be a problem. Lunchtime was a few hours away. Yaetherim took to the air. With a movement spell, he lifted one of the evidence boxes. He flew it over to Rakin's desk. Jorryn followed with the other. Then the two men set to work.

10

Confirmation

Tenora closed the boot of Mage Banoth's car. It only contained a few personal items and a tool set, just like the first three vehicles she'd searched. Nothing of interest.

After locking it, she turned to the next automobile. Its mudguards overhung the wheels by an inch. Leather trim covered the joins between panels, instead of brass or wood. Only one coachbuilder in town used it, and he worked with Locksmith Avora. A single set of keys bore the corresponding maker's mark. Tenora pulled them out and stepped around to the rear of the car. Like when assessing repairs, she'd start with the engine.

Whilst the boiler was sealed, the firebox wasn't. Without flames, 'twas just a large compartment. Working her way forward, she examined every nook and cranny. Yet her search found no sign of the connil hood. Two paper bags sat on the front seat, but these only held crumbs and spots of grease.

She walked around the car and opened the boot. An unmarked woven satchel lay in it, beside the standard tool set. It bulged in the middle. When Tenora picked it up, it drooped on both sides of her hand. Definitely some sort of clothes, then. Her heart pounded. She reached in, pulled out the garment inside, and blinked. Connil hoods didn't come in that shade of green. 'Twas merely a tunic tailored for a man. It would fit Kepan, and this was his vehicle.

Tenora re-folded the top and went to return it. Something else, much darker, lay at the bottom of the bag. Tenora put the tunic on the mudguard, then tipped the satchel over. A pair of brown goatskin boots fell into her hand. Her eyes narrowed. These seemed to be the latest fashion amongst town fairies. She'd noticed several of them wearing such footwear. Not what one would expect to find in a mage's car. Rychillans didn't even wear them.

"Arch-Mechanic Tenora?"

Tenora turned and found herself looking at another pair of goatskin boots, with the blue-skinned legs of a waterkind fairy in them. The fairy's bright blue eyes peered out from beneath a mop of vaguely combed red hair.

"It's Messenger Naeliya, isn't it? What brings you here?" Tenora asked in Fairic. Naeliya landed on the nearest mudguard and replied in the same language.

"I've got a message for you and Veritor Karis. Those letters you found at Jotol's house were being sent from a tower letterbox leased to the merchants' guild."

"What?"

"It's one they rented a couple of years ago. As far as we know, they haven't used it for anything else."

Tenora frowned. That couldn't be right. All merchants were at least rynil, if not tenil. But an earlier conversation with Karis came back to her. Every ganil and connil had started as a rynil. Just like rotten apples or bananas, they'd been identified and marked lower class, less trustworthy.

Before Tenora could reply, Karis joined them. Her hair covered her bone nubs once more. Naeliya repeated her message in Rychillan.

"Then it seems we shall have to question them, too," Karis said, once Naeliya had finished.

"Yaetherim's already taking care of that. Said he'd try to find Veritor Jorryn. He thinks there may be a connection to those thefts."

Karis' eyebrow emerged from behind her sunglasses.

"I see. Thank you, Messenger Naeliya."

"Do you have a reply for Yaetherim?"

Karis shook her head. Naeliya went to take off, but another sentence from

Tenora stopped her.

"Just a question, Messenger Naeliya."

Tenora held up the goatskin boots she'd found.

"What would these be worth to you? They seem to have cropped up around town like wheat at harvest time."

Naeliya flew in. She ran her fingers over the fabric.

"Well-made and brand-new. I'd say a couple of large favours. Where did you find them?"

Tenora just pointed to the open boot next to Naeliya. The fairy glanced in.

"Will that be all?" she asked. Tenora nodded, and Naeliya took off. Tenora returned the goatskin boots from whence they came and locked the vehicle. She glanced at Karis.

"That's Mage Kepan done. I've already searched those of Arch-Mage Darnith, Mage Banoth, and Mage Peran. Discovered nothing of interest in them," Tenora said. She put the keys in her pocket and drew the last set. A few quick steps brought her to the rear of Endra's car. She opened the engine and leaned in. Karis stepped around and joined her.

"Did you find anything in the college?" Tenora asked.

"No garments, nor a necklace that matches the crystal found beside Yaetherim. However, there is one thing of note. The office shared by Mages Kepan and Peran does not contain any spent crystals."

"Is that unusual?"

"Perhaps. That of Mages Endra and Banoth had used crystals in the rubbish bin. It could just be differing standards in tidiness. Yet the trash in Arch-Mage Darnith's room also contained spent crystals."

Tenora frowned. She extricated herself from the engine and tucked a stray lock of hair behind her ear.

"Mages Kepan and Peran? I wouldn't call either of them tidy. Both their cars are as clean as the floor of a barn. Kepan's had a couple of empty paper bags on the front seat, passenger side. Small ones with grease spots on them. Probably from a food cart. But no used crystals."

"I see," Karis replied. Tenora glanced over at the two vehicles she'd mentioned. The lack of spent crystals didn't necessarily mean anything.

While she kept her workshop tidy, she couldn't say the same about her shed at home. She resumed her search of the engine. Just like the others, it held nothing noteworthy.

"Aside from those goatskin boots, I have found no oddities so far. I even checked Apprentice Yerom's bicycle," she said. She closed the bonnet. Her hand flicked out towards the forest.

"A fairy patrol passed by, too. A Protector Captain named Charlys asked them to look out for those garments. They have not spotted them."

Karis made a note in her notebook. She snapped it shut.

"Even without it, we shall need to confirm what Mages Peran and Kepan told me."

Tenora nodded. A few minutes later, she finished searching. Like the others, it contained nothing relating to the murders.

After returning the keys, Tenora and Karis climbed into their car. Karis fired up the engine.

"Could Mage Peran explain where he was last night?" Tenora asked.

"Yes. At the harisyke courts in Amilyn Street. Not participating, but gambling."

"Betting on what?"

It wasn't unusual to bet on tournament games. Tenora had wagered a handful of kerlum like that herself. But she hadn't read of an ongoing competition in the newspaper recently.

"Those playing for recreation."

Karis reached over, disengaged the brakes, and shifted the car into gear. It moved off, and she steered it out of the carpark.

Tenora didn't reply. She and her friends often played harisyke, only for fun. But if people had bet on those matches, they'd have watched them closely. These games weren't shows for those with kerlum to throw around.

"Is that legal?"

"No," Karis replied. "Formal gambling is only allowed for tournaments and show contests."

Hence Peran's reluctance to discuss it in front of the other mages. Tenora pursed her lips. Whilst disappointing, betting barely matched murder in terms of depravity. Even so, she and her friends were not sheepdogs performing tricks for the amusement of others. They weren't there to win, but to have fun running around the court, hitting the ball back and forth across the net.

"He bet with a bookmaker named Polton Lonim," Karis added, "whom Arch-Veritor Rakin made ganil a few years ago. I believe it was for this same sort of illegal gambling."

Silence fell, save for the beat of the engine. Tenora gazed at Karis' left arm. It wasn't the terax marks that held her attention this time, but the limb that bore them. Toned and tanned, it showed Karis kept herself fit.

"Do you play much harisyke, Veritor Karis?"

"Not anymore," came the blunt reply. One of Karis' hands fiddled with the brooch on her tunic. Silence fell again. Tenora leaned against the door, her gaze landing upon the forest outside. It soon gave way to the bricks and cobblestones of Alkentoft.

Before long, they reached Shipwright's Tavern. It took only a few minutes to identify the waiter who'd served Kepan. He confirmed Kepan's testimony, right down to the choice of food.

* * *

Karis steered into the town hall's garage. They'd stopped at the guard barracks on the way, and Karis had given orders for Polton Lonim to be brought in for questioning. They climbed out and Tenora glanced back.

"I'm sorry, but I'll need ten minutes with that car. You've got a failing washer in one cylinder and the valve timing's a little off. It's been annoying me since we left here."

"Is it still safe to drive?"

"For the moment. You'll have to take it to a workshop to adjust the timing. But I can fix the rest now."

Karis stopped and turned around. She looked from Tenora to the car. Instead of a steely stare, she nodded.

"Please meet me in my office when you have finished."

Without another word, she strode off. Tenora reached for her tools and set to work. She soon found the affected washer. It only had a single split through the rubber. After removing it, Tenora conjured a flame. She held the washer to it. Once it softened, she pushed the crack closed.

It had just cooled off when Karis returned. Tenora glanced over her shoulder.

"I've only got to reinsert this."

"Very well," Karis replied. Tenora set about doing so.

"I gave orders to have all cars in town inspected," Karis added. "For those with stacked runes, the guard officers asked the drivers who last serviced them. I have just received the results."

"Who was it?"

"Only two names came up: Mechanic Jotol and Arch-Mechanic Warrett."

Tenora froze, her spanner halfway to her pocket. Warrett had been rather brusque that morning. If Karis was right, then he'd lied to her face.

"Shall I come with you?"

"Yes. I may need your expertise again."

"Good," Tenora replied. "I'd like to hear what Arch-Mechanic Warrett has to say for himself."

There'd been a note of reproach in her voice. Karis must have noticed, for she folded her arms.

"You told me Arch-Mechanic Warrett bears some hostility towards you. I must ask, is this because of any action on your part?"

"He was using reconditioned parts, without telling the clients. They don't last as long. He didn't take it well when I reported that to our guild."

Tenora paused and thought back.

"In hindsight, I think it got worse when I started courting Mechanic Seralyn, who works for him."

She sighed.

"Seralyn ended our courtship last year. Just after my promotion to Arch-Mechanic."

"I see," Karis replied.

Tenora finished her repair, and they climbed into the car. A brief drive brought them to Warrett's workshop. An aroma of engine grease and clanging of tools drifted through the doors. From somewhere within, a gramophone played *The Ballad of the Wandering Mage*.

Two steps through the door, Tenora found her path blocked. Ordan Kelish, Warrett's second-in-command, stared her down.

"Arch-Mechanic Warrett asked you to leave here this morning," he declared. Tenora stood up straight. It wasn't the first time Ordan had tried this. Without looking aside, she gestured to Karis.

"I'm working with Veritor Karis."

She paused and let that name hang in the air.

"We need to talk to Arch-Mechanic Warrett," Karis said. Ordan opened his mouth, but another voice spoke.

"I'll look after them, Ordan."

Seralyn stood a few feet away. Like Tenora, she'd tied her hair back and tucked it into her overalls.

"Very well," Ordan replied, "but it's your responsibility, Seralyn."

He strode off, and Seralyn turned to Tenora.

"Is the boss in trouble?"

"That depends on what he has to say," Karis answered. Seralyn glanced down at her boots.

"Where can we find him?" Tenora asked. Seralyn pointed to a small, beaten farm lorry halfway along the rear wall. A pair of overall-clad legs stuck out from under it.

They crossed the workshop. A dark, viscous liquid trickled out from beneath the truck, inching towards the nearest drain in the floor. Tenora frowned. Warrett should have used a drip tray. 'Twas careless to let oil run over the concrete like that. Especially for someone who'd described her as such, just that morning.

"Watch your step," Tenora said. Karis looked over and Tenora nodded to the oil. They reached the lorry. Tenora crouched beside it. She cleared her throat.

"Arch-Mechanic Warrett? It's Arch-Mechanic Tenora."

No reply came from beneath the truck. So he was giving her the silent treatment then. That was a fresh approach.

"Veritor Karis and I need to ask you about some runes," Tenora added, speaking louder. Again, no response. This was not like Warrett. He'd always been forthright with his thoughts. A nasty suspicion gripped Tenora. Her eyes fell upon the trickling liquid. From what she'd heard of Warrett, he wasn't careless either.

With her left thumb, she pressed on the crystal in her ring. It dug into her finger and energy skittered over her skin. She cast her spell. A flame flared into life, hovering level with her nose. A tweak of the magic turned it from orange to white.

Tenora leaned down. In the flame's light, the edges of the trickle appeared red. Dark red. Not the blue of used engine oil. Unfortunately, Tenora knew this colour, too.

"Veritor Karis, that, that's not oil," Tenora said, her voice shaking. She stood up and stepped back. Her breath came in quick gasps and her hands shook. With a flick of her fingers, she extinguished the flame. She cupped them to her mouth.

"Mechanic down! MECHANIC DOWN!"

Clunks and clangs sounded out as tools hit the floor. The rhythm of running footsteps filled the air. Ordan reached them first.

"What-?"

Tenora nodded to the blood.

"He's injured."

Ordan's eyes widened. Tenora pointed to the florakind crystal mounted in his bracelet.

"Could you lift the truck clear?"

Ordan extended a hand towards the lorry. It budged, then lifted, the wood body pulling the rest of the vehicle with it. Seralyn joined Ordan and added her own spell. They guided it out of the way. Below it, Warrett lay unmoving.

Silence fell.

Karis stepped in to examine Warrett. She crouched down, avoiding the stream of blood. She placed a finger on his wrist. Her lips moved, but no words passed between them. Tenora frowned. Karis must've been praying, not that Luxanke would be listening. She never did. When finished, Karis looked over her shoulder at the half-dozen mechanics standing around.

"I am sorry, but I must offer you my condolences," she said gently. Without waiting for a reply, she resumed her examination.

Tenora drew a cigarette and placed it in her mouth. It took her three tries to light it, her hands shook so. Her gaze passed from one mechanic to the next. Some stood with their mouths agape, others with heads bowed. Tenora's eyes met Ordan's. His look dropped to her cigarette. He gestured to it. She raised a hand, ready to put it out.

"Have you got another?" he asked. Tenora handed him one. This time, she lit it on the second go. Ordan nodded thanks, then stepped away. It may have been the light, but a tear appeared to roll down his cheek.

"Arch-Mechanic Tenora," Karis called. She beckoned Tenora over. Tenora joined her and crouched down. Her stomach turned.

"They stabbed him in the same manner as Jotol," Karis began. Tenora's heart jumped. A chill came over her. Stabbing Jotol in his house was one thing. But they had killed Warrett in the middle of a busy workshop, apparently with nobody noticing. Karis continued talking, her voice unwavering. Definitely a demeanour of steel. A second later, Tenora realised Karis was staring at her.

"What did you say? I didn't catch all of it."

"Can you please turn on the messenger lamp? I need to summon the town guard."

Tenora did so. Afterwards, she found Seralyn standing next to her. The other mechanic's face glistened with tears. Tenora reached out and put her hand on Seralyn's shoulder.

"We'll find who did this."

Seralyn nodded.

"What do you require from us?" she asked, her voice trembling. Tenora thought back to her encounter at Jotol's house.

"Did anyone see a hooded connil walking about?"

Seralyn stared at her.

"A hooded connil?"

"Yes."

"I'll ask."

Seralyn walked away, and Tenora took another drag of her cigarette. They had killed Jotol alone in his house. But that same person had entered this workshop full of mechanics and stabbed Warrett. Without being noticed. That totalled three killings, each increasing in audacity. This had to stop. She would see to it.

11

Lies & Alibis

Nothing. That's all they had to show for the last hour and a half of reviewing documents. Nothing. Yaetherim flicked aside the letter he'd just finished reading. A rather pointed missive, it chided Jorryn for his lack of progress on the thefts. It seemed Arch-Merchant Naltan did not dilute his words. Other letters were reports of robberies, or requests for updates. All from various merchants, Celys, Rynach, Naltan and others. But none stood out as particularly forceful.

Yaetherim glanced at the door. Jorryn had popped out to get tea. He'd left a few dozen heartbeats ago. Yaetherim turned his attention back to the papers. His wings drooped. Perhaps he was wrong. Those hoods could have vanished en route to the riverfarer docks. They'd have to investigate that if they couldn't find anything else amiss.

Footsteps approached, accompanied by voices speaking Rychillan.

"... nothing with these documents, so we'll need to check the original invoices for discrepancies," Jorryn said as he walked into the office. Tenora followed him through. Karis entered last and closed the door behind them. All three Rychillans held steaming mugs. Jorryn carried a second, fairy-sized one, which he handed to Yaetherim. The latter nodded thanks. Steam curled up from the mug, carrying an aroma of fresh tea with it.

"We received your message, Yaetherim," Karis added, "and I suspect those letters were being sent to Arch-Mechanic Warrett as well as Mechanic Jotol."

Yaetherim sipped his drink.

"Did you talk to him?"

"It's too late for that," Tenora said. Yaetherim went to reply, but the words died on his lips. She'd been crying. Her puffy, bloodshot eyes and moist cheeks gave that away. Yaetherim swore.

"They killed him too, didn't they?"

Tenora nodded. She reached up and wiped her eye.

"Stabbed in his workshop, with mechanics all around him. None of them noticed."

Yaetherim's wings twitched. The teacup tumbled from his hand. His fingers grabbed his stinger. Karis, Tenora, and Jorryn jumped back. Tea ran over the desk. Some seeped into the documents, the rest dripped to the floor. Yaetherim's breaths came rapidly. Cold sweat sprung up on his brow.

"Yaetherim, what's wrong?" Tenora asked in Fairic. Yaetherim opened and closed his mouth, words failing him. He hadn't left his hut for weeks after his attack. Scared his attackers may return, he'd found a sense of security within its walls. Naeviol and Charlys had coaxed him out after a month or so. With their help, he had pruned back that fear. Until now.

"You're in the veritor's office. No harm will befall you here," Tenora assured him. She crouched down, bringing her eyes level with Yaetherim. Words poured from him.

"How, how did they, you said unseen…"

"We believe the killer used a connil hood to masquerade as a cleaner," Karis replied. "Some mechanics saw one walk in."

"Yes, and they usually clean our workshops in the evenings. After we finish for the day," Tenora added.

That made sense. With that, a sense of relief washed over Yaetherim. His heart slowed. He unwrapped his fingers from his dagger. He glanced at the spilled tea.

"Sorry about the mess, I, ah…"

"I understand," Tenora said. Yaetherim blinked.

After cleaning up his spilled drink, Yaetherim returned to the desk. That simple task had steadied his nerves. Time to focus. The earlier they caught these killers, the sooner he could stop jumping at the fall of a twig. He cast his gaze over the three Rychillans. While he'd been cleaning, they'd arranged chairs and sat down.

"Right, that's one hood being worn by the merchant. Did you find the other?"

"No," Karis replied. She and Tenora recounted their investigation at the College of Mages. When they finished, Yaetherim leaned forward. His wings twitched.

"Veritor Karis, did you say Mage Kepan ate nistyr root or nistyr fruit?"

"Nistyr root. Waiter Otrai confirmed it."

That fitted with the cheese sauce and other vegetables. But it didn't match the diner. Yaetherim frowned.

"Have any of you actually tried that dish?"

Jorryn nodded. The others shook their heads. A knowing smirk curled Yaetherim's lips. Jorryn grimaced. He raised a hand to his stomach.

"Did it for a bet in school. I was ill for days afterwards."

"Exactly. It's like chillies for us fairies. Too much is fatal."

Jorryn's skin paled. Tenora blinked and turned to him.

"At school? Is that why we had that special assembly about wagers?"

Jorryn nodded and looked down. Yaetherim cleared his throat. This chatter wouldn't help catch the murderers.

"Did Mage Kepan seem unwell today?"

"No," Karis replied.

Silence fell while the implications sank in. Yaetherim cracked his knuckles. A Rychillan eating nistyr root with no ill-effects was unheard of.

"While this raises questions, we have not yet confirmed Mage Peran's alibi," Karis said.

"What about the merchants?" Tenora asked. Karis glanced at Jorryn.

"What have you found so far?"

"Not that much, I'm afraid."

Words stirred in Yaetherim's mind. Something he'd heard at the market hall. He turned to Jorryn.

"Didn't Merchant Celys say they always have a salvage team on standby when loading and unloading?"

Jorryn nodded. Tenora ran her fingers along the side of her head and tapped on the back of her neck. A frown creased her brow. Yaetherim paused. She'd probably realised what he was about to ask.

"But that's not what Merchant Rynach told me last night," she said. "He needed a couple of hours to organise a salvage team."

"Yet a ship was unloading there. You interrupted them," Karis pointed out.

"Then that Brial boat arrived and parked above the runaway car," Yaetherim replied. Three pairs of eyes fell upon him. Jorryn frowned.

"I guess I see what you're getting at."

"So do I," Tenora added, "but if Rynach was stalling me, he must've known the Brial ship would arrive then."

Tenora tucked a lock of hair behind her ear.

"One of the Brial tried to tell me something. But I couldn't understand him."

"Would you recognise them again? Veritor Jorryn knows Brialish," Karis said. Tenora nodded. A brief discussion followed, then Tenora and Jorryn departed for the harbour. Not only could Tenora identify the Brial, but she'd apparently dealt with fraudulent invoices before. Once they'd gone, Karis turned to Yaetherim.

"It will be upon us to confirm both Mage Peran's and Mage Kepan's whereabouts last night."

"You still think Mage Peran's involved with this? We already know Kepan lied about where he was."

"He may have another reason for lying."

Yaetherim blinked.

"Why else would he lie?"

"Several reasons and not all of them malicious. It could be a matter of illegal gambling, courting in secret, or associating with connil. Regardless of that, we should start at Shipwright's Tavern."

Yaetherim scoffed.

"Do you expect that waiter to admit he lied? To you, the steel veritor?"

Karis reached up and adjusted her hair. When she lowered her hands, two bone nubs poked through it. Yaetherim raised an eyebrow. Some people were intimidated by the Druhlac. He had more to fear from Rychillans.

"Perhaps I should talk to him alone. I'm no town guard. He may be a bit more candid with me."

Yaetherim found himself on the end of a steely stare.

"I take your point," Karis replied, "but you do not carry any authority."

Yaetherim shrugged.

"Nor do I bear your responsibilities. I don't have to care about anything else he's done."

Karis' hand fiddled with her brooch.

"Very well. I shall focus on the other lines of inquiry."

Karis departed. Yaetherim grabbed his satchel from Jorryn's desk where he'd left it earlier. Then he flew off to get lunch.

* * *

A short while later, Yaetherim arrived at the Shipwright's Tavern. As the name implied, it sat at the south end of the harbour. Sandwiched between a warehouse and a dry dock, one wall stood right on the shore. Pleasant aromas grew stronger as Yaetherim approached. His stomach growled.

Like most Rychillan shops, a window above the front door provided access for fairies. Yaetherim wasted no time flying through it. He hovered and watched until he identified Otrai. He appeared to be in his early twenties, about Yaetherim's age. After landing at one of Otrai's tables, Yaetherim ordered the dish Kepan had apparently eaten.

Otrai soon laid a plate before him. Several interesting aromas wafted up from it. Yaetherim tucked into it the moment the waiter stepped away. Not the way he would have cooked it, but satisfying anyway. After finishing it, he beckoned Otrai over.

"Is everything in order?" Otrai asked. Yaetherim nodded.

"Mage Kepan was right, it was delicious. Please pass my compliments to the chef."

"I'll do - I'm sorry? Did you say Mage Kepan?"

"That's correct."

Otrai shook his head.

"You must be mistaken. We don't serve nistyr root to Rychillans," Otrai added. "That is tavern policy."

Yaetherim gripped his dagger. He extended his wings, ready to take off.

"That isn't what you told Veritor Karis earlier."

Yaetherim's gaze didn't waver. Otrai cast a furtive glance around.

"Did you have some yourself?" Yaetherim asked. "You're looking a little pale."

"Not so loud. It's merely a small arrangement," Otrai murmured. He pulled up a chair and sat down. Yaetherim leaned in and whispered.

"I do not know what motivation he gave you to lie. Blackmail, or perhaps a bribe. Whatever it was, I don't care. You've already confirmed the fact of it."

Yaetherim nearly grimaced. He sounded like Karis.

"What's he supposed to have done?" Otrai asked.

"We suspect he's involved in the murder of a protector and two mechanics. Oh, and the attack that gave me these."

Yaetherim stretched his arms and wings out, showing his scars. Otrai's gaze ran down Yaetherim's arms, then flicked over his right shoulder.

"All I want from you is the truth," Yaetherim said.

"It was 850 kerlum. The bribe, I mean."

"Did he approach you last night or this morning?"

Otrai tilted his head.

"Four weeks ago. It's a standing arrangement. I'm to say he was dining here, should anyone ask."

Yaetherim raised an eyebrow. This agreement had started shortly before the disturbances in Cerrane.

"Do you know where he was?"

Otrai shrugged.

"Thank you."

Otrai got to his feet, and Yaetherim spoke again.

"One more thing. Nistyr root is a strange choice. Who suggested it?"

"Mage Kepan. I asked him what I should say if anyone sought those details."

With that, Otrai departed. Yaetherim flew out of the tavern, lost in thought. For someone allegedly innocent, Kepan had put a lot into this. After getting his bearings, Yaetherim made a beeline for the town hall.

* * *

Upon returning to the veritors' office, Yaetherim found it empty. Not that surprising. She may be the steel veritor, but Karis still needed to eat. He flew over to her desk. A single sheet of paper lay in the centre. Below his name, a few paragraphs of elegant Fairic writing contained news. The town guard hadn't located that bookmaker yet. But they'd spoken to the manager of the harisyke courts in Amilyn Street. She'd seen a mage visiting Bookmaker Palron multiple times, but she didn't know which one.

Yaetherim smirked. This confirmed Peran's story. Perhaps he now had the name of his attacker, Kepan Ardmoor. Must've been him. That water lance spell required skill in casting. A creak came from the office door. He folded the note and shoved it into his satchel.

Karis closed the door and slumped against it. Yaetherim leaned forward. His fingers curled around the handle of his stinger. Humans bled red, almost the same shade as their royal maroon. But no dark patch marred Karis' tunic. Instead of clutching at a wound, she rubbed her eyes.

Yaetherim doubted Karis meant for anyone to see her in such a state. So he cleared his throat. Karis' head whipped around like a startled bird. She met Yaetherim's gaze for a heartbeat, then looked down.

"Oh," she murmured, "you're here."

"Aye, I just read your note. Seems Peran has more of an alibi than Kepan. By which I mean he actually has one. That waiter, Otrai, took a bribe to claim Kepan was there."

Karis stared at him. Something shifted in her eyes. She pushed herself off the door and stood straight. Determination peppered her voice.

"We must see what Mage Kepan has to say for himself."

She extended a finger towards the evidence box on her desk.

"Please bring one crystal with you."

Yaetherim didn't need to be told twice. He retrieved a crystal and checked that the three scratches on it stood out. Then he joined Karis in the corridor. She turned and headed for the stairs. Yaetherim flew beside her.

"I visited the school," Karis said, "where I spoke to the students who had their magic classes this morning."

"You were talking to younglings? What about?"

Karis' left hand rose to her brooch. With her thumb, she stroked it.

"The attention of children often wanders, Yaetherim. Yet none of them saw a car leave the college during this morning's lessons."

"So the merchant did the stabbings. I thought we already knew that? I mean, with the underarm method and all that."

"Yes, and this confirms it. However, Mage Peran left the grounds."

"What? By bus?"

"No, by foot. Two students observed him enter the forest behind the college. He was carrying a cigarette."

"Is that all?"

"He returned several minutes later, without it. Aside from that, they saw nothing more of note."

Yaetherim pursed his lips.

"I hope he had that cigarette in his pocket. Its leftovers, I mean."

They reached the bottom of the stairs. Karis weaved through the Rychillans waiting in the lobby. Neither she nor Yaetherim spoke until they entered the garage.

"So you think Kepan is the mage involved, then? We know he lied about dining at the Shipwright's Tavern. He's got the means and opportunity to have gone to Cerrane, too."

"That appears to be the case," Karis replied.

Yaetherim crossed his arms. Again, Karis talked with the caution of a ranger approaching a bird's nest. All they'd learned pointed towards Kepan. Yet Veritor Karis seemed eager to make excuses.

"Appears to be? I suppose you'd say a tree only appears to have leaves, too. Everything is pointing to him!"

Karis climbed into a waiting car. Yaetherim joined her. Karis' hands moved over the levers. The engine hissed.

"Were you not a protector?"

"Aye."

"Then tell me, Yaetherim of Riala Village, what are the four key components of a conviction?"

"Means, motive, opportunity and evidence," Yaetherim replied. He held up his hand before Karis could reply.

"I know. We only have the first three."

"I agree these circumstances do point to Mage Kepan," Karis said, "but I must make a case such that it cannot have reasonable doubt cast upon it."

Silence fell. Another hiss came from the engine. Karis steered the car out of the garage. Yaetherim found himself lost in thought. Motive didn't need any further investigation. This rune capacity problem was a fallen tree blocking the path to stronger engines. Future generations would remember whoever solved it. Just like that Leinad chap he had read about. Not to mention the accolades and kerlum they'd receive. As for evidence, he'd have to see what they discovered.

Before long, they reached the College of Mages. A bus stood next to the building. Students poured out of it. Karis steered past and parked in a spare space. Yaetherim followed her inside.

She led him up the staircase, into a corridor with rooms on either side. A pair of brass plates hung on the nearest door to the left, bearing two names: Kepan Ardmoor and Peran Oaklon. Karis knocked. A blue-haired Rychillan emerged from the office. Crystals dangled from his necklace. One waterkind, the other airkind. Yaetherim flew in for a closer look. Only two prongs held each crystal. The mage's gaze flicked from Karis to Yaetherim and back.

"Veritor Karis? What can I do for you and, uh-"

"I'm Yaetherim of Riala Village, South Alken Forest."

Yaetherim gestured to the nameplates.

"I think I've met you or your colleague before. It wasn't pleasant."

The mage leaned in. Yaetherim flew backwards.

"Are you the fairy who got struck by the water lance?"

He'd spoken in something resembling Fairic. Yaetherim replied in Rychillan.

"The one who survived, aye. Paetobim was not so lucky."

"Lucky?"

"That spell's used to cut steel. What do you think it does to flesh and bone?"

The mage's gaze ran over Yaetherim's arms, then flicked down.

"I've read that too," he mumbled, "but to use it like that, well, um..."

Karis cleared her throat.

"We need to talk to Mage Kepan," she said. The man pointed down.

"He's teaching a class with Mage Banoth."

"Thank you, Mage Peran," Karis replied. She spun on her heel and led Yaetherim downstairs.

Voices came from the nearest classroom. Karis knocked on its door. A brown-haired Rychillan soon joined them. Nothing distinctive about him, aside from two terax marks. One showed he had been made ganil. A later mark indicated he'd redeemed himself and become a rynil once more. So he had done something unsavoury in the past, but not enough to be convicted and made connil.

Yaetherim pursed his lips. Before him stood a portly, balding, average Rychillan. Not what he expected of the figure who loomed in his nightmares. His earlier talk with Karis came back to him. They didn't yet know for certain if Kepan was guilty.

Yaetherim shook his head. He turned his attention to the two Rychillans.

"I'd rather not disclose where I was last night," Kepan said, "but it's not related to this murder."

"Aye, and we can certainly trust the word of one who's paid bribes," Yaetherim snarked. Kepan folded his arms and shot Yaetherim a glance.

"I don't need to justify myself to a flutterby."

Karis' expression darkened.

"Mind your tongue, Mage Kepan," she cautioned. "You should set a good example for your students."

Kepan frowned, but Yaetherim smirked. No wonder Kepan had picked such an obvious lie. Those who used that slur knew as much of Fairic culture as a lizard knows of steam engines.

"While Protector Yaetherim does not have jurisdiction," Karis said, "I do."

Kepan glanced down. Yaetherim checked the mage's neck. His gaze fell upon tanned skin where a necklace would've been. Instead, a silver bracelet on Kepan's wrist held two crystals. One waterkind, the other groundkind. That meant little. Kepan could've just switched jewellery.

"I have a reason for that. But as I said, it's something I'd rather not discuss," Kepan replied. He glanced over his shoulder. Karis merely stared at him. After a few heartbeats, Kepan shifted on his feet.

"Very well," Karis replied. "We will need to search your office."

Kepan shrugged.

"Again? If you have to."

Karis nodded, and Kepan returned to the classroom. The two investigators headed back upstairs. They explained to Peran what they needed. He frowned.

"Must you do it now? I have lessons to prepare. Besides, didn't you look in here earlier?"

"Yes. But we have received additional information since then. We shall not take over ten minutes."

Peran shrugged. He drew a cigarette case from his pocket.

"If you need me, I'll be outside."

With that, he strode off. Karis pushed the door open and gestured for Yaetherim to enter. He hovered above the two desks in the room. A faint aroma of spices hung in the air, along with a hint of tomato. No doubt it had come from the grease-stained paper bag on the desk beside the window. Yaetherim pointed to it.

"I take it that's Kepan's? Arch-Mechanic Tenora said she noticed some of those bags in his car."

"Indeed. He keeps his jewellery in the second drawer."

"Right," Yaetherim replied. He glanced up at the bookshelves running along the corridor wall. Kepan could have sneaked something up there.

"I checked there earlier," Karis said, "and found nothing."

Yaetherim took to the air. A few flaps of his wings brought him to the top shelf. Dust blanketed it. Some shot up, stirred by his wingbeats. A couple of sneezes escaped him. From behind him came some soft clinks and clanks. He joined Karis at Kepan's desk.

She closed the first drawer and slid open the next. Five silver bracelets and two rings sat in the front of it. Further back, a glistening splotch darkened the wood of its base. A drop of water fell, soaking into the discolouration. Yaetherim frowned. Desks didn't have plumbing. He landed next to the jewellery, shoved it aside and crouched down.

Yaetherim looked up and tilted his head. A chunk of ice hung off the underside of the top drawer. From its left dangled a gold chain. He straightened up and pointed.

"Veritor Karis, can you melt that? With a hot breeze or something?"

Karis leaned down and peered in.

"Please stand back."

Yaetherim did so, flying up and landing atop the desk. Karis lowered her hand. Her lips moved, but no words passed between them. Hot, humid air drifted up. A soft thunk came from the drawer. Karis reached in, then lay a gold necklace next to Yaetherim. Its pendant had three prongs, operated by a small clasp.

Yaetherim's heart jumped. Karis took the crystal Yaetherim had brought and placed it into the pendant. A flick of her fingers closed it. The prongs gripped the crystal. Each one aligned perfectly with its marks. Yaetherim leaned against an inkwell. His blood ran cold, and his breath raced.

"Veritor Karis," Yaetherim asked, "how likely is it for two pieces of jewellery to match that precisely?"

He already knew. But he needed to be certain.

"Not very. They are individually crafted," Karis replied.

Just as he'd thought. Yaetherim held his hand up.

"Means. Motive. Opportunity. Evidence," he said, counting each word on his fingers. "I think that's all the ingredients."

It all lined up. Kepan didn't have an alibi. But he did have the skills to cast a water lance spell and the necklace that matched the murderer's crystals. Yaetherim's pain and anguish now had a name attached. His wings flared and his heart pounded. With a few quick steps, he launched off the edge of the desk. His right hand closed around his stinger.

"Where are you going?" Karis asked. Yaetherim's head snapped over. How dare she interrupt? Just when he'd got the answer he sought.

"I have a few things to say to Mage Kepan," he growled. Even as the words left his mouth, his thoughts caught up with them. Kepan had nearly killed him last time. Confronting him alone would be stupid. He stopped and hovered.

"You will get your chance," Karis said, "but for now, we need to take him into custody. Please wait here."

Part of Yaetherim wanted to refuse. A few deep breaths dissipated his anger. He'd been yearning for this for months. It would be foolish to mess it up. He landed on Peran's desk.

Karis strode out of the room, carrying the necklace. Muffled conversation drifted through the wall from the next office. Silence followed. Then Karis called Yaetherim into the corridor. He flew out and found Karis waiting with two other mages, a man and a woman. The former's terax included the mark of one who'd become a chief of their profession. That made him the Arch-Mage, then. Yaetherim thought back to Tenora's account of her meeting with them. He recalled their names a few heartbeats later.

"I can't imagine Kepan would do something like this," said the Arch-Mage. Yaetherim folded his arms.

"From what I've heard, Arch-Mage Darnith, you'd find it impossible to believe any mage's involvement. But there's this thing called evidence," Yaetherim replied. Darnith jumped and looked around. Upon spotting Yaetherim, his mouth opened and closed a couple of times. He stared, then turned to Karis.

"Very well, let's get this done."

Karis led them downstairs. They headed for the classroom. Endra entered, and Kepan stepped out a few moments later. Yaetherim gritted his teeth. His hands curled into fists. On his right hand, his fingers itched for the handle of his dagger. Not yet. That may alert Kepan.

"Endra said you needed to see me, Veritor Karis?"

Karis held up the necklace. He only gave it a quick glance.

"We found this in your desk, with your other jewellery."

"And Paetobim had that crystal after you attacked him. If you look closely, there are still some smears of purple blood on it. Fell out of his hands while I was dressing his wounds," Yaetherim said. He didn't take his eyes away from Kepan. The colour faded from the latter's face.

"What? That's not mine."

Yaetherim folded his arms.

"So you usually keep other people's jewellery hidden in your desk, then?"

Kepan's mouth opened and closed a few times. Karis lowered the necklace. She stepped behind Kepan and placed one arm on his shoulder. Yaetherim drew his stinger.

"Put both hands back," Karis ordered. Kepan did so. Karis waved her hand over them. Beneath it, air solidified around Kepan's wrists. He tried to move them, but the solid air restrained them. A wave of relief washed over Yaetherim.

Karis spun Kepan by his shoulder. She undid his bracelet and lifted it off his wrist, revealing a band of pale skin below.

"Have you anything to say in your defence?" she asked. Kepan shook his head. He glared at Yaetherim.

"I will reserve that for my trial. I'll need to get witnesses together."

"Very well," Karis replied. She turned Kepan round and pushed him before her. Yaetherim flew around in front of Kepan. Dagger in hand, he flew backwards, staying a few arm lengths ahead. His nostrils flared and his hands shook. Kepan looked down.

"Oh, nay you don't! This is what you did. These scars are what you gave me. Do **not** think you may look away from them! I had to learn to fly again, thanks to you. I've spent eight months looking over my shoulder, wondering if you'd return to finish the job."

Kepan met Yaetherim's gaze.

"Last night," Yaetherim continued, his voice rising, "I comforted Taeperra, the sister of the protector you killed on Verbore Island. You've taken her brother from her and the other residents of their village. Not to mention the two mechanics your merchant accomplice stabbed today. Do you know what it's like to have someone shatter your life?"

Yaetherim punctuated the question with several choice words in Fairic and Rychillan. Anger, frustration and anxiety from the last eight months shot out with each expletive. By the time he finished, they'd exited the front door. He fell silent. Without saying another word, he flew over and landed on the nearest window ledge.

"Thank you, Veritor Karis," he mumbled, "I'm done. I'll meet you at the car in a couple of, um, minutes."

Karis just nodded. She marched Kepan over to her vehicle. As he watched them walk away, Yaetherim found his heart racing. He frowned. Gone was the relief of a few moments ago. Yet they'd identified and detained his attacker. Nor did his outburst bring him any shame. But once again, that unpleasant tickle stirred in his stomach.

It was something he'd seen during the arrest. He closed his eyes and thought back. Kepan had come out of the classroom, and Karis showed him the necklace. He had denied it was his. Karis then arrested him, removed his bracelet, and restrained him. Yaetherim sighed. He couldn't put his finger on it. He needed another look.

With that in mind, he flew to the car. Karis had the rear door open and was putting Kepan in. Inside, a wall of solid air separated the back from the front.

"Veritor Karis, may I have a moment?"

Karis stopped and glanced at him. Her eyes narrowed.

"Must it be now?"

"Aye. I'd like to get a good look at Mage Kepan. Need to be sure of something."

Karis pulled Kepan out of the car and turned him around. She kept one hand on his shoulder and the other on his arms. Yaetherim circled Kepan. Starting from the thinning hair, he ran his eyes down over the tailored tunic. His gaze passed over Kepan's hands, then flicked back. There it was, on the left wrist. A band of pale skin which hadn't done that tanning thing. Right where Kepan wore his bracelet. Yet no such lack of tan showed on his neck. Furthermore, the rest of the jewellery in Kepan's desk had been silver, with neither gold nor chain amongst it.

On its own, it meant little. Kepan could have just bought something outside his usual style and only worn it during those rune experiments. But Mage Peran, who shared his office, used a necklace to hold his crystals. He'd also gone into the forest for a simple cigarette break. Apparently.

"Have you seen what you need?" Karis asked. Yaetherim blinked and nodded. Without further ado, Karis bundled Kepan into the car. She closed the door and locked it. She beckoned Yaetherim over.

"Were you looking for something in particular?" she inquired.

"Aye, and nay. I think… I'd like to stay back here. I can't help feeling this dish is still missing an ingredient."

"It is. We have yet to find that connil hood."

"Two ingredients, then. I'll keep an eye out for that, too."

"Very well. Please join me in my office when you have finished."

Karis spun on her heel and climbed into the car. As she drove off, Yaetherim flew up onto the roof of the college. He landed on it and sat, legs crossed, in the shade of a nearby tree. With his eyes closed, he thought back. Memories flicked through his mind like leaves in a breeze. Several things stood out. The names on Peran and Kepan's office door. Grease-stained bags from a street cart. A plate of roasted nistyr root. That pair of goatskin boots and Armourer Dinsec hiding an illicit relationship.

Yaetherim's eyes snapped open. He blinked twice and shook his head. Warmth spread across his cheeks, and his wings drooped. Karis would've called his theory mere speculation. But it made sense. It explained almost everything. Even the goatskin boots in Kepan's car. But if he was correct, then they'd just arrested the wrong person. His attacker would still roam free.

He'd need to check a few things. With that in mind, he flew to the forest behind the college. Peran had been seen visiting there. It would be a good starting point.

12

Leads

Tenora stopped a few yards away from the Brial ship and ran her gaze over it. Whilst Rychillan ships were angular and functional, this ship's construction combined form and function. Each curve of the vessel served to push through air and water, rather than slice through them. 'Twas almost an artwork, a beautiful piece of engineering, and her eyes lingered upon it.

"Are you alright, Arch-Mechanic Tenora?" Jorryn asked. Tenora blinked. She had to focus. Despite repairs proceeding on the affected cars, she still had a job to do. Like any other troubleshooting, the root cause needed to be resolved. Those responsible would not stop of their own accord. Their flagrant disrespect towards life made that quite clear. Tenora nodded.

"Yes. Sorry, just my first chance to see one up close. It's an impressive work of shipbuilding."

A shrill whistle and series of chirps came from above. Tenora looked up. A Brial leaned over the ship's side. Deep green eyes stared into hers from above a sharp, mustard-yellow beak. The Brial warbled and tilted their head.

"He appreciates your kind words," Jorryn said. He turned to the Brial and raised his right arm, before stopping and lowering it. Instead, he cleared his throat and performed the introductions. Another series of chirps and whistles followed.

"Is he the Brial who tried to talk to you last night?" Jorryn asked. Tenora shook her head.

"No, they had paler feathers. Green, I think. Their beak had the same shade as a fresh ear of corn."

A torrent of trills and chirps came in reply. Jorryn moved his left arm up and down, as though waving a wing. The Brial leaned further down. He chittered and snapped his beak. Tenora jumped. Her hand dropped to her tool belt, fingers closing around a wrench.

"It's only laughter," Jorryn said, "that gesture's supposed to be for flight speed. First Mate Fenast there was talking rather quickly. But I caught one thing amongst all that. He asked if you talked to the Brial handling the ropes or the gangplank."

"The one dealing with the ropes. They tried to speak to me, but I don't understand Brialish."

Fenast spoke again. This time, his whistles and chirps were more subdued. Jorryn's frown deepened as he listened. Fenast finished, and Jorryn turned to Tenora.

"You talked to Able Seabird Fillan. He had an accident at the warehouse this morning. A shelf of goods toppled onto him."

Tenora's heart skipped a beat.

"A shelf of goods? Is he alright?"

"He's recovering aboard the ship, in their infirmary. But he asked to speak to the Rychillan woman with, ah, blue plumage, should she return."

Tenora blinked. That must have been her. She had seen no other women who shared her hair colour around the harbour last night. While natural, 'twas not the most common for Rychillans.

Jorryn turned back to Fenast.

"May we please come aboard to talk to him?"

A few whistles came in reply. Then Fenast said something to his crewmates. Two of them lowered the gangplank. Fenast greeted Tenora and Jorryn at the top of it and escorted them below-deck. Tenora's eyes darted around, taking in details. Most of the edges were rounded, which would reduce injuries in rough water. But their layout still maximised the space available aboard.

About halfway along, Fenast led them down a flight of stairs. Another few steps brought them to the infirmary. A Brial sat behind a desk to the right. They stood as the others entered, then resumed their seat after a few whistles from Fenast. Around the room, four beds hung off the walls. Only one was occupied.

Broken, pale green feathers poked out from a dressing on the occupant's left wing. A bandage covered the join between upper beak and face, just below closed eyes. Tenora rubbed the bridge of her nose. Faint pain, a memory of her own injury there, flared up for a second. Even now, a slight bump marked the break. She wouldn't ask Fillan too much, lest the movement of his beak aggravate his injuries.

Tenora stopped a few paces away. Fillan's eyelids snapped open. He leaned forward. Brial and Rychillan stared at each other.

"Please don't strain yourself," Tenora said. "I'm Arch-Mechanic Tenora Perskel. I think you wanted to speak to me?"

Fillan nodded. He uttered a stream of whistles and clicks, similar to what they'd heard from the first mate. Tenora turned an inquiring gaze to Jorryn. His expression matched that which she'd seen on rookie mechanics, usually after learning something the hard way. Jorryn tapped his fingers against each other.

"Merchant Rynach said this ship arrived early, didn't he?"

"Yes, and that this was the only suitable berth for it."

Jorryn cleared his throat.

"The Brial got here right on time, despite having engine trouble a couple of dozen miles after leaving. It's a point of honour for them, keeping to their promise like that. And they sent word ahead. Both when they had the problem and when they resolved it."

Tenora stared at Jorryn.

"Could you, um, say that again?"

He did so. Tenora reached for her cigarette case but stopped herself. She'd not seen a single Brial smoking aboard, nor any ashtrays. Instead, she settled for running her hand along the side of her head. It helped, despite no errant hair needing such tidying.

Rynach could have an innocent explanation. Perhaps he'd merely assumed they'd be late. Tenora hoped that was the case. Else, he had lied and obstructed her. Her blood ran cold as another realisation hit. It had been the merchant involved who'd killed Warrett and Jotol.

"Was Merchant Rynach in the warehouse when you had your accident?"

That question garnered a short, three-tone whistle from Fillan.

"That's a yes," Jorryn translated.

"Thank you," he said to Fillan. "We should let you rest now."

He turned to Tenora.

"Arch-Mechanic Tenora, do you have any more questions?"

Tenora shook her head.

"Not that I can think of. I'd like to hear Merchant Rynach's explanation for this."

"So would I," Jorryn replied. Fillan leaned back into the pillow and closed his eyes. Both Rychillans headed for the door. Just as they reached it, more whistles and clicks came from the bed. Jorryn paused and looked over his shoulder.

"Thank you. We wish you a speedy recovery."

Presumably Fillan had wished them good luck, if not the blessings of whatever deity he worshipped. Tenora hoped it was the former. Even her own god didn't listen. She sighed. At least he'd meant well.

A short walk brought them to the warehouse. Tenora held back and let Jorryn do the talking. Yet she paid attention. Merchant Rynach had been in and out all morning, doing errands. They weren't sure if he was there at the moment. Tenora frowned at that. Such tasks were easily delegated, and the merchants' guild was one of the biggest in Alkentoft. Surely the manager of their main warehouse could organise his time better than that.

One merchant went to find Rynach, and another led Jorryn and Tenora inside. Despite the questions raised, they still needed to check the original invoices for these thefts. They headed to the rear of the building, weaving between crates. These changed to rows of shelves, each laden. Sunlight from the windows gave way to illumination from overhead lanterns. An acrid odour assaulted Tenora's nose. She sneezed and sniffled, trying to clear the familiar stench. Jorryn coughed and blinked twice. He shot a look at the corked glass jars shelved beside them.

"'Tis a cleaning mixture," Tenora said, "Connil use it to clean workshop floors."

"Does it have to be that foul?"

Tenora shrugged.

"It does a good job of getting grease out of concrete. We open all the windows and have airkinds ventilate the building when it's used."

Jorryn moved over, away from the glass jars. They soon reached a door in the rear wall of the warehouse. Their escort unlocked it and ushered them in.

"You'll find our active records for this year in here. We store those from previous years at the market hall."

Jorryn nodded.

"Thank you."

The merchant left, and Tenora followed Jorryn into the room. Sunlight streamed in from a window opposite the door. Below it stood a table, with a single chair tucked in under it. A row of four-drawer filing cabinets ran the length of the wall to the right. Each drawer bore a label on the front, showing dates four or five weeks apart.

Jorryn stepped over to the cabinets. He opened a drawer dated 31 weeks ago. From the folders within, he pulled three documents and held them out. Tenora wiped her fingers on a rag from her overalls, checked they were clean, then took the papers.

"These were the first ones. Can you spot anything amiss with them?"

Tenora sat at the table and lay the invoices out before her. She thought back to those greedy junior mechanics whom she'd caught red-handed. Minor details had revealed their alterations, some of which also appeared on the documents before her. Her finger traced over the lines of the letters and numbers, pausing at each inconsistency.

"There are a few things amiss, Veritor Jorryn."

Jorryn joined her.

"The ink's colour doesn't match, here and here," Tenora said. She pointed out the discrepancies.

"Couldn't they have run out while writing?"

Tenora shook her head.

"Then I'd expect all the following text to have the same ink. It's like the paint we use for bodywork repairs. Batches differ slightly, so the patched-up parts don't quite match."

"Oh."

Tenora tapped the page, her finger on one of the suspicious numbers.

"Without those alterations, this invoice would show only five bushels of sugarcane sold, not eight. Did this shipment have three bushels stolen?"

Jorryn snatched up the paper and held it close to his face. Tenora took a deep breath and let it out. Sweat formed on her brow, not just from the humidity. Rynach had lied to her about that ship, and to Jorryn about the thefts. He had planned this.

"Yes, it did. At least-"

A crash sounded out, the splintering of wood-on-wood. Tenora jumped to her feet. A set of shelves slammed into the doorframe. The walls shook. Two jars tumbled into the room. Wood splintered and glass tinkled. Tenora threw her arm up. Several shards grazed her skin. Cleaning fluid sloshed over the floor.

Jorryn ran for the door. Tenora dashed to the window and swore. 'Twas mounted in the wall, with no latch or hinges allowing it to open. Fumes from the spilled mixture clawed at her throat. Behind her, Jorryn started coughing. Tenora's eyes watered. With one hand, she rubbed them. The other closed around her wrench. Each breath burned. She glanced back. Jorryn stood vainly trying to clear the doorway.

Tenora swung the wrench with all her strength. It thudded into the window. A few cracks appeared. She swung it again, putting her hip into it. The fractures spread, but the glass held. She cursed. Of course, a warehouse would have secure windows. The wrench fell from her hand. Energy crackled up from her ring. A simple spell shot from her lips.

Orange and yellow flames flickered through the cracks she'd made. Around them, the glass melted. Tenora coughed. She blinked, trying to clear her eyes. This was too slow. More magic skittered over her skin.

"Ha!"

She clenched her fingers. Flames flared, almost as high as the window itself. Heat washed over her.

The glass exploded.

Shards shot outwards. Tenora stopped casting. The flames vanished, but some sparks smouldered in the wooden frame. Fresh air flowed in through the opening. Tenora extinguished the embers, grasped her wrench and smashed out the remaining glass. Now softened and broken, it gave way. The moment it was clear, she turned and grabbed Jorryn. He did his best to stand. She helped him over to the window.

"Breathe," she ordered. He did. After a few moments, his breathing slowed. Tenora let go. Jorryn staggered, then stood.

"Are you okay?" Tenora asked.

"Yes, the door's-"

Several coughs interrupted his words.

"Blocked?" Tenora said. Jorryn nodded. Tenora gestured out the window.

"We shouldn't stay in here. Come on."

She helped him through and followed him outside. For a few moments, they just breathed. Despite the salty scent of the sea, each breath brought welcome refreshment.

Shouts came from within the warehouse. Nearby, the beat of an engine drifted through the air. It grew louder. After a few seconds, a car drove around the building. Tenora stepped forward and waved to get the driver's attention.

Steam surged from its funnel, and it sped up. It veered towards Tenora. She jumped back. Wood and steel flashed past. Air solidified and slammed into her. She staggered and recovered. Her hand flicked out at the disappearing vehicle. Magic skittered over her skin. An extinguishing spell shot from her lips.

Maybe the spell had hit, maybe it hadn't. The beats didn't falter, only growing fainter as the car drove away. If her spell had worked, it should lose power within a couple of blocks. Tenora swore and clenched her fist. 'Twas all she could do. Hopefully, the town guard could find the driver who'd tried to run her down.

"Did you see that?" Tenora asked.

"Yes, it was Merchant Rynach."

Like steam into the morning air, the last of Tenora's doubts evaporated.

"Falling shelves crushed that Brial, Fillan, didn't they?" she inquired. Jorryn nodded. He narrowed his eyes.

"It'd just take a blast of wind directed at the top to topple them. And Merchant Rynach is an airkind," Jorryn finished. He pointed along the dockside.

"There's a guard post down there," he said. "I'll go raise the alarm."

"It was a blue car. Steel-bodied, wood footboards. Looked like Coach-builder Meston's work."

"Thank you," Jorryn replied. Tenora frowned. Jorryn had a wheeze in his voice and panted as he walked off. No surprise there. Tenora was still short of breath herself. But it wasn't as bad as her first encounter with that cleaning fluid. She'd grown used to it since.

A shout from inside the warehouse caught Tenora's attention. Voices spilled from the window, people calling out. Tenora spun on her heel. They'd been lucky. Others could've been hurt.

She strode along the side of the building. Upon reaching the front, she had to pause for breath. At least she no longer had that scratchy feeling in her throat. It'd be a couple of hours 'til all effects of those fumes wore off.

A few paces from the warehouse door, a blue and orange shape swooped down. Tenora stopped. She blinked and peered at the fairy hovering before her. Naeliya smiled, relief in her eyes.

"Good, there you are. They're trying to get into the archive room."

"We got out through the window. Were you looking for me?"

"Yes, I'm here with Veritor Karis. She's arrested Mage Kepan."

"What?"

"She and Yaetherim found the necklace that matched the crystals. It was hidden in his desk."

"Well, that's some comfort."

"You can say that again. Anyway, we came to help with this side of it. Me and Karis, I mean. Yaetherim's stayed at the college to check a few things."

Tenora pinched the bridge of her nose.

"It's Merchant Rynach. He's got away. Tried to run me down behind the warehouse."

Naeliya's eyes widened. She flicked her hand over her shoulder.

"You'd better talk to Veritor Karis, then. She's this way."

Without waiting for a reply, Naeliya flew around. Tenora followed her inside.

On first glance, the goods appeared undamaged. That changed when they reached the last two rows of shelves. They lay toppled over like dominoes. Bottles and boxes sat strewn beneath them, their former contents splattered across the floor. Merchants moved to-and-fro, cleaning up. Tenora listened, but couldn't hear any moans or groans.

"Is anyone injured?" she asked.

"No, but we've a couple of visitors in the archive room," replied one merchant. Tenora let out a sigh of relief and shook her head.

"We escaped through the window. Veritor Jorryn's gone to raise the alarm."

The merchant stopped. Before he could speak, another voice spoke from behind Tenora.

"Arch-Mechanic Tenora, are you injured? You have blood on your arms."

Tenora glanced down. A dozen or so flecks of red dotted her forearm.

"Just scratches, Veritor Karis. From shattered glass."

Tenora turned and looked up, meeting Karis' gaze. She explained what had happened since their arrival at the harbour. When she finished, Karis surveyed the wreckage.

"To have one accident is a misfortune. To have two in a day strikes me as questionable."

"That's what we thought," Tenora replied, "and they're both beneficial for Merchant Rynach."

Karis nodded.

"That had occurred to me."

She glanced at Naeliya, hovering nearby.

"Messenger Naeliya, can you please find Veritor Jorryn and ask him to join us? We will be in Merchant Rynach's office."

Naeliya flew off, and Karis turned to Tenora.

"Arch-Mechanic Tenora, I appreciate your assistance with this investigation."

Tenora pursed her lips and folded her arms. She knew where this was going.

"I'd like to see this through, Veritor Karis."

"You are not one of the town guard."

"You're worried about the danger? 'Twas I who made our escape when we were trapped just now."

Karis' eyes narrowed. Silence hung between them for several moments.

"Please stay close to me for the time being," Karis said. Tenora nodded.

Karis accosted a nearby merchant. After a few minutes, she stepped away with a key to Rynach's office. She led Tenora to the right of the warehouse.

At this end of the building, a second storey stood out from the wall, halfway between floor and roof. It extended far enough to hold some offices and a walkway to reach them. A falling shelf had struck one of its supports. Tenora peered at it. It hadn't buckled.

They reached Rynach's office a few moments later. Tenora paused on the balcony and glanced out over the warehouse below. From here, she could identify the merchants moving about. It was an ideal spot for a manager to supervise things. Such as who arrived and departed.

With that in mind, she joined Karis in the office. Karis stood behind a desk on the right, rummaging through the top drawer. Above it, a window looked out over the harbour. To the left, a set of shelves held various trinkets and some dust. Tenora frowned. An ornate mug and a handwritten Fairic book sat on the middle shelf, a conspicuous gap between them. Tenora stepped over for a closer look. A dagger-shaped patch lay clear of dust.

"That matches the scabbard of a seven-inch blade. Such a scabbard could hold the weapon used on Mechanic Jotol and Arch-Mechanic Warrett," said Karis. Tenora turned.

"You didn't find it in there?" she asked. Karis shook her head.

"Not in the top drawer. The bottom one is locked."

Karis' gaze dropped to the pockets on the front of Tenora's overalls.

"Arch-Mage Darnith told me you threatened to break into their cars, should they not hand over their keys."

Tenora's cheeks flushed, and she glanced down.

"I wasn't going to, I mean, not without your say-so. Just wanted to avoid delays."

"I trust that was not an idle boast?"

Tenora folded her arms.

"I never joke about my work, Veritor Karis. Be it professional matters or recreational tinkering."

Karis stepped back from the desk and gestured to the bottom drawer.

"Then can you please open this?"

Tenora strode over. She crouched down, drew her precision screwdrivers, and started. Her hands moved steadily, guided by instinct as much as thought. After a few moments, the lock gave a satisfying click. A final twist of the screwdriver retracted the bolt, and she stepped back. 'Twas Karis who actually had the authority for this search.

Karis slid the drawer open. A few sheets of paper lay within, below a dagger in a scabbard. Karis grabbed the latter. Holding the edges of the handle, she drew it from the scabbard. With a faint rasping sound, it came free. A foul metallic odour hit Tenora's nose. Her gut heaved. She did not need Karis to tell her what red, half-dry substance coated the blade.

"We should be able to get some fingerprints from this," Karis said. Tenora didn't reply. She crossed to the window, threw it open, and leaned out. Her gaze fell upon the Brial ship, moored almost directly opposite. She focused on it until her stomach settled.

To Tenora's relief, Karis had sheathed the dagger by the time she stepped back. Instead, the veritor stood over the desk, examining two documents, side-by-side. A series of elegant, flowing swirls and loops, which meant nothing to Tenora, covered both pages.

"Is that Brialish?"

Karis nodded. She placed her hand on one document.

"This is the first letter you mentioned, advising of their engine trouble." She pointed to the other.

"They sent this half an hour later. It states that they had resolved the problem, and that they are steaming at full speed to ensure they arrive on time."

Tenora pursed her lips. Her heart thumped. The memory of Fillan, lying bandaged in the infirmary, came back to her. He had attempted to warn her, and Rynach had tried to kill him. Just like how he'd killed Jotol and Warrett. He must have the blood of a lizard, to take lives in such a manner. Acting only in his own self-interest. Tenora let out a sigh through clenched teeth. Karis was saying something.

"... have no doubts this dagger is the murder weapon," Karis said. "It is a Druhlashi drogeste blade, for use in a ceremony of marriage. It should never see blood."

Tenora glanced at the weapon.

"Seems stupid of him to leave it here."

Karis looked up. Her expression shifted, her lips flicking ever so slightly upward.

"When the threat of arrest is near, the guilty tend to panic. You said yourself he was in a hurry."

That would explain a lot. Now that she thought about it, Tenora could imagine what had happened. Rynach must have seen her and Jorryn board the Brial ship from the window. He'd panicked. Despite her anger, she couldn't help smirking. She knew this situation. It was just like troubleshooting an errant engine. They'd examined the effects, worked back, and found the root cause of the problem.

Tenora went to speak, but stopped as Naeliya flew in, alone. The latter landed on the desk, between the two letters. Karis glanced at the door, then fixed Naeliya with an inquiring stare. Naeliya gestured out the window, along the harbour.

"Veritor Jorryn collapsed after reaching the guard post. They've sent for a healer."

Karis leaned forward. She fidgeted with her brooch. A frown furrowed her brow.

"Do you mean he's passed out?" she asked.

"He was awake when I got there. Was telling them about Merchant Rynach. Wanted to help find him."

Karis shook her head.

"No, not when he is indisposed."

She turned to Tenora.

"This is because of those fumes, is it not?"

Tenora nodded.

"He'll need to rest. Should be right tomorrow. That's what worked for me, first time around."

"Then I will see he gets it," Karis replied. "Messenger Naeliya, can you please come with me? I shall require your help to coordinate the search for Merchant Rynach."

Tenora didn't hear Naeliya's reply. Memories stirred, details blossoming from them. Tenora blinked and looked over.

"About that, Veritor Karis. His car has a new left-front mudguard. The paint doesn't quite match up. It also has rust on the rear door, just above the running board. Two spots, one above the other, about the size of a kerlo coin. Behind them is another, kerlar-sized spot. The car itself is metal-bodied, the only wood is the running boards."

Karis nodded and jotted a reminder in her notepad.

"What about Yaetherim?" Naeliya asked. "He is still at the College of Mages."

"I cannot spare any people. Rynach is an active threat to the peace of Alkentoft."

"I can stop by your office to see if he's sent a message, Veritor Karis. If that would help. I mean, with Veritor Jorryn ill, well, I've been short-staffed myself," Tenora said. She received a steely stare in reply.

"That would be helpful. It is crucial we overlook nothing. Others may also try to reach me there."

"I understand," Tenora replied. Karis nodded.

"Thank you. We shall start north and work our way south, should you need to find me."

Following a brief discussion of details, Karis and Naeliya headed off. Tenora returned to the car she and Jorryn had arrived in. Although it wasn't much, she was still helping. 'Twas all she could do at the moment. She smiled a second later. No, it wasn't everything she could do. A check of her watch confirmed the time. In about an hour, some of her mechanics would start delivering repaired cars back to their owners.

Instead of the town hall, she drove to her workshop. Upon arrival, she changed into a spare set of overalls, cleaned the blood and sweat off, and gathered her mechanics around. She gave them the same details she'd told Karis and asked them to keep their eyes out whilst delivering the vehicles.

That done, she headed off. She now knew who had killed her colleagues and attacked those fairies. If she had anything to do with it, Rynach Reulo would not get away again.

13

Names

Scents of plant saps and resins wafted up from the broken branches and crushed leaves below. Yaetherim flew above them, following the trail they marked through the forest. From behind the College of Mages, it followed the creek downstream. His eyes flicked side-to-side, his right hand resting upon the hilt of his stinger.

It had first appeared six months before, according to a passing protector patrol. Yet there hadn't been signs of poaching since. A wry smirk crossed Yaetherim's face. Starting such a trail took some effort. Why bother doing so without stealing from the forest? It could've merely been children exploring. But the half-green leaves showed it was still in use.

There'd been no sightings of Rychillans using this path. Either they'd been lucky to remain unseen, or they knew when patrols would pass. Before parting ways, Yaetherim had asked that patrol to deliver a message to their colleagues. Merely a simple question, little more than a hunch.

After about a sixth of a mile, he reached a dead palm tree. Half-fallen, it leaned against a live one between the trail and creek. Dislodged dirt and exposed roots at its base showed someone had twisted it out of the way. Just beyond, the stream widened, and its flow slowed. The path veered left and ended at the bank. Several flat, mossy stones poked out of the water. Specks of sunlight fell on them, from gaps in the leaves and branches above. Yaetherim landed on the nearest, a fairy's footstep away from the shore.

His nose crinkled. This creek stank from what had been washed into it. Fortunately, the stench was not as strong as the ocean.

Yaetherim's wings ached. Best to rest them now, while he still could. He surveyed the clearing. The rocks lay before him like plates on a table. Several bore bare spots where moss had been scraped off. Marks about the size of a human shoe. He smirked. As in Cerrane, moss again provided guidance.

Leaping from rock-to-rock, he followed the path of scuffed footprints. After a half-dozen jumps, the trail ended at a large rock in the middle of the stream. Easily big enough to hold two humans.

A whistle sounded through the trees. Fingers closed around his stinger. That wasn't birdsong.

"Yaetherim? Where are you?"

Yaetherim released the dagger. He cupped his hands to his mouth.

"Charlys, down here!"

Yaetherim paced along the edge of the rock. His eyes didn't leave the creek. He stopped on the far side. Water flowed smoothly round every other rock. But here, between it and the next rock away from the bank, it rolled over itself. Just like in a boiling pot. He held his hand above it. No heat rose from it. But something must cause that. This wasn't a stage actor. It couldn't pretend.

Behind him, a dull slap sounded out. Wood on moss, from a pair of backless sandals. Yaetherim turned around. Charlys stood a couple of arm lengths away, her blue wings twitching. No smile curved her lips. Despite this, his stomach fluttered for a heartbeat or two.

"Hello Sunbird. I take it you got my message?"

"You asked about a protector courting a mage?"

"Oh, aye," Yaetherim said. He sat down and patted the moss beside him. "It's a bit of a story."

Charlys joined Yaetherim. She folded her wings back and tilted her head slightly. One eyebrow almost vanished under her hair. Within her hazel eyes, curiosity burned.

"I'd imagine so," she replied. "Sounds like quite a leap from what you told me this morning."

"We've just arrested Mage Kepan Ardmoor for the murder of Protector Paetobim, the attack on me and all the rest."

Charlys grinned, revealing that cute gap between her top teeth. But Yaetherim did not return it. Instead, he folded his arms. Charlys' grin vanished.

"But I don't think he did it," Yaetherim added.

"So, why did you arrest him?"

"I didn't, Veritor Karis did."

Charlys shot him a look. One eyebrow raised, the other slightly dipped. Just the barest hint of a smile on her lips. He'd seen that expression dozens of times.

"I'm not being silly," he said.

"You know what I meant," Charlys replied. "Besides, she's a veritor. I doubt she'd arrest someone without reason."

"Two reasons. First, he won't say where he was last night. Bribed a waiter to claim he was dining at Shipwright's Tavern. Second, we found the necklace that matched those crystals. Hidden in his desk, concealed by ice."

Charlys whistled.

"That does sound incriminating to me."

"That's what I thought. Remember those parrot poachers a year ago?"

"Aye. Oh, your gut feeling again?"

Yaetherim nodded. His cheeks flushed, and he hoped Charlys hadn't noticed.

"All his other pieces of jewellery are silver. Not a necklace amongst them. But Mage Peran wears his crystals in a gold one. He also happens to share Mage Kepan's office."

Something Karis had said stirred in Yaetherim's memory.

"And some students spotted him heading into the forest. Possibly sneaking off down this trail while having a cigarette."

"Are those the only points in Mage Kepan's favour? You did say he'd bribed a waiter."

"True. But I think I've figured out why he's staying silent. Have you seen those goatskin boots that the town fairies have?"

Charlys glanced at her feet.

"Aye, I hear they're the latest fashion. Some protectors wear them."

"Any in the North Alken Stewardship?"

"Two or three of them."

"Do any of them require a new pair and also enjoy roasted nistyr root in cheese sauce?"

Charlys let out an upward sigh. Her hair flopped up and flipped back down. Yaetherim shrugged.

"Thought it may've come up in conversation. Most patrols are boring."

"You don't need to remind me, Therry," Charlys said. She flicked Yaetherim a frown.

"You've just described Taesonith of Wileth Village, Elori Forest. Now that I think about it, she does frequently volunteer to patrol around here."

"I'd like to talk to her if that doesn't interfere with her duties."

Charlys glanced towards the College of Mages. Her wings twitched.

"A waterkind mage has attacked two protectors. 'Tis enough of a threat for us to act on."

Yaetherim got to his feet. Charlys took his hand, and he helped her up. She slowly withdrew it, her fingers running lightly over his palm. A couple of steps brought them to the edge of the rock. Yaetherim pointed out the rolling water he'd noticed earlier.

"Here's something else we'll need to check. Did you spot the trail through the forest?"

"Aye, we have been keeping watch on it."

"It starts at the clearing behind the College of Mages," he said, "and we've not found the connil hoods. Veritor Karis and Arch-Mechanic Tenora searched the whole of the building, grounds and cars between them. I believe the latter even checked Apprentice Yerom's bicycle."

Charlys took off and flew above the rock. Before Yaetherim could speak, she swooped down. She grabbed a fallen leaf from beneath a wild banana tree. Holding it, she returned and hovered low over the water.

"Therry, could you grab that end?"

Yaetherim did so, and Charlys wedged the tip of the leaf between two rocks.

Now Yaetherim understood. He lowered his end into the creek, upstream of the rock. The stream caught it and pushed it against both rocks. With the makeshift dam in place, the rolling water settled.

Yaetherim crouched down and peered in. Odours of various saps and plant residues wafted up. But despite these clouding the water, he could make out some item sitting below it. He smirked. Earlier, he'd wondered why someone would form a trail yet not take anything. Now he had his answer: to leave something.

It sat beneath a dome of shimmering air. A walling spell, cast from airkind magic. Not groundkind. Yaetherim uttered a few choice words in Rychillan. Charlys chuckled.

"You really can be quite colourful, Therry," she said. Warmth spread over Yaetherim's cheeks. His wings twitched, and he glanced away.

"I wasn't aware you spoke that much Rychillan."

Charlys just tilted her head. Her smile slid sideways into a smirk.

"Aye, I know," Yaetherim replied. Nokinds may not have magic, but they didn't necessarily lack anything else. He turned back to the water. Perhaps he'd sworn too soon. An airkind rune could also create such a barrier. Furthermore, Mage Kepan had bribed a waiter. Another deception wouldn't be past him.

"I'll get Taesonith," Charlys said. "Is there any more you need to check?"

Yaetherim shook his head. Charlys took off. Yaetherim watched her go until the blue of her wings vanished amongst the browns and greens of the forest. He would have to thank her once this was over. She would insist he didn't owe her anything. But he'd record a large favour owing in their village's ledger of favours, anyway. Least he could do, after all she'd done for him.

But for now, he had something more urgent to report. He pulled a notepad and pen from his satchel. For several minutes Yaetherim wrote, outlining his deductions about the jewellery and the two mages. He had just finished when sandals slapped on the rock again. That would be Charlys. Since he'd been attacked, she had developed a habit of landing heavily.

Yaetherim got up and turned around. Charlys stood behind him, a stranger beside her. The latter's ember-red eyes met Yaetherim's. Then she glanced down. Silver ear cuffs sat on the tips of her ears, poking through her charcoal-black hair. Goatskin boots covered her legs from the knees down. At least, where the holes in them didn't show the dark-orange skin beneath.

It may have been the breeze, but this firekind's wings seemed to tremble. Yaetherim kept a straight face. Her manner had already answered one key question.

"Protector Taesonith, of Wileth Village?" Yaetherim asked. She nodded and Yaetherim introduced himself. With a flick and a spell, he pulled the banana leaf onto the rock beside him. The water resumed rolling over itself. Yaetherim pointed to it.

"I understand you patrol round here often. Does that usually happen?"

"Most of the time, yes. Thought it was rock or the like."

"Well, there is something there."

With another flick of his fingers, Yaetherim put the banana leaf in place. He gestured to the becalmed water.

"What do you make of that? I can't get a clear view of it myself."

Taesonith leaned over.

"Stand back."

She held her arm over the stream. Her lips moved, whispered words passing from them. Orange and yellow flickered under the water. It started bubbling again. Yaetherim and Charlys exchanged a look. This time, steam rose. Yaetherim smirked. His hand shot out. Energy skittered along his arm. A movement spell brought another banana leaf over. With this one, he blocked the flow from downstream.

A few minutes later, the water between the leaves had boiled off. Taesonith stopped casting and stepped back. Yaetherim peered over the edge of the rock. Before him, a dome of solid air sat on the mud. A neatly folded connil hood lay below it, dry. Beneath that rested a human-sized leather satchel. Yaetherim smirked. Then he beckoned the others over.

"Can you two see any runes down there?"

He certainly couldn't. Both protectors confirmed it.

"Very ingenious, Protector Taesonith. Thank you. I've seen what I need,"

Yaetherim said. He stopped casting, and the water rolled in once more. No longer held, both banana leaves drifted away. Taesonith smiled.

"I'm glad I could help," she replied. Yaetherim nodded.

"How long have you been courting Kepan?" he asked.

"We're not courting! I only run errands for him from time to time."

Taesonith broke off. Her left hand shot up to her mouth, and her wings flared. She crouched, ready to launch into flight. Half a sentence escaped her.

"How did you-?"

A smirk threatened to curl Yaetherim's lips, but he pushed it aside. It had just been a guess, but it had borne results. He gestured towards the College of Mages.

"Mage Kepan is fond of food from street carts and has a few of their empty bags lying around. But he claimed he was eating roasted nistyr root in cheese sauce with potatoes and carrots at a certain tavern last night. Even for us, that's an acquired taste. And his arrangement with Waiter Otrai is ongoing. As though he wouldn't know when it'd be needed."

Taesonith frowned. Her eyes narrowed.

"But that doesn't mean he would not have tried our cuisine."

Yaetherim shook his head.

"He referred to me as a 'flutterby' when talking to Veritor Karis earlier today. Not the type of person who'd willingly try Fairic food."

Charlys folded her arms. Yaetherim didn't look away from Taesonith.

"Mage Kepan bribed a waiter to say that. Just some dish that could sound plausible. Now those street carts don't serve much Fairic fare, but he must've heard about that recipe somewhere. I hear it's one of your favourites."

Taesonith's cheeks flushed purple. Her wings drooped and her gaze took root at her feet.

"That's what I was about to mention," Yaetherim continued, "your goatskin boots. They're a recent fashion, I understand. Yet that pair's almost falling apart. You could use new ones. Like the pair Arch-Mechanic Tenora found in Mage Kepan's car. Just the thing for a payment or lover's gift. I mean, we forest fairies have little need for kerlum."

"Oh."

Charlys cleared her throat.

"Were you running these messages when you were on patrol?" she demanded. Taesonith's left hand rose and fiddled with her ear cuff. Her fingers ran over the intricate floral design in the silver.

"Nay, only in my off time. Kepan's compensation was adequate for the effort."

Yaetherim pointed to the cuff.

"I should think so. Are those part of it too? They are rather well-detailed. Not to mention valuable. And not an obvious payment. Just the thing for someone who wants to be discreet."

Taesonith's hands dropped to her side.

"Speaking of jewellery," Yaetherim continued, "does Mage Kepan wear gold often?"

Taesonith shook her head. She didn't look up.

"Nay, it hurts his skin. Makes it itchy and red. He had me return a couple of pieces to Bookmaker Polton because of that."

Yaetherim blinked. He's heard that name earlier.

"Bookmaker Polton Lonim?"

"Aye. I believe they were gambling payments."

Yaetherim raised an eyebrow. Surely kerlum or crystals would be more suitable for that. But those would also be more obvious. Jewellery still had value amongst Rychillans. Kepan must have been trying to keep this secret. Yet Peran, who shared his office, claimed to be betting with the same bookmaker.

"Is Mage Peran aware of this?" he asked. Taesonith shrugged.

"It's possible. He's walked in on us discussing it."

"Did Mage Kepan seem comfortable with that?"

"Nay, he immediately changed the topic."

Yaetherim smirked. Kepan hadn't recommended the bookmaker to Peran, then. Perhaps Peran had borrowed his colleague's excuse when talking to Karis.

"Thank you, Protector Taesonith," Yaetherim said. "You've been very helpful."

"Indeed. A little too helpful. Protector Taesonith, you can consider yourself suspended from duty. There will be a full inquiry into this," Charlys declared.

Taesonith just nodded. She took off and headed for the College of Mages. Yaetherim whistled, and she looked around.

"You won't find Mage Kepan there," he signed. "We arrested him for murder earlier."

Taesonith dipped in the air. She quickly signed back.

"What? Whose murder?"

"Protector Paetobim, on Verbore Island yesterday evening. Two Rychillan mechanics today."

Taesonith shook her head.

"Nay, he was meeting with Bookmaker Polton last night. He had me arrange that."

"Then you'd better let Veritor Karis know."

"Where can I find this veritor? Alkentoft guard barracks? Town hall?"

Yaetherim pulled out the letter he'd written. He added a few more sentences to it, then held it out.

"She'll be in the veritor's office, top level of town hall. Please take this to her. It explains who the actual murderer is. Her desk's the one facing the door."

Taesonith snatched the paper out of his hand and flew off. Yaetherim rubbed his palms together and turned to Charlys.

"Now that's sorted, I'd like to keep watch on Mage Peran until Veritor Karis gets here."

Charlys stepped forward and took Yaetherim's hands in hers. Her hazel eyes met his. The beat of his heart slowed.

"Therry. Yaetherim. I appreciate what this means to you. But are you certain Mage Peran is guilty?" Charlys asked softly. Yaetherim went to reply. The words withered on his lips. She had a point. They had arrested the wrong man.

"It makes more sense than Kepan. A few things indicate it."

"Such as?"

"You know how humans turn darker in the sun? Tanning, I think it's called."

Charlys nodded.

"It doesn't happen where clothes or jewellery shield their skin from sunlight. Mage Kepan had a smooth tan around his neck, and none below his bracelet. So he usually wears bracelets instead of necklaces. Then there's the necklace itself," Yaetherim said.

"Aye, you mentioned that earlier. I see what you're getting at," Charlys replied. She glanced to the right.

"I'll arrange some protectors to help."

Yaetherim blinked.

"Really?"

Charlys put her hand on his left shoulder. She stood up on her toes, bringing her eyes level with his.

"Therry, if you are correct, he's already got the better of you once. Do you think Naeviol, Paechalor, or I want to see you bleeding again? Or worse? You won't be on your own this time."

That last sentence hit Yaetherim like a falling tree. A tear rolled down his face. Charlys reached up and wiped it off.

"Thank you," he whispered. She nodded.

"Besides, he's attacked other protectors. That's a threat we need to deal with."

Yaetherim gestured towards the College of Mages.

"Thanks. I'll be waiting on the roof."

The two fairies went their separate ways. Charlys' earlier question came back to Yaetherim. He had been positive Kepan was guilty. Everything had pointed to him. Now it all seemed to indicate Peran. He needed to be certain this time. Karis wouldn't take too kindly to a second mistaken arrest. Recent memories percolated into his mind. A smirk crossed his face. He knew how to make sure.

Yaetherim reached the college. He discreetly checked through the windows and spotted Mage Peran teaching in the middle classroom. That done, he circled the building. He took note of the doors. Six on the bottom level, front and rear for each room. A couple on top, one at each end. He landed on the roof, above the front right door. This led to the staircase upstairs. From here, the driveway and front yard lay before him. To his left, the carpark filled the space between brick wall and forest.

A shrill whistle sounded out. Yaetherim turned. Charlys touched down on the tiles, flanked by three other protectors. She performed introductions. Yaetherim explained his plan. Then they sent one protector down to the main road to keep watch. The others remained on the roof with Yaetherim. Charlys flew around the rear of the college and knocked on the end office window. Voices drifted up a moment later.

"Arch-Mage Darnith, I'm Protector Captain Charlys. We've found a trail leading into the forest from the clearing behind your building. Looks like someone's been trespassing regularly."

Yaetherim tilted his head. He'd not heard Charlys speaking Rychillan before. It rolled off her tongue, albeit with a bit of an accent.

"You're certain it's someone from the college?"

"That trail only leads to here. It could be students sneaking off. I'm afraid this is a formal request, sir. Please ask all the mages to watch for anyone going down there. There's already been enough damage done to the forest."

"Do you require us to report it to you?"

"Any member of the North Alken Stewardship will do."

"Very well, Captain Charlys."

The window thudded closed a few heartbeats later. Charlys rejoined Yaetherim on the roof. He looked closely at her.

"Your Rychillan's pretty good. I mean, I still sometimes stumble over verb tenses."

Charlys blushed and glanced down.

"Oh, it's just practice," she replied, "so did that sound alright?"

"Yes, as long as Arch-Mage Darnith tells Mage Peran."

With that, Yaetherim strode to the edge of the roof. He sat, his feet resting in the gutter. For a little while, nothing much happened. Some messengers stopped by the college. On the border of the forest, an occasional protector patrol passed by.

After about an hour, a shrill whistle sounded out. A bus lumbered up the driveway and parked beside the building. Students piled out, their shrieks and laughter filling the air. Peran and another mage escorted a similar group out. Once the younglings climbed aboard, Peran turned to his colleague.

"You and Endra are taking this one, aren't you?"

The other mage nodded. Peran flicked his arm over his shoulder.

"I'm having a smoke, then."

Without waiting for a reply, he spun and headed behind the building. Up on the roof, Yaetherim strode along the edge. He didn't take his eyes off Peran. He could be going for a cigarette. But it may be a convenient excuse. Peran paused at the rear of the carpark and looked around furtively. Yaetherim smirked. The latter, then.

"Did he see you?" Charlys whispered. Yaetherim shook his head. He leaned over. Peran walked over to the broken bushes marking the start of the trail.

"I think we know where he's going."

Yaetherim launched himself off the roof and soared above the forests. Charlys joined him a heartbeat later. Below, the forest canopy thinned out, leaving the gaps that gave the speckled rocks their pattern. The fairies swooped through a gap. Footsteps and crunching leaves drifted through trees. They grew closer and closer. Yaetherim's heart raced. Like in Cerrane, that icy hand closed around his chest once more. But it was different this time. He knew what to expect.

Yaetherim landed on a wild banana tree. Charlys touched down next to him. He raised a finger to his lips, and she nodded. They took cover behind a large leaf. Huddled up, their wings brushed together. A pleasant shiver shot down Yaetherim's spine. He ignored it and remained still. His scars spoke of the consequences should they be discovered.

A couple of heartbeats later, Peran pushed his way through the forest. He reached the stream and stepped from each rock to the next. Every footstep landed on a bare patch. It only took him a few moments to reach the rock next to the hidden hood. Yaetherim smirked as Peran crouched down and peered through the water. No doubt about it now, Peran was the mage involved. Yaetherim shifted slightly to get a better view.

Peran sat down. From one pocket, he drew a rectangular metal case. He flipped it open. One side held about a dozen cigarettes. The other bore a firekind crystal in a narrow clip. Below it, three engraved runes led to a scorched spot.

Peran flicked the clip, touching the crystal down to the engraving beneath it. A short flame flared up at the other end of the runes. He went to light a cigarette, then stopped. His gaze shot from tree to tree. Yaetherim sucked his breath through his teeth. His heart raced. Seemed his plan had worked. Peran was indeed worried. Sweat formed on Yaetherim's brow, and not from the humidity.

Charlys pushed her fingers between his. She squeezed his hand. Yaetherim glanced down, meeting her eyes. His heartbeat slowed. He wasn't alone this time. While some comfort, Peran could attack both of them. Slice them up with that water lance, like carrots on a chopping board.

"Okay. Okay, okay," Peran said. Yaetherim looked around. Only a few animals ran about. Peran must be talking to himself. Humans did that sometimes. Yaetherim leaned in slightly. Charlys moved with him and glanced over. Yaetherim held his finger to his mouth. Peran took a deep breath.

"Okay. We need to get away unseen. That's all," Peran muttered. He leaned down. Water and solid air both parted. Peran stood a few heartbeats later, both satchel and hood in hand. Yaetherim pursed his lips. With that garment, Peran could pass unnoticed amongst Rychillans. Jotol and Warrett's murders had made that clear enough. He intended to flee. Yaetherim's fist clenched. Peran sought to escape the consequences of his actions. Just as he had for eight months. They couldn't have that.

Magic crackled over Yaetherim's skin. His movement spell latched onto a coconut. It detached a moment later. Peran still stood upon the rock, fiddling with his satchel. Yaetherim moved the coconut above the mage. It was a rather large one, enough to feed a half-dozen fairies. While not a water lance, it would give Peran a taste of what he'd done to others. Something unexpected he couldn't escape. Perhaps an injury would prevent him from fleeing.

"Therry?" Charlys whispered.

Yaetherim blinked, as though she'd slapped him across the face. His cheeks flushed. He had thought his anger behind him after unleashing it upon Kepan. Attacking Peran in the forest, unannounced with malice, would only repeat what the mage had done to him.

A flick of his fingers flung the coconut aside. It plunged into the creek. Water flew up. Some splashed Peran. He flinched and leaped back. One hand flicked out. Water formed in front of it. A lance shot out, then stopped.

"Who's there?" Peran shouted. Yaetherim and Charlys exchanged a look. Neither answered. Peran's gaze jumped from tree to tree. From the bank came a rustle. A lizard scurried out from the undergrowth. It gazed at Peran for a second, then lowered its head and lapped up some creek water.

Peran dropped his hand. He let out a sigh and shoved the hood into the satchel. Without missing a step, he crossed the rocks to the shore.

Yaetherim leaned in, his lips a finger-width from the tip of Charlys' ear.

"I'll take the lead," he whispered, his voice barely louder than breeze between trees.

Charlys nodded. Yaetherim jumped back off the branch and spread his wings. He drew his stinger. From tree to tree he flew, keeping leaves and branches between himself and Peran. Behind him, Charlys did the same. Yaetherim's heart pounded, each beat thumping in his ears. Before each move, he glanced ahead to ensure Peran didn't spot them.

That worked, at first. But just as Yaetherim emerged from behind a branch, Peran stopped. He turned and leaned against the half-fallen palm tree beside the trail. Yaetherim dived. His feet thudded onto the ground. His eyes shot up. Peran wasn't looking at him, nor had he spotted Charlys. Instead, the mage had his cigarette case in hand. After lighting a cigarette, he put it to his mouth.

Within moments, a haze of tobacco smoke hung in the air. With a spell, Peran pushed it back down the path. Yaetherim's stomach turned. It didn't make him cough any more. He'd spent enough time around Rychillans for that. Charlys hadn't.

With a wave, Yaetherim got her attention. He signed quickly.

"You'll need to get clear. Fly above the canopy, we'll meet at the college."

Without waiting for a reply, he shot a spell at the leaning palm tree. It creaked, tumbled, and splashed into the creek. Peran yelped and staggered. Then he regained his balance and stood. Above, leaves rustled. Yaetherim glanced up. No sign or sound of Charlys. Yaetherim's wings sagged, and his heart slowed. Charlys was safe.

Looking back, Yaetherim found Peran checking the path in both directions. Yaetherim dived under a bush. For several heartbeats, only birdsong filled the air. A metallic snap sounded out. Yaetherim peeked out. Peran slipped the cigarette case into his pocket.

Peran strode off. Yaetherim quickly took flight. The smoke scratched at his throat. But he didn't cough.

They soon reached the end of the trail, and Peran paused again. After checking the clearing, he crossed to a car in the parking lot. With one quick movement, he opened the luggage compartment at the front, threw the satchel in and closed it.

Once Peran returned to the college, Yaetherim emerged from the trees. He landed on the car's boot and tried the latch. It didn't move. He frowned. Peran had put in a significant effort to hide that bag. Nothing legitimate would need that.

A slap sounded from the roof of the car. Yaetherim glanced up, meeting a familiar pair of eyes.

"It's locked, Sunbird," he said. He punctuated his words with a glance at the college building. For his talk of getting away unnoticed, Peran wasn't doing much about it. He could have easily climbed into this vehicle and driven off.

Yaetherim cracked his knuckles and took flight. A frown crossed his face. Three fairies stood on the roof. Two protectors, and a red-haired waterkind. Given the latter's town garb, he could guess who she was.

"Sunbird, I've mentioned Naeliya, haven't I?"

Charlys frowned and pursed her lips.

190

"After your last couple of visits to Alkentoft, I think."

"You're about to meet her."

He landed. Charlys touched down beside him. Yaetherim performed the introductions.

"So what brings you here, Messenger Naeliya?" Charlys asked pointedly. She folded her arms. Naeliya pointed northeast.

"Veritor Karis sent me. She's searching the town, and wanted to check if you'd found anything."

"Didn't she get my note?" Yaetherim said. Naeliya shook her head.

"Not if you addressed it to her office. Arch-Mechanic Tenora's going there, to handle that sort of thing."

Yaetherim frowned.

"Shouldn't that be a veritor's job?"

"Aye, but Veritor Karis is searching for Merchant Rynach Reulo. Veritor Jorryn's indisposed, and Arch-Veritor Rakin is on the night shift this week."

Yaetherim blinked.

"Wait, what happened to Veritor Jorryn?"

"Merchant Rynach tried to kill him and Arch-Mechanic Tenora," Naeliya replied. She explained what had taken place at the warehouse. Her tale horrified the other fairies.

"Are they alright?" Yaetherim asked, once Naeliya had finished. She nodded.

"Arch-Mechanic Tenora didn't seem that affected. Connil use that stuff to clean her workshop, so she's used to it. That wasn't the case for Veritor Jorryn. Veritor Karis ordered him home to rest."

Yaetherim pinched the bridge of his nose. He understood how Jorryn must feel. Helpless and frustrated. Maybe even afraid, lying in bed, worrying if his attackers would try to finish the job. That same fear which had loomed over Yaetherim for eight months. But now Yaetherim had their measure. They were cowards. He laughed. Just a sharp snort. Both Charlys and Naeliya shot him baffled looks.

"Therry?" Charlys asked. Yaetherim waved his hand reassuringly.

"Aye, I'm alright. Naeliya, does Merchant Rynach know Mages Kepan or

Peran at all?"

"He's known Mage Peran for years. I've been carrying messages between them since I started as a messenger. They were friends in school, I think."

A smirk twisted Yaetherim's lips. Now it made sense. Peran's words in the clearing, his remaining here, it all added up.

"Merchant Rynach is on the run," Yaetherim said, "and his old friend, his partner in crime, is here. That's why Peran's not fleeing. He's waiting."

Charlys' breath whistled through the gap in her teeth.

"That does make sense, assuming Veritor Karis doesn't get him. Messenger Naeliya, would you recognise Merchant Rynach?"

"Aye."

"That makes one of us," Yaetherim replied. He shot a look at Charlys. She nodded and gave an order to another protector. The latter took flight and headed northeast, towards Alkentoft. Charlys flew off a moment later, to Taselo Village. They'd need a change of protectors.

Charlys soon returned and landed next to Yaetherim. She looked around. Her gaze fell upon Naeliya, who'd found a spot in the shade. She lay on her back, eyes closed and wings spread. Charlys folded her arms and shot her a look from beneath a frown.

"At least some of us are still awake," she said. Before Yaetherim could reply, one of Naeliya's eyelids popped open.

"I don't know how long your patrol paths are," she replied, "but I suspect they're less than the length or breadth of Alkentoft. When you cover that distance several times a day, you learn to conserve your energy. Besides, you will need me to notify Veritor Karis as quickly as possible when Merchant Rynach gets here, won't you?"

Charlys didn't reply. Yaetherim looked from one to the other. Naeliya wasn't drunk. In fact, he'd never seen her this sober. While he understood Charlys' worries, they did not cause him concern. They could rely on Naeliya.

A soft 'thud' sounded out, that of the protector returning from Alkentoft. He shot an apologetic look at Charlys.

"I'm sorry, ma'am. Veritor Karis isn't available at the moment. She's leading the search in Alkentoft itself. They can't spare any constables."

Yaetherim didn't reply. He nearly swore. Instead, he let out a sigh. Finally, he had the Rychillan who had attacked him. After eight months, he knew who'd scarred him and where to find him. Below his feet. No mistake this time. Yet town guard inaction could still allow Peran to escape.

"Of course they'd prioritise Rynach. He's killed Rychillans," Yaetherim spat, his voice dripping with sarcasm.

Charlys tilted her head, and a half-smile crossed her lips. Again, she wore that look indicating he should know better. He opened his mouth to speak, but the words died on his tongue. Rynach had murdered two Rychillans. Humans the same size as him, not fairies one-sixth his size. Had done so in broad daylight, unnoticed. He had attempted a couple more murders, too. In comparison, Peran had only killed a single fairy and wounded another.

Yaetherim blinked. It was as though he'd just taken off a pair of goggles. He met Charlys' gaze. A smirk crossed his lips. He stood up straighter and folded his wings back. Charlys smiled.

"You've got something in mind, haven't you, Therry?"

"Aye. You know, I read through the Accord of Reiksoft several times while recovering."

Charlys raised an eyebrow.

"Is it that interesting?"

"Boring as watching plants grow. Thought it might provide answers. But for all it covers, there's a lot it doesn't," Yaetherim replied. He explained his plan. Charlys nodded when he'd finished.

"We should be able to handle that," she said. She turned to the protector beside her.

"Please deliver a message to Taselo Village," she ordered. "All protectors coming here need to be armed with crossbows. Ask them to send airkinds, if possible. Then you can consider yourself off-duty, after all that flying about."

"Aye, ma'am. Thank you."

With that, the protector took flight and headed for Taselo Village. Yaetherim strode over and sat on the edge of the roof. His legs dangled over the gutter. His gaze fell upon the cars parked below. Now it was just a question of waiting and acting if needed.

14

Regrouping

Tenora rubbed her eyes as she strode down the corridor. The aroma of coffee drifted up from the cup in her hand. She'd bought it from a food cart outside town hall, her last stop on the way in. After leaving her workshop, she had decided to take up Seralyn's earlier offer of help. So she had stopped by Warrett's shop and given the mechanics there the description of Rynach's car. Even Mechanic Ordan had been willing to watch out for it. She pursed her lips. More watchers meant more chances of locating Rynach. Hopefully, before he could hurt anyone else.

With that in mind, Tenora sipped her coffee. Finding Rynach may take minutes or hours, she didn't know for sure. But with fatigue encroaching like kudzu, she needed to stay awake.

She reached the veritors' office. 'Twas unlocked and she slipped inside. Karis had advised the town hall staff Tenora would be acting on her behalf. No surprise there.

That changed two steps through the door. A hooded figure stood between her and Karis' desk. The stench of cleaning fluid wafted from their bucket. Her heartbeat raced, pounding in her ears. Her free hand closed round her wrench, as the impossibility of the situation crossed her mind. Rynach could not have known she was coming here.

"Please turn around, slowly," she said, managing to keep her voice level. The connil did so. Tenora let out a sigh. A stranger peered out from beneath the hood. A genuinely repentant Rychillan. Not just someone taking advantage of society's blindness towards that class. 'Twas a man's face, his brown eyes surrounded by blue hair mixed with a few strands of white.

"My apologies," he said. "I was tidying."

It took her a moment to believe those words. This man, whoever he was, wouldn't have been marked untrustworthy without good reason. Another whiff of the cleaning fluid hit her. Her stomach heaved. She cleared her throat.

"Could you please return later?" she asked. He nodded.

"Again, I apologise, ma'am."

With that, he left. Tenora found herself alone. She let go of the wrench. Her hands shook as she put a cigarette in her mouth and lit it. Moments before, she'd reached for a tool to defend herself. Here, in the office of those who kept the kingdom's peace. She had jumped to a conclusion when her entire career revolved around logical diagnosis from facts. Rynach couldn't possibly have known she would be here. Furthermore, she always tried to give repentant connil the benefit of the doubt. They'd seen the error of their ways, that's why they undertook repentance. She frowned. That fracas at the warehouse had indeed sown weeds amongst her thoughts.

With one well-practised motion, she removed her cigarette and sipped her coffee. Steam curled up, carrying a pleasant, smoky aroma. Tenora closed her eyes and let it wash over her lips. It ran down her throat, taking some of her dread with it. Each breath came easier than the last.

A second sip of coffee prompted an additional realisation. For her, this business had only lasted a couple of days. Scant comparison to Yaetherim's eight months. Thirty-two weeks of walking about in fear. Little wonder he'd been so offhand about his injuries. Yet another reason to find Rynach, not that Tenora needed one. With Kepan already under arrest, this dangerous affair should soon be at an end.

After extinguishing the cigarette, she tossed it into a rubbish bin. Standing around smoking and sipping wouldn't help track down the murderous merchant. She stepped behind Karis' desk. Two neat stacks of paper sat atop the desk, one on either side. An inkwell stood to the left. Beside this display of order lay a page ripped from a notebook, with a fairy-sized sheet clipped under it. Only a few sentences comprised the top note. Apparently, a protector named Taesonith had delivered the letter pinned to it. She could also provide corroborating testimony.

Her curiosity piqued, Tenora opened the other message. Angular, Fairic script covered the page. Slightly messy, but written large enough for a human to read. 'Twas fortunate, for Tenora had to do so twice. She swore. Moments before, she'd thought this on the verge of resolution. But this report from Yaetherim belied that. It put forth a compelling case and had a witness to back it up. If he were indeed correct, the wrong mage now languished in a holding cell.

A few steps brought Tenora to the call lever on the wall between bookshelves. It slid smoothly into place and a fairy arrived within minutes. Tenora gave him both notes and gestured north.

"Veritor Karis is searching the town. She needs to see these right away. Can you please deliver them to her?" she asked in Fairic. She held out four kerlum coins and two kerlar. The messenger took one of each. Tenora jiggled her hand, and the others clinked together.

"I know it's not that expensive," she said, "but you'll need to locate Veritor Karis. I'm not sure exactly where to find her. But she's working south from the airship terminal."

The fairy stared, then glanced at Tenora's terax. He raised an eyebrow.

"Is it about that car thing? There're a few rumours going around."

"It is. This will help end it."

"I'll ensure Veritor Karis gets these. Who shall I say forwarded them, Arch-Mechanic...?"

"Tenora Perskel."

The messenger nodded and departed.

Over the next few hours, Rychillans and fairies stopped by with messages for Karis. Most weren't relevant to this case, and so Tenora lay them aside for later perusal. Some updates from Karis came in, too.

After a short while, another fairy arrived. He wore clothes woven from leaves. Typical forest garb, rather than the stitched fabric of one who lived in town. Above his left elbow, he bore the armband of a protector. Tenora gestured to the desk, and he landed.

"I've got a message for Veritor Karis, from Protector Captain Charlys and, um, Ex-protector Yaetherim."

Tenora leaned forward, being careful not to loom over him.

"What is it?" she asked in Fairic. He started talking, and Tenora's eyes widened. She listened closely, nodding every sentence or two. Yaetherim and Charlys had seen Peran retrieve the connil hood. He'd hidden it in the forest, under some running water. Tenora couldn't help but raise an eyebrow. 'Twas a rather ingenious hiding spot. Once the protector had finished, he glanced out the window.

"Under the Accord of Reiksoft, we'll have to ask your town guard to arrest him."

Tenora sighed. Karis had given her instructions, should an eventuality like this arise.

"We will do what we can," she replied, "but Veritor Karis and all the guards are busy searching for Merchant Rynach."

The protector folded his arms. Tenora pressed her hands together, then lay them flat on the desk before her. Not exactly lowering a pair of wings, but the best imitation she could do.

"We'll get someone there as soon as we can," Tenora added apologetically. The protector just nodded and flew off. Tenora watched him go. A sigh escaped her, and her stomach gurgled. She checked her watch. It was getting on for the nineteenth hour. Slightly early for dinner, but it had been a big day. She headed downstairs.

A brief walk later, Tenora returned with a paper bag from a food cart. Nothing fancy, simply a ham-and-cheese sandwich and some dried fruits. Upon returning, she heard two voices coming from within the veritors' office. One belonged to a man, the other she'd once known intimately.

"... asked us to report any sightings to her here," Seralyn said.

"She's probably not too far away. 'Tis getting on for dinnertime, and there are several food carts in the town square. Speaking of which, have you eaten?"

"Not yet. I'll grab something once I've spoken to Tenora."

A pang of guilt shot through Tenora. Although she had a valid reason, she had left her post. But she'd not expected Seralyn to drop by at this moment. She opened the door and entered the office.

Seralyn stood between the desks. A silver-haired gentleman sat behind the desk to the right. Some strands of white showed in his hair and his face bore a few lines of age. His terax spoke of a career in the town guard, rising to the rank of veritor. A few marks above that was one Tenora had also earned: chief of profession. She swallowed. This had merely been a question of malfunctioning engines when she'd woken this morning. Now, she was addressing the officer-in-charge of the town guard for Alkentoft. Second only to the governor in terms of authority.

"Good evening," Tenora said. "You must be Arch-Veritor Rakin. Hello Seralyn."

The other Rychillans turned to her. Tenora held her left arm out, terax forward. Rakin read it and Seralyn gave her a small nod.

"My apologies," Tenora added. "I just went out to get some dinner."

She met Seralyn's gaze, expecting some harsh remark about timing. It wouldn't be the first time. Instead, the other woman glanced down.

"You're correct," Rakin replied, "and you must be Arch-Mechanic Tenora Perskel. Karis sent me a note to expect you."

Tenora ran her empty hand along the side of her head and over her ear.

"Seralyn, did you find something?"

"I was returning Acolyte Kemus' car to him and spotted the one you described."

"What? Where?"

"Two-and-a-half blocks from the temple, south of the river."

Tenora's stomach fluttered, as though butterflies flew within it. That was it. Rynach must be around there somewhere. Priests and acolytes managed the repentance of connil. With his hood, Rynach could hide amongst them until the search had died down.

"That makes sense. Mage Peran is waiting at the College of Mages. It's to the southwest of the town. Just like that temple," Tenora replied. Both of the other Rychillans blinked.

"May I ask where that information came from?" Rakin asked. Tenora repeated what the protector had reported earlier. When she finished, Seralyn nodded.

"I think Yaetherim is correct," she said. "They might be planning to meet up."

"If it is the same vehicle," Rakin added. "Arch-Mechanic Tenora, what was its number plate?"

"I only got the briefest of glimpses. Rust and repaired panels were the key details I spotted. But that sort of wear is common. I'd recognise the pattern if I saw it again."

Rakin leaned forward and clasped his hands, his elbows resting on the desk.

"If Mechanic Seralyn is correct, there is a risk Rynach may see you."

"Tenora's got an eye for detail, sir," Seralyn said. "She'd be able to identify it from only a drive-by."

Tenora's cheeks flushed. Whilst she would certainly try to do so, she couldn't make any guarantees.

"Very well," Rakin replied. He met Tenora's gaze. Instead of steel, 'twas concern which greeted her.

"I'll send word of this to Karis and await further messages here. But please be careful," he said. Tenora nodded. She strode out of the office, with Seralyn behind her.

They headed downstairs, Tenora munching on her sandwich. She finished the last few crumbs as they reached Seralyn's car. A few moments later, they were underway. Tenora drew a cigarette, then stopped. Seralyn kept looking over, her gaze flicking from the windscreen to Tenora.

"Please watch the road, for the sake of us both."

"Sorry, I'm just... Tenora, why did you not get the number plate? It's not like you to miss that sort of thing."

"I didn't have much choice," Tenora replied. She recounted what had happened at the harbour, from her meeting with Fillan through to her arrival at the town hall. When she finished, Seralyn gasped. She lay a palm on Tenora's knee. Warmth washed over Tenora, and she sucked her breath through her teeth.

"Tennie," Seralyn said, "you could have been injured, or..."

Tenora sighed.

"I know. But I couldn't sit back. Others may have been hurt."

Tenora lifted the other woman's hand off her leg and placed it on the steering wheel.

"Please don't call me 'Tennie'," she chided, "it was you who ended our courtship, remember?"

Seralyn blushed and turned her attention to the road. Awkward silence filled the car.

Fortunately, the drive only lasted a few minutes more. Seralyn turned right once they'd crossed the river. Two blocks of houses went past, followed by another of forest. Surrounded by a wooden fence, one of Alkentoft's three fairy villages sat amongst its branches. Halfway along this block, Seralyn reduced the throttle and braked. She nodded forwards.

"It's still there, on the left."

Tenora peered out the window. A car stood in the shadow of a mail tower. Its construction and colour matched the one she sought. Blue, metal body, varnished wood running boards.

"Can you please pull over up ahead? I'll need to check the other side."

Seralyn parked against the kerb. Both mechanics climbed out. Tenora looked around. Aside from the temple and fairy village, only houses lined the streets. A few people walked along the footpaths.

Tenora circled the suspect car and crouched by the left-front mudguard. Sure enough, it bore a shade of blue lighter than the rest. On the rear door, three spots of rust marred the paint. Two the size of a kerlo coin, one above the other, and a kerlar-sized spot behind them. Tenora's breath came quickly. She stepped around to get a clear view of the number plate. She thought back to those few moments at the warehouse. With them fresh in her mind, she took another look. Yes, this was Rynach's vehicle. Those spots of rust, the mudguard, what she could recall of the number plate, they all matched.

Rynach may be nearby. Tenora frowned. She put her palm on the side of the engine. No heat came from within.

"Arch-Mechanic Tenora?"

Tenora jumped. Her ponytail whipped around as she looked back. Karis stood on the footpath, a constable behind her. A town guard car sat parked half a block away. Tenora placed her hand on her heart, which thumped like a fairy playing a drum.

"Pardon me, Veritor Karis. I didn't hear you there."

"My apologies. I did not mean to startle you."

Tenora shook her head.

"It's not you who worries me. This is Merchant Rynach's vehicle. It matches the one that ran me down," Tenora replied. She gestured to Seralyn.

"Mechanic Seralyn here found it while returning an acolyte's car."

"I see," Karis said. Seralyn cleared her throat.

"We, ah, think Merchant Rynach may be lying low in the temple. Amongst the connil."

Karis' lips tightened, and her eyes narrowed.

"Do you need any more from me, Veritor Karis?" Seralyn asked.

"No," Karis replied, "but thank you for your help."

Seralyn nodded. She bade farewell to Tenora and strode off. Karis turned to the guard constable.

"Stay here," she ordered, "and ensure no-one uses this car."

"Yes, ma'am."

She glanced down the road.

"Arch-Mechanic Tenora, I will need your assistance."

Tenora looked down. Tears welled up in her eyes. Her fingers half-curled into a fist, and it took an effort to relax them. It had been about a year since she'd last set foot inside a temple. There was a reason for that.

"Perhaps I should check if there are any messages from Yaetherim. Rynach might head for the College of Mages," she said. Somehow, she kept her voice level. A sheet of paper entered her vision. Only a few sentences covered it.

"Please take these orders to Guard Sergeant Palron on your way. Last I saw, he was in Jobin Street."

Tenora took the page and now met Karis' eyes. She pointed to the guard car.

"May I borrow that? Seralyn gave me a lift here."

Karis nodded and handed over the keys. She turned and headed for the temple. Tenora quickly reached the guard car and brought it up to steam. As she drove off, relief washed over her. A slight smile curved her lips. Rynach wouldn't be able to get far on foot. Either Karis would find him, or Yaetherim would be waiting with some protectors. But however it worked out, it would soon be over.

15

Stalling

aylight had started to give way to dusk. Most of the mages had gone home, but Peran had remained. He was working on lesson plans, or so they'd overheard. So Yaetherim and Charlys kept watch from atop the college. Naeliya continued to conserve her energy. Charlys shot a look at her.

"At least we've got fresh protectors," she commented. Before Yaetherim could reply, the fairy stationed at the front of the building motioned rapidly. Barely had she signed one word before her fingers formed the next. Yaetherim's eyes widened. A connil was walking up the driveway. He'd just passed the protector by the road. Yaetherim's hand dropped to his stinger. His thoughts caught up with his instinct a heartbeat later. This newcomer may simply be the cleaner.

He strode over and tapped Naeliya on the shoulder. She sprang to her feet. Several quick steps brought them to the edge of the roof. Yaetherim frowned. Few connil could afford clothes as well-tailored as this visitor's. This Rychillan also bore the symbol of a merchant, tattooed down by his left wrist.

"I can't see a connil's terax mark on him," Yaetherim whispered, "can you?"

"Nay," Naeliya replied with a shake of her head.

At the top of the driveway, the newcomer paused. He looked around, then reached up and lowered his hood. Purple eyes peered out from beneath neatly combed hair. Yaetherim glanced over at Naeliya. Her hands formed two words, "Merchant Rynach." Yaetherim signed back. Naeliya nodded and took off. She flew high, heading down to the road.

Yaetherim did not look away from Rynach. His wings twitched. A couple of deep breaths helped calm him. They didn't need to confront Rynach and Peran. All they had to do was delay them until the town guard arrived.

Below, a door thudded closed at the front-right of the building. So not a classroom. It had barely faded before Charlys gave orders. A single protector to act as a lookout on each corner of the roof and another down by the road. But keeping watch was one thing. Holding these killers here was a different matter.

His gaze fell upon the car sitting in the parking lot. Steam curled up from its funnel. Peran had fired it up a short while ago. While the vehicle's body was wood, the engine was metal. Florakind magic couldn't disable it.

Yaetherim caught Charlys' attention and pointed down. She nodded. He strode to the front of the roof, dived and hovered outside the rightmost door. Cut from a solid piece of timber, it appeared to open inward. A growth spell wouldn't work. It had been dead too long.

Yaetherim's hand flicked out. An incantation spurted from his lips. From the forest came a sharp snap. A still-green vine sailed through the air. Yaetherim planted it against the doorsill. He took a deep breath. Energy raced over his arm and poured into the plant. It shot up, wrapping itself around the handle. Tendrils grabbed the door and frame, binding them together.

Yaetherim leaned forward, as though that would boost the speed of the spell. He stopped only when the vine hit the top of the doorway. His skin itched. He had never cast that intensely. But he couldn't help smirking. This web of vines would ensure no escape this way. With that done, he swapped out the crystal in his belt with a fresh one from his satchel.

He glanced at the single lit window on the upper level. Shadows moved behind a closed curtain. The Rychillans inside could still get out via the back door. Yaetherim pursed his lips. A few fast flaps of his wings brought him onto the roof. He perched on the peak. Charlys joined him a heartbeat later.

"I've sealed the front exit," he said. "We'll have to watch the rear."

"All three of them?"

"Nay, only the one at this end. The others are the classrooms."

He gestured towards the road. The distant beat of a car engine drifted through the air. It could have been coming from Alkentoft, or nearer.

"Any sign of Veritor Karis?"

"Not yet."

Yaetherim nodded and dived off the roof. He touched down on the verandah. Two soft slaps sounded out. From his left, Charlys shot Yaetherim an inquiring look. He held his finger up to his lips, then led Charlys around to the front of the building. They stopped halfway along.

With a movement spell, he tugged open the window above them. Just far enough for voices to escape. Peran's voice drifted out.

"I have little to worry about. They arrested Kepan for my part of it."

"Then you're lucky. They found my car. I had to flee on foot," Rynach replied. Yaetherim folded his arms. The merchant's words carried a distinct note of outrage. Almost as if being held accountable for his actions was beneath him.

"Yes, it's a fine mess you've landed us in," Peran retorted.

"Me? Those runes were your idea."

"Who insisted on field testing them in the cars, hmm? You even used your contacts to identify willing mechanics."

Silence fell for a moment.

"Come on, we'd better be going before they find me," Rynach grumbled.

Yaetherim flexed his wings. That was all he needed to hear. He took flight and looped around the building. With Charlys behind him, he hovered outside the rear carpark end door. After a few moments, muffled thumps sounded from inside. Yaetherim drew his stinger.

"Try it again!"

Yaetherim smirked. No indignation flavoured Rynach's voice this time. Instead, his words carried a hint of panic. Another thump came.

"I'm telling you, it's jammed!"

"They... they know. They know we're here!"

Yaetherim's smirk grew. Now they knew how he'd felt.

"Not necessarily, Rynach. Calm down. That door seizes up sometimes, especially during the rainy season. There's a reason we keep it ajar during the day."

That may have been true. But Peran's tone lacked confidence.

"Right. What about the rear exit, then?"

Yaetherim flew back. Beside him, Charlys brought her crossbow up. She aimed high, where a Rychillan's face would be. Yaetherim threw his stinger. With a spell, he caught it by the wood inlay. He held it at the height of a human's eyes.

To his left, Charlys backed off. Her free hand moved. Not signing, merely beckoning. Another protector joined them, also armed. Just in time, too. A soft click came from the door. It swung open. Peran stepped through, his head turned back.

"... we've nothing to worry about."

"Actually, you do," Yaetherim said. Behind Peran, Rynach stopped. Peran looked forward. His eyes fell upon the stinger, then jumped to the hovering fairies. Yaetherim slowly rolled the dagger. The last hints of daylight glinted on its blade.

"Be careful, Mage Peran," he snarked, "getting cut up won't give you a clean getaway. Or a clean anything."

His free hand pointed to the crossbows borne by Charlys and the other protector.

"A lesson you taught me, by the way. It took three waterkinds to wash the blood and dirt off, when they found me in Oato Clearing. Now, you know what we fairies are like with favours and debts. I learned something from you, and it's time that was repaid."

Peran's face paled, almost matching the bark of a paperbark tree. He looked down.

"You don't need to say any more, Yaetherim. I heard what you said to Kepan earlier. I've spent the last eight months looking over my shoulder, too. Wondering when the town guard would arrest me for a moment of panic."

Peran continued to speak, but his words just flowed past like water. Each of Yaetherim's muscles trembled. The stinger shook. Peran took a step back. When Yaetherim spoke, his tone could have formed ice in a fresh cup of tea.

"A moment of panic? Do you think I'd have trouble finding a landing spot in a clearing, Murderer Peran? You're as remorseful as a spider catching a fly."

"No, I-"

"Your guilt didn't prevent you from doing it again, did it? And when you heard Charlys and me by the speckled rocks today, you cast a water lance, sight unseen. You also tried to smoke us out with your cigarette. Not something someone does on the spur of the moment."

Peran's cheeks flushed. Yaetherim held his arms out, scars forward. Peran looked away.

"Go on, study your handiwork. I had to learn to fly again, thanks to you. Even now, I can't feel about a quarter of that wing. The Verbore Islanders are mourning. You killed one of them! All for some stupid, ineffective runes."

Peran leaned in. Yaetherim raised the stinger, aiming it at the mage's left eye. He wouldn't wish injury upon anyone, not after all he'd experienced. Not now. But Peran didn't know that.

"Stay back," Yaetherim growled.

"I never intended to hurt anybody. We just needed somewhere to experiment."

"Then why did you not try to bribe me eight months ago?"

Peran's eyes widened. From behind, Charlys gasped.

"You'd have taken a pay-off?" Peran asked. Yaetherim shook his head.

"Of course not! But you didn't even ask. I was on my own. Nobody would have known. Yet you just went straight to that water lance. An attempt to kill me. You succeeded with Paetobim."

Peran ran his hand through his hair. His shoes suddenly caught his attention. Yaetherim folded his arms. At least this one had the decency to feel some guilt. He shot a look at Rynach, who'd remained conspicuously silent.

"Was it the same with Mechanic Jotol and Arch-Mechanic Warrett? Panic in the heat of the moment? When you hid under a hood, sneaked up and killed them?"

Rynach shrugged.

"They knew too much," he stated.

"I see. Well, good news. You are going to wear those hoods you're keen on, once Veritor Karis…"

"Therry, watch out!"

Charlys' warning came too late. Air blasted Yaetherim. He tumbled, recovered, and swooped around. The door banged shut. A crossbow bolt thudded into it. Yaetherim lunged for the handle. He found it locked. From inside, footsteps thundered up the stairs.

Yaetherim sheathed his stinger. He flew back. Peran's car was waiting underneath the balcony.

"Come on!"

He didn't wait for a reply. Wisps of steam still drifted up from the vehicle's funnel. Above it, a section of air grew opaque. Yaetherim swore. Just a simple airkind walling spell, cast to provide a ramp down. That's what would determine if his attackers would escape or not.

Above, the air finished solidifying. A grunt sounded out. Yaetherim's wings burned, but he didn't care. They would not get away. Not now. He soared up. Ahead, Rynach hurled himself onto the ramp. With one motion, Yaetherim drew his stinger and threw it. Even guided by his magic, it missed.

Summoned back, the stinger slammed into Yaetherim's hand. Beside him, Charlys fired as Peran slid down. A grunt from the mage indicated she'd hit something. Steam hissed from the car. Peran thumped onto its roof. He jumped in. Before he'd closed the door, the vehicle moved off.

Yaetherim swore. With no sign of Karis or the town guard, the killers would escape.

16

Escape

Bricks had given way to trees several minutes before. Having not found any messages waiting at the town hall, Tenora had taken her roadster to check at the College of Mages itself. The fairies had stationed a sentry by the road there. That's what that protector had said. More to the point, the sooner Karis knew of Rynach's whereabouts, the less chance he had of escape.

Ahead, a gap in the forest marked the college's driveway. Tenora pulled over and engaged the parking brake. With the roof folded down, she had a clear view of the trees above. Calling out would be indiscreet. Instead, she stretched her arms up. A few quick words in signed Fairic conveyed her intentions. At least, she hoped that was the case. She was better at speaking it than signing.

For a few moments, only the birdsong and dusk surrounded her. Two taps rang out from the windscreen. Tenora blinked. A fairy stood on the boot of her car. His feathered wings marked him as an airkind. Clad in clothes woven from leaves, he wore the armband of a protector. He held a loaded crossbow, which was aimed down. Tenora introduced herself.

"Has Merchant Rynach gone past?" she asked.

"What's your interest in him?"

"I am working with Veritor Karis to catch him."

The sentry's frown deepened. Before he could reply, a blue-skinned, red-haired fairy swooped in. Recognition dawned, but Naeliya spoke first.

"Arch-Mechanic Tenora? What brings you here?"

"I wanted to check if Merchant Rynach had arrived."

"He has. I'm on my way to notify Veritor Karis."

Tenora's breath caught in her throat. To realise the possibility was one thing. 'Twas another to have it made real. She glanced over her shoulder.

"You'll find her at the southern temple," she said, her words running together. She paused.

"They're checking the connil there. We found his car parked nearby."

Tenora reached for her cigarette case. Her hand brushed against her wrench. The familiar touch of cool metal sparked an idea.

"Messenger Naeliya, are there any cars at the college?"

"One, I think it's Mage Peran's."

"Thank you."

Naeliya flew off. Tenora pursed her lips. She didn't have to worry about notifying Karis. Naeliya would see to that.

"You're trying to keep them here 'til the town guard arrive, aren't you?" she asked the protector.

"Aye, that's the idea."

That was all Tenora needed to hear. She flicked a knob beside the throttle. At the front of the car, the headlights flickered out. Dusk encroached upon her. She dropped the fire and vented the leftover steam. After jumping out, she pulled up the roof and locked the doors behind her. In less than a minute, she'd removed both crystals from the engine. She slipped them into a pocket. Those murderers wouldn't escape in this vehicle. Now to ensure they couldn't use theirs, either.

She strode up the driveway towards the college. With one hand, she pressed her overalls against her, lest the tools clank and give her away. They dug into her, but she didn't slow.

A twisted mess of tendrils and leaves covered the right-front door. Only a few spots of paint showed through it. It shook as she drew closer. Muffled voices came from behind it, punctuated by thumps.

"Try it again!"

"I'm telling you, it's jammed!"

"They... they know. They know we're here!"

Tenora didn't wait for more. She dashed over to the car in the parking lot. Steam rose from its funnel, and a faint hiss escaped its cylinders. Only a fool would open a running engine. Even if she dropped its fire, she wouldn't have time to vent it.

Tenora crouched next to the front wheel. Staying low, she kept the car's body between herself and the college. She set to work on the lug nuts. One, two, three, four, each came undone in seconds. She moved to the rear.

Words drifted through the air, Rychillan with an unmistakable Fairic lilt. 'Twas a tone which could turn steel brittle. It must've been Yaetherim, else another fairy had survived an encounter with the killers. A second voice called out.

"Therry, watch out!"

Tenora's heart skipped a beat. She glanced up. The protectors on the roof stood with their weapons drawn. Beside the building, air solidified.

Quicker than before, she set to work. Within seconds, the rear wheel's lug nuts joined the others. Her pulse raced. The image of Jotol slumped dead careened through her thoughts. She'd rather not end up the same.

Tenora jumped to her feet. She sprinted for the front doors of the college. Once there, she pressed herself against the first classroom door. Her breath came in quick gasps. She resisted the urge to light a cigarette. Now was not the time.

Steam hissed, followed by colourful Fairic cursing. The car picked up speed. Rynach sat at the wheel, Peran in the back seat. Three fairies flew in pursuit. Yaetherim in the lead, a nokind and an airkind behind him. 'Twas the fastest Tenora had ever seen a fairy fly. She cleared her throat.

"Don't worry! They won't get too far," she called in Fairic. Yaetherim spun around. Crossbows flicked towards her. She stepped back. Yaetherim pushed the weapons down. Tenora raised her hands. The lug nuts glinted in the moonlight. Yaetherim peered at them.

"Are those-"

A screech split the air. Sparks flew. Bare axles bounced off the cobbles, each impact punctuated by a thud. To the left, bushes shook as the loose wheels slammed into them. Tenora winced. Necessary, it may have been. But that had been a functional vehicle before she'd sabotaged it. Days of work by mechanics and coachbuilders, undone in moments by her.

The car skidded to a halt. Tenora broke into a run. Furious flapping of fairy wings came from behind her. Both killers extricated themselves. Peran held his head. Rynach dashed around. He grabbed the mage by the shoulder.

"Come on!"

They turned and ran. Tenora's hand shot out. Energy crackled. A wall of fire erupted, cutting off the fleeing Rychillans. They skidded to a halt. Tenora twisted her wrist. A flower of flames bloomed, surrounding the killers. Both were sweating. On Peran's arm, it mixed with the trickle of blood flowing from a cut on his shoulder. Tenora pursed her lips. She doubted they were simply feeling the heat.

Tenora slowed and stopped before the warmth became uncomfortable. She glanced to the left, where Yaetherim flew an arm's length away. His two friends hovered behind, crossbows ready.

"Where did you think you were going?" Tenora demanded. Rynach glared at her, but Peran smiled sheepishly.

"We were just trying..."

"I know what you sought to do. Escape the consequences of your own actions. Did you believe I was joking when I spoke of the responsibility we share, Mage Peran? A duty of care to our clients. A duty you threw away like a used cigarette."

"All for some stupid runes," Yaetherim said. "You killed and maimed for something you should have damn well known wouldn't work. A paper bag is more responsible than either of you."

Tenora wasn't sure of her own expression. But if looks could inflict harm, Yaetherim's would have ended Peran and Rynach then and there. Rynach folded his arms.

"They worked, to a degree. We had to test them in real-world conditions. Surely you understand that, Arch-Mechanic Tenora. Isn't that what you were doing when you spotted that runaway car?"

Tenora glared at the merchant.

"I experiment on a single vehicle. The only risk is to myself," she said. "Did you not consider trying that?"

"What, and get noticed?"

Yaetherim scoffed.

"You mean misbehaving cars and boiler explosions don't attract attention? What does, then?"

Another glare came from Rynach.

"They didn't point at us. Kept it at arm's length."

"Then you severed that arm by murdering my colleagues," Tenora snarled. The flames flared, punctuating her words. Peran's hand shot up. Air blasted out, shoving the fire towards Tenora and the fairies. Heat washed over them. Tenora dived aside. Instinct took over, and she fired off an extinguishing spell. Rynach shoved Peran forward and ran.

Tenora chased the fleeing murderers. Her boots beat against the driveway, each step quicker than the last. They would not escape.

She went to cast another fire wall. Before she could, a bark-covered branch burst out of the forest. It skipped over the cobblestones and slammed into Peran and Rynach. They stumbled and tumbled. With a gut-wrenching crunch, they fell. Tenora dashed around and cut them off. To each side hovered a fairy, crossbow at the ready. Yaetherim flew behind the killers, his stinger drawn. Tenora stretched her hand towards the sprawled murderers. Her thumb pushed on the crystal in her ring. Magic tingled, primed for casting.

"Would you care to try that again?" Yaetherim asked.

Peran stood up. Energy crackled over Tenora's skin. One more step and another wall of fire would contain them. Rynach tried to stand. His left leg buckled, and an anguished cry escaped him. Peran caught the falling merchant. He met Tenora's gaze. No hubris filled his eyes. Instead, he seemed to plead.

"I think his leg's broken."

Tenora lowered her hand. That anguish had been genuine. Rynach wasn't going anywhere. Before she could reply, Yaetherim piped up.

"Oh, calm down. Not like he's been left to bleed to death in a forest clearing."

Tenora resisted the urge to glance at the fairy. Never had she heard such bitterness with a Fairic accent.

"You've made your point. Can you get him some first aid?" Peran asked. A muttered sentence escaped Rynach, too quiet to hear. Tenora tensed. But it was Peran who exploded.

"For Luxanke's sake! Can't you see it's over? You're in no condition to run."

A whistle split the air. Tenora glanced back. A town guard car stopped at the end of the driveway. Karis climbed out, along with three guard constables and a waterkind fairy.

"Don't worry about that," Tenora replied, "I think your ride has just arrived."

Karis and the others reached them a few moments later. The veritor's face was a mask of impassivity. She ran her eyes over the scene before her.

"I received your message, Protector Yaetherim," Karis said in Fairic. She gestured to the tree branch lying beneath Rynach.

"I hope these injuries were not intentional."

Yaetherim shook his head.

"Just meant to stop them running."

Tenora nodded in agreement. Karis turned. Tenora found herself on the end of a steely stare. She brushed aside a lock of hair.

"Messenger Naeliya told me you came to check with the sentry."

Karis glanced at the wrecked car a dozen yards up the driveway.

"Is this what you call checking for messages?"

Tenora blushed.

"I only meant to stop them from escaping."

"They would have done, without her intervention," Yaetherim added. Karis held Tenora's gaze a moment longer, then turned to Yaetherim.

"I have ordered Mage Kepan's release," she said, "and I hope you have the correct people this time."

Yaetherim smirked.

"They admitted it, Veritor Karis. You can ask the protectors who were with me."

Karis turned her stare upon the two killers before her.

"Mage Peran Oaklon and Merchant Rynach Reulo, you are under arrest for murder on three counts, one count of assault, twenty-three counts of rune tampering, eighteen counts of forging documents, and two counts of violating the Accord of Reiksoft."

"That we know of," Yaetherim added.

"Thank you, Protector Yaetherim," Karis said. Without looking back, she gestured to the guard constables.

"Take them into custody. See that Merchant Rynach's leg is healed. He will need to be capable of facing trial."

The constables did so. Karis stepped over to Yaetherim and the other fairies. But their words passed by Tenora.

Rynach and Peran wouldn't hurt anybody else. Thanks to the town guard, the affected cars had been identified. Twenty-three counts of rune tampering, Karis had said. That number sent a shiver down Tenora's spine. At least that many people had been at risk. But not any more.

Tenora went weak at the knees. She leaned her back against a tree beside the driveway. She panted, and a rivulet of sweat rolled down her face. No longer did the goatgrass of unanswered questions prickle her thoughts. It was over.

"Are you all right, Arch-Mechanic Tenora?"

That question had come from Yaetherim, hovering a couple of feet away. Tenora nodded.

"Yes, it's a massive relief."

Yaetherim smiled. Not the smirk she'd seen earlier, but a genuine smile. His eyes softened and shoulders dropped. For a heartbeat, 'twere as though a different fairy hovered before her.

"It is that," he said. "It'll take a bit of getting used to."

He looked up the driveway. Karis and the protector captain conversed, the former taking notes.

"Figured I'd let them sort out the bureaucratic side of it. Sunbird, I mean,

Charlys, is good with that type of thing."

Tenora glanced over. She'd seen the fury in that nokind captain's eyes. Now here was Yaetherim calling her by a nickname.

"It sounds like you can depend on her. Must've been some comfort for you," Tenora observed. Yaetherim nodded.

"Aye. But there are also some Rychillans I can rely on, it seems."

Tenora pulled out a cigarette. She stopped with it halfway to her lips. Yaetherim shrugged.

"Go ahead, I don't mind. I've smelled worse at Cropper's Crony."

Tenora returned the cigarette to the case. Despite her exhaustion, worry no longer prickled her thoughts. Instead, she peered at Yaetherim. Even now, a slight smile curved his lips. She didn't need to ask if he'd obtained what he sought. Before either of them could say more, Karis joined them.

"I must convey my gratitude for your help," she began, "and request just one more thing of you both. We shall hold the trial the day after tomorrow. Will you be available to testify?"

"Yes," Tenora replied.

"Of course," Yaetherim said, "you'll find me at Cropper's Crony."

"Are you staying there tonight?" Tenora asked.

"Aye, I'll be there for a few days. I help in the kitchen to pay for my food and board."

Tenora nodded down the driveway.

"Would you like a lift, then?"

Yaetherim nodded. He flew over to the protectors. Tenora strode down to her car and replaced the crystals in the engine. She let out a sigh. It had been a big day. They'd still have to testify at the trial. But for now, they could relax.

17

No Worries

Yaetherim's wings drooped. He rested his right arm over the side of the fairy notch in the front seat of Tenora's car. Despite the day's events, fatigue didn't weigh him down. He shot a casual glance out the back window. Tenora leaned over the engine. She'd mentioned returning the crystals before they could get going.

The vehicle bobbed. Tenora sat next to Yaetherim and shifted some control levers. After a few dozen heartbeats, a soft hiss sounded from the rear. Tenora steered the car towards Alkentoft. It bounced onto the cobblestone road.

Tenora coughed. Yaetherim looked up, his gaze landing on the rag tied around her ear. Unlike Jorryn or Karis, this arch-mechanic had no duty to investigate these crimes. Yet she'd twice put herself at risk doing so. She had run into danger the first time, seeking to contain that boiler explosion. Yaetherim wasn't sure if he would've done the same.

He stretched his wings and cracked his knuckles. Now that he thought about it, most of the Rychillans he'd worked with had conducted themselves sincerely. Even Jorryn had helped where he could. Like with Tenora, it had put his health at risk. Yaetherim sighed. Perhaps he had misjudged them.

"Are you all right?" Tenora asked in Fairic.

"Aye, just thinking," Yaetherim replied. He glanced out the window.

"And I'm thinking I owe you a large favour, Arch-Mechanic Tenora

Perskel."

She shook her head without hesitation.

"Not at all, Yaetherim. I didn't want anyone else to get hurt."

A smile curled Yaetherim's lips. Favours aside, he owed her his respect, too.

"Okay. Tell me, have you testified at one of these trials before?"

"No, but we learned about them in school. Veritor Karis will present the case and she'll call us to testify. After that, those accused shall be given a chance to defend themselves."

She'd almost spat the last few words out.

"They may question parts of our testimony. After that, if they haven't refuted the argument against them, Veritor Karis will sentence them."

"Seems straightforward," Yaetherim replied. Silence fell for a few heartbeats.

"Do you understand Brialish, by any chance?" Tenora asked. Yaetherim frowned.

"Nay, I've never needed it. Does that injured Brial also need to testify?"

Tenora shook her head.

"Trials aren't open to the public, but there's at least one reporter present. Those with a stake in the crimes committed may observe. Merchant Rynach attacked Able Seabird Fillan to keep him quiet. I suspect he'd like to see justice done."

Yaetherim nodded. He should send a message to Verbore Island, then. Taeperra deserved the same. Perhaps the trial would answer some, if not all, of her questions. At least she wouldn't need to wait eight months for the complete story.

Silence fell again. Yaetherim stared at the improvised bandage on Tenora's left ear. Where it had been tomato red, it now appeared the colour of an unpeeled beetroot. Human blood darkened when dry, as did that of fairies. She hadn't changed that dressing at all.

"Arch-Mechanic Tenora, have you had a wound like that before?"

"You can call me Tenora, and no. This is my first time."

"I thought so. May I offer some advice?"

"Of course."

"Keep it clean. I didn't."

Yaetherim ran a finger over the single scar on his left arm. He shivered, thinking of what could've been.

"Forgot about one dressing, the least painful. Had to slap a poultice on it when it turned foul."

Even now, the skin surrounding that scar bore a faint discolouration. Tenora shuddered.

"Thank you," she said. "I'll keep watch on that."

Silence fell and Yaetherim closed his eyes. Not to rest. There'd be time for that soon. Instead, he thought back over the events of the last eight months. Peran and Rynach would be given a chance to challenge the facts against them. He'd have to ensure his testimony stood as firm as an ironwood tree.

Neither of them spoke until Tenora parked outside Cropper's Crony.

"Thank you, Tenora."

"You're welcome. Do you know how to get to the guard barracks? That's where the trial will be."

"It's just up from the town hall, isn't it?"

"Yes, one block north."

"Thanks."

With that, they made their farewells and Yaetherim headed into the inn. Despite the day's events, sleep did not come easily to him. As usual.

* * *

From his perch on the front edge of the witness box, Yaetherim stared across the courtroom at the two killers. Surrounded by iron bars running from floor to ceiling, they stood with the life and lean of fallen trees. Rynach leant on the rear of the cell with a plaster cast wrapped around his leg. A walking stick under his left arm propped him up. Beside him, Peran sagged against the side of the cage. For a heartbeat, his eyes met Yaetherim's, then they dropped. Yaetherim's hand twitched and almost reached for his stinger.

Yaetherim glanced back into the witness box. Tenora sat on a bench built across it. Unlike the other day, she wore a yellow dress and bore only the faintest smudges of grease. To Yaetherim's left, Charlys rested with her legs dangling over the carpeted floor. All three of them had already given their testimony.

Even with Charlys beside him, Yaetherim's heart raced. Aye, Karis had indeed arrested these two killers. But they'd have a right to reply once she finished her summing-up. Some sly words may yet see them walk unpunished.

"… after we took you into custody," Karis said, "we examined the satchel and connil hood you placed in your car. The latter matched the hood discovered in Merchant Rynach's house, in terms of wear and dye shade. This indicates they were made and stolen together. The bag contained a notebook with several drawn rune sequences, one per page. Each depicted overlaid runes, instead of side-by-side. One page had been torn out, but the tear fitted the top of the sheet found by Protector Captain Kaetarpen and Protector Yaetherim in Cerrane. Finally, the fingerprints found at the scene of Mechanic Jotol's murder match those of Merchant Rynach. These are also present on the dagger found in Merchant Rynach's office."

Murmurs came from Yaetherim's right, in multiple languages. He glanced at the viewing gallery. A variety of faces, mostly Fairic and Rychillan, filled them. Taeperra and Kaetarpen sat amongst them, as did Kepan and Darnith. A Brial with a bandaged wing watched from the front row. Next to him, a Rychillan man scrawled in a notepad. A reporter, according to his terax.

"As such," Karis continued, "this evidence, along with the testimony you have heard, links you to these crimes. Three murders, twenty-three counts of rune tampering, fourteen unregulated rune sequences and one assault-"

Karis broke off. A heartbeat later, Yaetherim found her gaze upon him.

"Protector Yaetherim, would you say that attack robbed you of your purpose?"

Yaetherim blinked. His wings flicked forward. Such a personal question was the last thing he'd expected in a courtroom.

"Throughout this investigation and trial, Veritor Karis, you have used my former title. But the fact is, I am no longer a protector."

Yaetherim stood and turned. He extended his right wing for everyone to see. As usual, three dozen points of pain tugged upon it.

"This wound, more so than the others, meant I couldn't continue my duties as a forest protector. Even after learning to fly again. So, I've been helping my brother with his role as our village apothecary. It's like cooking, in a way, but doesn't allow much experimentation."

He sat and shot a glare at the two murderers.

"Just to be clear," he added, "when I say experimentation, I mean safely testing new mixtures of ingredients."

"Thank you, Protector Yaetherim," Karis said. "That testimony is sufficient."

She turned back to Peran and Rynach.

"One assault resulting in severe injuries and deprivation of a fairy's purpose. Whilst this deprivation is not codified, it is a factor which must be considered. That is the case against you, Mage Peran Oaklon and Merchant Rynach Reulo. What have you to say in your defence?"

Silence fell over the courtroom. Yaetherim squirmed. Fingers intertwined with his. They squeezed his hand gently. Yaetherim smiled.

"Thanks, Sunbird," he whispered. Across the courtroom, Peran and Rynach exchanged a look. The latter gave a small nod. Peran turned and addressed Karis.

"Veritor Karis, I hope you may take our intent into account. Lack of rune capacity is a growing problem, and we simply sought to solve it, via means of magic."

A snort came from the witness box behind Yaetherim. Peran shot a glare across the courtroom, then continued.

"Engines cannot keep expanding in order to provide more power. This would lead to a vehicle which is all engine and no cargo. Which, I'm sure you realise, is not practical. We conducted our initial experiments in the forest, for the same reason the College of Mages is located there. So accidents wouldn't injure too many."

Yaetherim scoffed. He folded his arms. This was the first he'd heard of their concern about injuries.

"I didn't mean to kill anyone," Peran continued, "I only acted in moments of panic-"

"Do you think we only sprouted yesterday? We've been over this already!"

Warmth spread through Yaetherim's cheeks. Were his skin a lighter tone, they'd have flushed purple. Those words had just slipped from his mouth. He'd not meant to interrupt. Charlys' hand clenched. Several pairs of eyes watched from the viewing gallery.

"Do you have something to add, Protector Yaetherim?" Karis asked. Yaetherim shrugged. If she was asking, he may as well contribute. He shot Peran a look which would strip leaves from branches.

"Tell me, what caused you to panic when you hid that necklace in Mage Kepan's desk? I'm no waterkind, but surely it would take some time to conjure ice to conceal it. Then there's that gambit you tried with the cigarette smoke when leaving the speckled rocks. Those are actions that require forethought."

Yaetherim folded his arms and glanced at Karis.

"To be fair, Rychillan isn't my first language. Your word 'panic' means being startled and afraid, does it not?"

Karis nodded.

"Indeed, it does. Your points are noted."

She turned back to the killers.

"Do you have more to state in your defence?"

Peran shook his head. He slumped against the iron bars. All eyes fell upon Karis. Yaetherim's heart raced. After a few moments, Karis spoke.

"Peran Oaklon and Rynach Reulo, you have shown a significant lack of responsibility in the execution of your experiments. Furthermore, no Rychillan may take the life of another, regardless of race or species, except in extenuating circumstances. No such factors are present here. Not only have you failed to refute the claims against you, you have attempted to justify your crimes. As such, this court finds you guilty on all charges."

Yaetherim leaned forward. Now he'd see how seriously the Rychillans took this.

"You are to be made connil," Karis continued, "with no path to atonement.

Additionally, you may no longer claim any protection from the laws of the kingdom. Both this outlawry and your status shall be recorded on your teraxes."

She nodded to the guard constables surrounding the iron cage. One opened it, then they escorted the convicted killers away. Yaetherim leaned back. A grin curled his lips. With such a record, no Rychillan would help them. They'd have to completely fend for themselves.

From beside him tinkled a laugh. Turning, he found a familiar pair of hazel eyes watching him. Below them, a smile showed that cute gap between Charlys' front teeth.

"You've got a lovely smile, Therry. It's good to see it again."

Warmth spread through Yaetherim's cheeks. Once more, he was glad for his bark-brown skin.

"Strange," he replied, "I was just thinking the same about you."

Charlys' smile broadened. Behind them, wood thudded on wood as Tenora exited the witness box.

"So what now?" Charlys asked. Yaetherim went to reply, but words failed him. He hadn't thought that far ahead. So he simply shrugged.

"I'm sure I'll figure out something."

"Cropper's Crony for the next few days, then?"

"Aye. Don't fret. I will be home soon."

Charlys glanced at the courtroom door. The observers were leaving through it.

"I should get going."

"I'll tell our elders the full story when I return."

Her smile vanished. A frown took its place.

"Yaetherim."

"Don't worry, Sunbird. Just the facts. Those alone should make my point."

"Aye, I shall let them know. Take care, Therry."

With that, she launched herself towards the door. Yaetherim watched her go, then followed.

In the corridor outside, he found Taeperra and Kaetarpen waiting for him. They both insisted on owing him large favours, the latter on behalf of the elders of Mirost Village. After bidding them farewell, he flew to Cropper's Crony. He immediately joined Chef Tarlon and threw himself into cooking. But this time, he didn't need it to distract him from his worries. When the day's work was done, he retired to his room.

Yaetherim slept well that night.

About the Author

D.T. Bella is an Australian author who writes detective-fantasy fiction. He lives in South-East Queensland, and finds the local scenery quite inspirational. In his spare time when he's not writing, he enjoys model railroading and cooking.

You can connect with me on:
- https://rychilla.com
- https://twitter.com/Rychilla
- https://www.facebook.com/rychillacases